STAGES OF GREY

Graduate student Dulcie Schwartz finds herself in the front row of a murder in the latest instalment of the Dulcie Schwartz feline mystery series.

When Dulcie's friends drag her to see a disco version of Ovid's Metamorphosis, the grad student finds herself in the front row of a murder. Was jealousy the reason for the death? Money? Or darker secrets? And what role does Gus, the troupe's feline mascot, play? Dulcie must untangle the truth before she also gets caught up in deadly illusion.

A Selection of Recent Titles by Clea Simon

MEW IS FOR MURDER
CATTERY ROW
CRIES AND WHISKERS
PROBABLE CLAWS
SHADES OF GREY *
GREY MATTERS *
GREY ZONE *
GREY EXPECTATIONS *
TRUE GREY *
GREY DAWN *
GREY HOWL *
STAGES OF GREY *

* *available from Severn House*

STAGES OF GREY

A Dulcie Schwartz feline mystery

Clea Simon

Severn House Large Print
London & New York

This first large print edition published 2015
in Great Britain and the USA by
SEVERN HOUSE PUBLISHERS LTD of
19 Cedar Road, Sutton, Surrey, England, SM2 5DA.
First world regular print edition published 2014 by
Severn House Publishers Ltd., London and New York.

British Library Cataloguing in Publication Data

Simon, Clea author.
  Stages of grey.
  1. Schwartz, Dulcie (Fictitious character)--Fiction.
  2. Theatrical companies--Fiction. 3. Murder--
  Investigation--Fiction. 4. Cats--Fiction. 5. Detective
  and mystery stories. 6. Large type books.
  I. Title
  813.6-dc23

  ISBN-13: 9780727897862

Severn House Publishers support the Forest Stewardship Council™
[FSC™], the leading international forest certification organisation. All
our titles that are printed on FSC certified paper carry the FSC logo.

MIX
Paper from
responsible sources
FSC
www.fsc.org   FSC® C013056

Printed and bound in Great Britain by
T J International, Padstow, Cornwall.

ACKNOWLEDGMENTS

This particular story came about on a starlit night on a walk through Provincetown with Jon S. Garelick, and for that, as well as many other gifts, I thank him here. Readers and supporters including Brett Milano, Vicki Constantine Croke, Sophie Garelick, Frank Garelick, and Lisa Jones kept me going as well, as did my wonderfully supportive agent, Colleen Mohyde of the Doe Coover Agency. Many thanks as well to John McDonough, for the ins and outs of computer crime and police work. Any and all errors are despite his good work, not because of it. Finally, editor Rachel Simpson and her staff remain wonderful to work with. I could not ask for better. Purrs out, people.

ONE

'I have reason to believe my boyfriend is a wolf.'

There, she'd said it. The words were out. Not that she got any response. In fact, the small black and white cat whom Dulcie had addressed looked particularly unfazed by her human's strange pronouncement.

'I'm talking about Chris, Esmé,' Dulcie tried again. 'I seriously think that Chris might be a wolf.'

She didn't dare raise her voice. It was still early, and a Monday, and her boyfriend was asleep in the other room. Sound asleep, from what she could tell, after another late night out on some unspecified errand. But Dulcie didn't want to risk waking him. And so even as the sun warmed the tiny kitchen of their shared apartment, she kept her voice to a whisper as she opened a can for Esmé.

'Meh.' The little cat seemed uninterested in anything except the dish Dulcie was holding.

'Sorry.' Dulcie placed it on the mat. 'But, Esmé, don't you care?'

The only response was the sound of lapping. Dulcie had rarely felt more alone.

'Wolves. I am surrounded by wolves.' Dulcie

tried the thought out again as she walked into the Square. Coffee in hand, the dim winter sun taking the edge off the cold, she didn't find the idea quite so horrific any more. 'Still,' she said to herself as she trudged down the cold winter street, 'it could be a lot worse.'

At the sound of her own words, Dulcie laughed, her breath visible in the frigid air. Chris, she had realized, would understand in a moment what she meant. As a fifth-year graduate student at one of the world's most prestigious universities, Dulcie had known competition at its most brutal. Fellow students, desperate faculty, and vengeful ex-lovers all had done their worst if not to her, then in front of her, leading her to see academia as something one shade darker than a Jacobean drama.

Still, Dulcie had been lucky in her friends – from her former room-mate Suze to her department mates Trista and Lloyd – and in several of her colleagues, like the librarian Thomas Griddlehaus. While she wasn't crazy about her thesis adviser, she was developing a good working relationship with a senior scholar at another university, and she had hopes that that scholar, Professor Renée Showalter, might soon be offered a position here. And she had Chris, the most supportive and loving boyfriend she could hope for. Considering what else was out there – in terms of cut-throat, back-stabbing, crazy rivals – she knew she had it good. If one or maybe two of those closest to her were werewolves, well, at least they were on her side.

'Unlike the review committee,' she muttered,

watching her breath steam.

It felt good to get it out, and she was still far enough from the university that she was pretty sure nobody would have overheard her. Still, she glanced around to make sure – it was instinct at this point. Once she got within sight of the departmental offices, she'd have to go into full-on political mode. Yes, she was grateful for the feedback. No, she'd have no trouble revising her paper once again. Of course, she would consider incorporating the review committee member's own work as a source. This was all part and parcel of getting her paper into an academic journal. No wonder a couple of wolves seemed benign in comparison.

'Good morning, Dulcie.' The friendly voice broke into Dulcie's reverie as she entered the little clapboard house that served as the offices for the Department of English and American Literatures and Language. Nancy, the departmental secretary, was an anomaly in academia. Always warm and cheerful, she also managed to be briskly efficient. 'Are you looking for your mail?'

'Yes, please.' Dulcie felt her own mood lifting as the motherly secretary reached across her desk to pick up a thick bunch of envelopes. 'Here's hoping.'

'I haven't sorted through these yet,' Nancy said as she began leafing through the stack of envelopes. Dulcie bit her lip. Most of her mail went to her apartment, of course. But some of the academic journals to which she had submitted proposals would be responding to her via the department. It was their offhand way of checking her credentials, she knew, and that meant that they hadn't heard of her. Still, she was too excited to be insulted. That was a big pile of envelopes.

'Here, I knew there was one.' Nancy pulled a business-sized missive from the pack and handed it to Dulcie.

'One?' Dulcie looked over at the pile. 'And those others?'

'I'm sorry, Dulcie.' Nancy's voice was solicitous. 'These are largely for Mr Thorpe. The rest, well, they're for other students.'

'One.' Dulcie felt herself deflating as she looked at the slim envelope in her hands. Well, one was better than none – and the return address on this one was a box office in New Haven. She carefully lifted the flap and removed the single sheet.

Tired of paying such high rates for student loans?

'Great.'

'Dulcie?' Nancy looked concerned and was rising from her desk. 'Is it ... bad news?'

'No.' Dulcie forced what she hoped was a reassuring smile. 'Just junk mail. I'm sorry, Nancy. It's just that I was hoping ... You know, after presenting at the conference and all...'

'But your paper has been accepted for the ELLA journal.' Count on Nancy to find a bright side.

'Pending revisions,' was all Dulcie could add. She shook her head. 'I can't think about this any more. Is he in?'

Nancy nodded, clearly happy to let the matter drop. 'Would you like more coffee?' It was the only consolation she could offer at this point, but Dulcie was grateful for it. Nancy did make great coffee.

'For this relief, much thanks.' Her travel mug full, Dulcie went to face her thesis adviser.

Ten minutes later, she was back on the street, and it wasn't only the stinging wind that was bringing tears to her eyes. Thorpe couldn't help it, she told herself. Her thesis adviser – and the acting head of the department – didn't mean to be insensitive. But the moment she had walked into his office, he'd been after her about her revisions.

'You have to keep up, Dulcie,' he'd said, an unusually stern note creeping into his voice. 'If the panel doesn't like your progress on the revisions, word will get out, you know.'

'But...' She'd wanted to argue. She'd presented the paper already, at one of the biggest conferences in her field. Plus, it had already been vetted not only by Thorpe himself but also by her unofficial mentor, Showalter. Shouldn't the publication process be getting easier by now? She didn't dare ask that. Instead, she had ventured a tentative thought. 'They wouldn't actually reject it at this point, would they?'

'You heard what happened to Timothy Lemuel, didn't you?'

'Timothy Lemuel?' She felt so out of it. 'No. I'm sorry. I don't know him.'

'Exactly,' Thorpe said, looking down at a paper on his desk. 'Now, where are we on your latest chapter?'

It was a wonder she made it out of the offices without breaking down. Not that she had time to. Not only did she have the latest revisions – rewrite requests that directly contradicted the last set she'd done – but Thorpe had made it clear that he expected her next chapter by month's end.

'Plan on bringing me some pages by Friday,' he'd added, almost as an aside. 'If you can't multitask...' He'd left the sentence open-ended, intentionally. At least, Dulcie thought he did. Since he was reaching down into his desk drawer as he spoke, she couldn't be entirely sure.

Now she blinked away the tears and looked at the brochure he'd handed her when he'd sat back up. *Time Management for Academics: A Seminar.*

TWO

'You don't need another seminar.' Trista was fuming. 'What you need is some fun!'

Dulcie was too tired by then to put up much of a fight. It had been a long day. Still, she lifted her head enough to protest weakly. 'I have fun.'

Her blonde friend snorted in derision. 'Racing over to meet us for a drink after the library closes does not constitute fun.'

Dulcie was about to argue. She had, after all, run straight from her carrel – where she had written very little – to join her friends. But before she could defend herself, Trista continued. 'Opening night at a new bar – right in the Square, no less – and I have to nearly drag you out. I know Chris would agree with me. Now that he's not working nights, he must want to go out sometimes.'

Dulcie simply nodded, trying to keep her dismay from showing on her face. It was hopeless, anyway. Trista was not only more of a party girl than Dulcie would ever be, she had also finished her thesis. Could she have forgotten so quickly what it was like? Maybe she had, because she kept talking – and Dulcie snuck a peek at her cell phone. She'd called Chris on her way over to the bar, but had gotten his voicemail. Maybe, she decided, she should text him. Unlike their old,

13

familiar hang-out, this place was crowded and loud. He could be on the other side of the room, and she wouldn't know it.

Even as she was typing, a message came in. But, no, it was from Renée Showalter. *I understand how discouraging it can be.* Dulcie smiled. Only a professor would actually type out complete words. *But this is only one of many publications to come.*

Thx, Dulcie typed back – and then corrected herself. *Thank you.* It wouldn't hurt her to emulate her role model.

'Are you in, Dulcie?' She looked up to find Trista and their assembled friends looking at her.

'Sorry, what?'

'Tickets,' Trista said.

'To that new theater,' Raleigh stepped in to explain. 'Trista said they're doing a disco interpretation of Ovid. She says it's really fun.'

Dulcie opened her mouth and closed it again, unsure of how to respond. Lloyd, Raleigh's boyfriend and Dulcie's office mate, laughed.

'It's not that bad, Dulcie,' he said. 'At least, it's not supposed to be.'

'The actors are top notch,' Trista chimed in. 'And they're in great shape. There's one act in which they're supposedly only wearing body make-up.'

Dulcie looked around. Jerry, Trista's long-time boyfriend, had not joined the crowd. That didn't mean anything – Chris wasn't here yet, either. But Dulcie felt her heart sinking. She liked Jerry. And she liked Trista less when she was in this mode, all flirty and full of herself.

14

'Come on, Dulcie.' Trista looked like she could read her friend's mind. 'Even Jerry wants to go. Some buddy of his from the Boston software coalition can get us tickets at, like, half price.'

Theater even computer geeks could love? Dulcie bit back the temptation to voice her thoughts out loud.

'Clark said it was pretty good, and he's in Classics.' Raleigh read her look correctly.

'It would be a chance to see that new theater,' Lloyd chimed in. 'The URT.'

'Is this the one that took over from the book-store?' Dulcie considered this another reason to boycott.

'That old place, yeah.' Clearly, Trista did not. 'I don't know how they got the smell out.'

Dulcie opened her mouth to protest, then decided against it. True enough, Revolt! had been a bit close, though unlike many, she had always assumed its mustiness came from the stacks of used books – 'donated by the people, for the people' – rather than the rotating crew of volunteers who staffed the place.

'I'm just sorry they're gone.' That was honest, as well as diplomatic. 'They did fill a niche.'

Trista's raised eyebrow – accentuated by her latest piercing – was response enough.

'Tell us about the new production, Tris.' Raleigh stepped once more into the breach. 'Clark only told me a little.'

'It's called *Changes*, and everyone says it's brilliant.' Trista sat back, happy to have won. 'The director – I think he's British – is reinter-preting the *Metamorphosis*. Taking it back to

15

basics.'

'It's not going to be like that *Hamlet* that just closed, is it?' Lloyd still looked skeptical. Dulcie turned in astonishment, and he pointed to Raleigh. 'She keeps up with the New York scene.'

'Lord, no.' Trista chuckled. 'That was a fiasco. But that wasn't the fault of the interpretation.'

'I heard it was pretty out there.' Raleigh would always be the voice of reason. 'Even for Off-Off Broadway.'

Trista was shaking her head. 'No, from what I read, it was the lead – the Hamlet – some newbie named Harvey Brenkham. Everyone said Brenkham looked the part: dark and brooding. But on opening night he lost it. Total stage fright. Squeaky voice. Forgetting his lines.'

'Poor guy.' Despite herself, Dulcie was drawn in.

'Pity the rest of the cast, not him.' Trista snorted. 'Halfway through the ghost scene, he took off – ran off the stage and out of the theater. I gather the audience thought it was part of the production, but it wasn't. They had to vamp their way through the rest of the scene and then wait while the understudy got in costume. Brenkham's never going to work again.'

'Well, that might be something to see.' Lloyd looked intrigued, at least until Raleigh elbowed him. 'Or not. But I'd be up for the URT thing.'

'Me too, if the price is right.' Chris's familiar voice came from behind her. Dulcie turned to see her boyfriend and Jerry, both shedding their parkas as they pulled up chairs. 'Dulcie, you interested?'

'Maybe.' Her smile had more to do with his arrival than their plans, but so be it. Besides, Trista might have a point about Chris wanting to go out. Dulcie liked to think that she and Chris had a special bond, but her blonde friend knew more about men than Dulcie did. Jerry still hung around, despite what Dulcie suspected were at least heavy flirtations on his girlfriend's part. Besides, ever since she had begun to question Chris's odd disappearances, Dulcie had found herself wondering about their relationship as well. Because if he wasn't a ... well, what she feared he might be, then where was he disappearing to at night? If he were a wolf, she would rather he be the faithful kind.

'Tomorrow?' Trista wasn't wasting any time.

'Maybe if I can get more work done tonight.' Before Trista could argue, Dulcie turned to her boyfriend, who was reaching for the communal pitcher of beer. 'You don't mind, do you?'

She caught her boyfriend mid-swallow. 'Let me finish this, and I'll walk you.'

'Don't be silly.' She stood, pulling her own coat from the seat-back as she rose. 'You just got here. Hang out a bit.'

'You sure?' He'd already put his glass down. If they were at the People's Republik, they'd have full-size pints.

'Yeah.' She wasn't. Not at all. In fact, if anything, she was sure of the opposite – that she wanted to sit with her boyfriend and unwind with her friends. But if they were going to go out tomorrow – an actual date, if you counted hanging out with a half-dozen other graduate students a date – then she knew what she needed to do. 'Stay. Have fun.'

'I should go, too.' Lloyd rose. 'I'll walk with you, Dulcie.' Raleigh got up as well.

'Don't be silly.' Her smile was genuine now. She might not want to leave, but the show of loyalty made it almost worthwhile. 'Enjoy the night while you can. You're both so much better with deadlines.'

With a quick kiss for Chris, she started for the door. Any longer and her resolve would weaken.

'That is a woman who is ready to finish her thesis,' she heard Trista say as she walked away. 'Frankly, I'm glad. She's been dallying with it for long enough.'

THREE

Suze, you around?

Texting and walking wasn't the smartest idea. Dulcie wasn't really afraid of street crime – she was still in the Square, with its bright lights and crowds – but Cambridge's brick sidewalks could make walking treacherous, even without the distraction.

Call me?

Tonight, though, she needed a little positive reinforcement. Suze and Dulcie had been roommates for years – since they were both sophomores. Recently they'd drifted, a natural enough occurrence, Dulcie figured. Suze was working and studying for the bar, while Dulcie was still in school. But at times like this, Dulcie really missed her no-nonsense friend. Trista might be in her discipline – a Victorian, but still a lit major – but she had changed. Some of it was status – the multiply pierced blonde had successfully defended her own dissertation and had landed a prestigious post-doc. Some of it was ... Dulcie shook her head. She didn't know. Only that Trista had become more and more set on dominating their little social group, or at least on telling Dulcie how to run her life. And that crack about finishing her thesis. Didn't she remember?

Trista had gotten so caught up in her own dissertation that she'd given them all a scare, not that long ago, disappearing without a trace for several days.

Besides, it wasn't that Dulcie didn't *want* to finish. Of course she did. It was more that she wanted to make sure she did it right. By the time she defended her thesis, she wanted to know everything about the anonymous author she was studying. She may have started wanting to write a simple exegesis of one book, *The Ravages of Umbria*. But she was way past that now. And, really, with so much material waiting to be examined, how could she stop?

It was unfair to say she was stalling. It was also, she admitted, possibly partially true. It *was* scary to contemplate what she would do after she'd gotten her degree. And if that was the case, could Trista's other complaints hold water?

'Maybe I am too much of a hippy.' Dulcie remembered one of Trista's criticisms. 'Lucy would love that.' Lucy, Dulcie's mom, still lived on the commune where she had taken her daughter nearly twenty years before. The commune – although Lucy insisted on calling it an arts colony – was far from perfect. If Dulcie never ate another bean casserole in her life, it would be too soon. But its focus on cooperative government, while highly inefficient, had left Dulcie resistant to leaders of any kind.

Suze would understand, and shivering in the wind, Dulcie thought about texting her friend again. But, no, she checked her phone. Suze hadn't responded. Besides, if she were really

20

being honest, Dulcie would admit to herself that it wasn't only Trista who was bothering her. It was Chris. Chris and the idea that he just might be...

She shook her head and reached up to button her collar higher. Just the thought made the night seem colder.

It wasn't the kind of thing she could ask about. She'd tried, once before. Come right out and told Chris that she thought he might be at least partly not human. There had been a lot going on, and he'd responded with confusion, so she had let it go.

She tried to tell herself it didn't matter. She, Dulcie Schwartz, was many things. A doctoral candidate. The only child of a slightly nutty mother. The possible descendent of a brilliant Gothic author. All of these were part of her, and if somebody only focused on one facet – say, that she was able to communicate with the spirit of her late, great cat, Mr Grey – well, they might think she was a bit odd, as well. So what if her boyfriend were a werewolf. Did that really matter?

It wasn't as if he killed people.

He hadn't, had he?

As Dulcie made her way through the Square, she found herself pondering the possibility. A wolf, by its nature, was a hunter. Chris was certainly a carnivore. Dulcie could distinctly recall some choice comments on the subject when one of their friends – it must have been Trista – had gone, briefly, vegan and invited them all to a meal featuring seitan. It had not been pretty.

21

Unbidden, the image of what had happened on the way home came to her. Pizza – with sausage and pepperoni – devoured almost wordlessly. If she closed her eyes, she could still see his teeth...

'Hey, lady!'

Startled out of her memory, Dulcie stopped short, just in time to keep herself from walking into the man in front of her. Tall and lean, he looked down at her with a frown.

'Sorry.' She shrugged. 'I was thinking of something.'

His only response was to arch his eyebrows and shake what Dulcie now saw was a shoulder-length gold mane.

'I said I was sorry,' Dulcie barely mumbled the words as he passed her by, leaning away from her as they passed on the narrow sidewalk. It was a bit theatrical, but she couldn't really be angry with the leonine stranger. He'd probably been trying to dodge her as she had walked into him. Still, she didn't need some random passer-by making her feel any less secure. Not when she had so many questions about the real man in her life.

As if on cue, her phone rang.

'Dulcie? Where are you?' It was Chris, and Dulcie stopped walking again.

'Why? What is it?' Something was wrong, she could hear it in his voice.

'I shouldn't have let you leave like that.' Behind him, she could hear the noise of the bar. Trista, she thought, was still talking, though maybe she was imagining that. 'It's not safe and, well, I'd rather spend my time with you. I'm

22

coming to get you.'

A wave of relief swept over her, warming her despite the bitter wind. 'Thanks, sweetie.' She felt honor-bound to add: 'You don't have to, you know.'

'I know. I want to.' The bar noise was gone, and she imagined him on the street outside. 'So, where are you?'

She looked up. 'Down by that new hotel. The one that used to be the gas station?'

'Got it. Wait there, sweetie.' He hung up before she could protest again. He was such a sweetheart. Really, her suspicions were crazy. So maybe he had a dark side. Dulcie pushed her hands deeper into the pockets of the oversized sweater that served as her winter coat and stared at the building across the street. Since she didn't drive – none of them could afford cars – she'd never had reason to patronize the old-fashioned service station that had stood on the corner for as long as she had been in town. Still, it had been a surprise when it had been torn down. Didn't people need to buy gas any more? And when a sign appeared, announcing a hotel to be opened on the same spot, she'd found it confusing.

'Why don't they just call it Gas?' Trista had quipped, when it first opened. This was back when Trista was still interacting rather than pronouncing.

'The Fill-Up,' Lloyd had offered, prompting Raleigh to respond with, 'The Pump,' and then a blush, as the rest of them had filled in the off-color possibilities for a no-tell hotel.

The result had been anything but – it was a

small boutique hotel simply called 'H'.

'It's too pricey for my parents,' Suze had reported. She had been the first one to check it out. 'I'm thinking the university will use it for visiting bigwigs.'

'I guess,' Dulcie had said, strangely saddened. Another sign that the college town she had fallen in love with nearly ten years before was outgrowing its old counterculture ways.

'Things change,' Chris had thrown in, picking up on her melancholy. Standing on the corner, waiting for him, Dulcie told herself that wasn't all bad.

She was also, she told herself after another arctic blast, an idiot. The H might be too expensive for Suze's parents – and that meant it was certainly out of Lucy's budget, if her mother ever did manage to come east. But that didn't mean she couldn't avail herself of the lobby. Rather than standing on the sidewalk looking in at the warm glow of shaded lamps on leather sofas, she could be waiting inside.

She pulled her phone out again. 'Chris?' No, her call went straight to voicemail. 'Chris, I'm going to wait inside the lobby of the new hotel. Okay?'

He'd find her, wouldn't he? Stepping into the street, Dulcie paused to peer back down the way she'd come. A cab went by, and a couple huddled close. She took another step. No sign of her boyfriend. Retreating back to the sidewalk, she tried his phone again. Nothing, and just to be on the safe side, she texted him: *In H lobby. Find me!*

24

She'd had a few minutes' head start, but not that long. When she'd texted Suze, she'd stopped walking – a lesson she should have remembered when she nearly collided with the gold-maned stranger. And Chris had much longer legs. Plus, he knew she was waiting, out here in the cold. She looked down the street. Nothing.

There was no point in worrying. Maybe he'd stopped for a slice. That wouldn't be too surprising. Dulcie could imagine him ducking in, thinking he would grab one and go – and then realizing that he could bring a whole pie back to the apartment. That would add a minute or two, but it would be worth it, she told herself. He was a generous man, even if he might be a bit careless. And, really, if she were waiting for him inside, where it was warm, she wouldn't mind a few more minutes.

Resisting the urge to check her phone – or to call – one more time, she stepped off the curb. And wheeled around as a horrific cry rent the air.

'No!' A man's voice – she thought it was a man's – rang out, somewhere in the direction of the Square.

'Chris!' She called his name out loud as she turned and ran toward the noise. 'Chris!'

'No!' A small crowd had gathered at the next corner, but she pushed her way through. There, under an abnormally bright street light, she saw him. Not Chris, but the handsome stranger. Only those strong, regular features weren't handsome any more. Instead, they were contorted, his wide mouth stretched open in a wordless cry, long

25

blond hair thrown back. The wolves had gotten him. They were dragging him down, taking him into the shadows.

FOUR

'Wait, no!' The voice sounded familiar, but Dulcie didn't pause. She pushed ahead, toward that scream, toward the shadow. And then suddenly she wasn't going forward, as hands wrapped around her, pulling her back. Desperate to help, she jerked herself free – and felt herself fall, the grey stone of the curb rushing up to meet her.

'Dulcie? Are you okay?' The voice was familiar but faint. She was deep, deep under the sea. 'Dulcie?'

'Stand back, please.' Another voice, breaking in. 'Stand back. Coming through.'

'Dulcie?' She opened her eyes to see Chris, his face drawn and more pale than usual under the blue-white street lights. Around him, five or six other faces leaned in. 'Are you okay?'

'What?' Before she could properly respond, Chris disappeared. A burly stranger took his place, blocking out the others.

'Don't try to get up, Miss. Just relax.'

'Wait...' Where had Chris gone? Dulcie sat up, only to be hit by a wave of dizziness and nausea.

'Steady there.' Hands like catcher's mitts wrapped around her upper arms.

'Dulcie!' Chris's face popped up over the

27

broad man's shoulder, his dark eyes wide.

'Chris.' The nausea was replaced by relief, and she reached out to him. 'Give me a hand?'

'Miss, don't.' The stranger held on, and she turned toward him.

'Do you mind?' She channeled her best Thorpe and reached forward, taking Chris's outstretched glove.

'Dulcie, are you all right?' He pulled her to her feet, and she fought another wave of dizziness.

'Of course.' She nodded. A mistake. 'I think so. What happened?'

'You fell and hit your head.' Chris was shaking his. 'I heard you yell.'

'Miss, you really should come with us.' The big stranger – who, Dulcie now noticed, was wearing an EMT jacket, size XXL – started to nudge Chris back among the other bystanders.

'No, wait.' It was coming back to her, and she turned toward her boyfriend. 'Someone grabbed me. I was ... what happened to the wolves?'

'Miss.' With a nod to Chris, the EMT wrapped a thick arm around Dulcie. 'Let's go—'

'*No!*' Dulcie shook free. 'I know what I'm talking about. The reason I was running – the reason I fell – was that I saw someone – a man with long hair – being attacked.' She looked up at Chris. 'I did.'

'I believe you, honey.' He turned to the EMT. 'She sounds like herself. Can I just take her home?'

The tech didn't look pleased, but before he could object another voice chimed in. 'Phil, there's another call.'

'Well, okay then. I'm writing this one down as non-compliant.' With a grumble like rocks rolling down a mountain, he turned and disappeared into the crowd.

'Maybe we should go to the university health services.' Chris was by her side, and she leaned on him. 'I mean, you were out cold.'

'Was I?' Now that the drama was gone, along with the ambulance, the small crowd was dispersing as well. 'Chris, that man – the one who was attacked – what happened to him?'

Her boyfriend only shook his head. 'I don't know what you're talking about, Dulcie. There's nobody here.'

She pushed past him and stared down the street. The blue-white light put the pavement and sidewalks in high relief, and she ran down to the break in the buildings, to stare down into the shadowed alleyway where she was sure...

There was nothing. Not even a garbage can. The buildings on both sides ran back about twenty feet to a dead end: a solid brick wall that lacked even a door. Not that wolves could open a door. Though if the wolves were really...

'Dulcie?' Chris called from the sidewalk and started walking toward her.

Quickly she dropped to the pavement and ran her hand along the asphalt. No blood, not that she could see, although there was a strange faint glitter to the dark surface.

'Dulcie?' Chris was kneeling beside her now, taking her hand in his. 'Maybe we should go now? I think you should see a doctor after all.'

FIVE

Dulcie knew enough to keep her mouth shut. Even as the doctor shone his light into her eyes, asking her to tell him what had happened, she both tried not to blink and to sound coherent. Talking about a pack of wolves in Harvard Square wouldn't help her case at all.

Chris, however, ratted her out. 'She was talking about wolves, Doctor.' He had cornered the tired-looking physician as he'd started to leave the room. But if Chris thought that Dulcie couldn't hear him, he was mistaken. 'About a wolf pack taking down some blond guy.'

'It must have been the shadows, Chris,' Dulcie called over. Whatever she had seen, she wouldn't be able to follow up if they locked her in here. 'Or something.'

'Wolves?' The young doctor – he couldn't be any older than they were – turned, tired eyes blinking. 'You didn't say anything about that.'

'I have realized I must have been mistaken.' Dulcie tried to sound as clear as she could. Only as the words came out did she realize that they were stilted, as if she was indeed only barely holding madness at bay. 'I was out there alone, and it was cold. And where were you anyway, Chris?' She hadn't meant to turn the conversation toward him. However, it was a useful strategy. 'I kept looking down the street and you didn't show.'

'I was a little delayed.' He paused, but didn't explain further. 'I'm sorry.'

'Because when I first heard a man screaming...' Dulcie stopped too late. 'That is, when I *thought* I heard someone yell.'

'Maybe we should admit you.' The doctor had woken up now. 'Let me get the attending.'

'Please.' Dulcie jumped off the examining table. She wasn't sure what her rights were, but surely they couldn't – wouldn't – detain her on the basis of something her boyfriend said. 'Maybe I misinterpreted something I saw, but really, I'm fine.'

He paused, considering her request. 'Well.' He looked at Chris. 'Will you be with her?'

Chris nodded.

'I'd like you to come in again tomorrow,' the young doctor said finally. 'I would simply have you under observation for tonight anyway. But you–' he turned back toward Chris – 'you've got to keep checking on her. If she seems to be sleeping too heavily or you have any trouble waking her at any point, call nine one one.'

Dulcie was pulling her boyfriend through the door before he could reconsider. 'Chris, please,' she said as soon as she got him outside. 'We've got to go to the police.'

'Dulcie, what?' He seemed about to turn back into the brightly lit health center, when she grabbed his hand. 'I'm worried about you.'

'And I'm worried about that man I saw.' She

31

stopped, trying to figure out how best to explain what she saw, and then just launched into it. 'So, no, I don't understand it,' she finally concluded. 'But I know what I saw and more to the point, I know what I heard.' She shuddered, remembering that blood-curdling shriek, and looking up at her boyfriend found herself once again contemplating the unthinkable. 'What gets me is that you didn't hear anything.'

Chris only shook his head. But since he was no longer protesting, Dulcie took his hand and started walking up Garden Street to where the campus police were based. They were only a few blocks away when he found his voice.

'Dulce, I don't think this is the best idea.'

She didn't stop walking. For one thing, it was too cold.

'Dulcie, will you think about it for a minute?'

'Think about what?' She glanced over. Despite the bright moonlight, he didn't look lupine. 'About not reporting a crime?'

'You don't know what you saw.' His legs were so much longer than hers, he didn't have to strain to keep up, but Dulcie still thought he was a bit too out of breath. 'Dulcie, please?'

'Chris.' She stopped now and turned toward him. 'Do you have something you want to tell me?'

'Just that I don't want you to get hurt.' He looked so sad suddenly that Dulcie wavered. So what if he was ... not what she had first thought him to be. She still loved him.

But that didn't mean she could stop being a responsible citizen. And so she walked that last block and pushed the door open. He could follow or not; she didn't turn to see.

'Hello.' She walked up to the uniformed officer at the counter. 'I would like to report a crime.'

Twenty minutes later, she was grateful that Chris had in fact followed her into the building. In between trying to explain what she had seen and heard and why she had run toward what had appeared to be a horrible situation, she'd become dizzy again.

'She hit her head when she fell.' Chris must have seen her swaying and helped lower her into a chair. 'The doctor at the health services wanted her to stay overnight.'

'Maybe that would have been a good idea,' the uniformed cop answered drily. 'Better than rushing into a wild-dog attack.'

'They weren't ... oh, never mind.' Dulcie lean-ed forward, hoping the nausea would pass. When she sat back up, Chris and the cop seemed to have come to an agreement.

'Thanks.' She saw Chris mouth the word as the cop picked up the phone.

'What?' Dulcie didn't have the energy for any more words.

'He's called a cab for us, Dulcie.' He helped her to her feet. 'We're going home.'

It took the last bit of her strength to get up the stairs, but the greeting she got from Esmé made it worthwhile.

'Wow,' said the little cat, rubbing against her ankles. Dulcie couldn't resist. She scooped Esmé into her arms and buried her face in thick fur.

The deep rumble of her purr was more than soothing; it felt like a validation that she had not only been brave, earlier that evening, but right.

'You understand, don't you, Esmé?' Chris had gone to get her a glass of water, leaving her alone with their pet. 'I know what I saw – and I had to try.'

'I know, little one.' The voice that responded was deeper than that purr. Older, too. *'But we have senses other than sight, and sometimes even the heart may be misled.'*

SIX

The Howl pursued her like a beast possessed, breaking into her solitude as a warning of the fiend to come. Like a cry from Hell, that demonic Wail echoed in the night, an aggrieved Bay that drew strength from the Thunder, seeming to grow in volume e'en as it rose, like a soul in agony. E'en as it sounded again and again. The wolves were coming. The damn'd Beasts were at the Gate. She could hear their Cry, the howling. Shaking her...

Even without the nightmare, Dulcie would have slept badly. Chris seemed intent on waking her every few minutes. And although he cited the doctor's warning – *don't let her slip into a deep sleep* – Dulcie thought him a bit overzealous in its practice.

'Chris, I'm allowed to get some sleep,' she protested finally, after he once again shook her back to consciousness.

'You were tossing and turning,' Chris answered, looking concerned.

'I was dreaming.' She buried her face in the pillow. 'Let me sleep,' she mumbled.

Whether or not he could make out her words, her intent must have been clear because he lay down next to her and she could hear him sigh. She should apologize, she knew that. He was only doing what he thought was right. If only that last dream hadn't been quite so vivid. If only she hadn't woken to the thought that one of the wolves was pawing at her.

'*Is being touched so bad?*' She started at the voice and felt Chris stir beside her.

'Mr Grey?' She barely whispered his name. If Chris had already fallen back to sleep, she shouldn't wake him. Besides, she treasured the idea of having a private conversation with her spectral visitor. 'That is you, isn't it?'

The low rumble of a purr greeted her, and she smiled.

'*You welcome some contact.*' The rebuke was clear, despite the voice's warmth. '*What difference lies in the touch?*'

The image of a paw came into Dulcie's mind. She could almost feel the cool leather pad against her cheek.

'That's different, Mr Grey.' She didn't want to argue, but he had to understand. 'A house cat and a wolf...' She paused, unsure how to continue.

'*Mrrrup?*' The question was clear.

'I know, Mr Grey. Even if Chris is a wolf, he's still Chris.' She stopped, unsure of how to continue. 'At least, I think that's what you're trying to say. Is that it?'

But before her feline visitor could respond, Chris had turned. Flinging one arm over her, he nestled in beside her. Even through the pillow, she could hear his gentle snoring. Or was that a purr?

By the time Esmé joined them, curling up on the bed beside them, Dulcie was sound asleep.

36

SEVEN

After the previous night's fiasco, Dulcie didn't expect anything from the police. In fact, at first she suspected the voice on the phone to be pulling a prank.

'You're who?' She blinked at the receiver, which she'd grabbed on the first ring. Chris was still snoring gently.

'Officer Tomley. I took your report last night?' She vaguely recalled a portly young man in a uniform. 'I have some photos I'd like you to look at.'

'Today?' Photos of what, was what she had meant to ask. Surely they wouldn't expect her to ID a victim. To look at horrible wounds...

'At your convenience.' The voice on the other end of the line didn't sound distressed or hurried. 'I'm on duty until ten, but if that doesn't work for you, I'm sure the next desk officer will be able to help.'

His lack of concern as much as anything else woke her fully. Promising to be there within the hour, she slid out from under the covers to start the day.

'Mrrup?' Esmé met her in the kitchen.

'Yes, of course.' Dulcie had been reaching for her own cereal bowl, but she put it down to get

37

the cat's dish.

'Plus ça change...'

Dulcie was so startled, she nearly dropped the can. 'Esmé?'

'Oui?' The wide green eyes that looked up at her couldn't be more innocent.

'Did you just speak French to me?'

In response, the little cat simply rubbed against her shins and purred. And so Dulcie popped the can's lid, emptied it into the dish, and set it on the floor.

'What did you mean, anyway?' she asked. 'The more things change? I haven't been doing anything different around here.'

Esmé ignored her, intent on her food.

'I haven't.' Dulcie couldn't help feeling a little defensive. 'If anything, it's Chris who is changing.'

Nothing. But since she no longer had any appetite for her own breakfast, Dulcie donned her coat and headed out into the cold.

She was halfway into the Square when her phone rang. Hoping it was Suze, she reached into her bag. She paused to pull her glove off with her teeth before noting that the caller wasn't her friend. Instead, it was departmental headquarters, which meant – most probably – Thorpe.

'Good morning, Mr Thorpe.' She pulled the glove from her mouth and struggled to keep her voice even. If he was calling to see if she'd signed up for that seminar, she was going to lose it.

'Ms Schwartz.' In the pause that followed,

Dulcie pulled a strand of wool from her lip. 'You sound a bit ... fuzzy.'

'Sorry.' She wiped her mouth with the back of her hand. 'Is that better?'

'We need to talk about this spring.' His non-answer was his response. 'About Commencement.'

'Commencement?' Dulcie didn't mean to sound dim, but it was hard to think about the June ceremony on this frigid winter day.

'Is there an echo on this line?'

Dulcie couldn't tell if her adviser was seriously asking or simply being rude, and so she held her tongue.

'Because, if you expect to be part of the ceremony, we really should begin to talk about your defense.'

At that, Dulcie could no longer be silent. 'Defense? But Mr Thorpe, this spring is too—'

'Yes, yes.' Her adviser sounded as if she had already made her case. 'We've been through this before, Ms Schwartz. It's only natural to be a bit nervous.'

'But that's not...' She heard herself sputtering. 'It's not that I'm not ready. I mean, I'm not, but it's because the work isn't ready—'

'As I've said, it's quite natural—'

'No!' She was yelling now. A cyclist looked over, concerned. 'I'm not done yet! I still have work to do.'

'Well, then.' Thorpe didn't sound fazed by her outburst. 'You really ought to get cracking then, Ms Schwartz. Have you considered that seminar?'

It was only through an extreme force of will that Dulcie was able to be civil after that. It helped that she was nearing the Square by this point and was able to plead a more pressing engagement. At least, it should have helped.

'More pressing than your dissertation, Ms Schwartz?' Thorpe's voice positively dripped disbelief. 'I doubt anything in your present day is more pressing than your entire academic future.'

'I'm due at the campus police headquarters.' Never before would she have thought she'd be relieved to say such a thing. 'I've been called in as a witness.'

So grateful was Dulcie for the escape that she momentarily forgot her dread about the upcoming meeting. For while she didn't understand what had happened, she knew what she had seen. Could a pack of feral dogs – she didn't dare say the word 'wolves' aloud, not in the light of day – carry a man off without leaving even a trace? Had that poor man, or some part of him, been found?

EIGHT

It must be the job. Dulcie could conjure no other explanation for why she had been greeted with a smile once she made her way into the police headquarters and asked for Officer Tomley.

'Right this way.' Tomley had led her in without any kind of warning or show of concern. Fatigue, she told herself. Or simply the wear and tear of too many violent interactions. The man must have lost any natural sense of shock or horror years before. 'Please.' He motioned to a chair in one of the small interview rooms she knew too well. 'Take a seat.'

Dulcie did and removed her gloves. Her hands had gotten unaccountably cold since she had arrived, but it seemed wrong to keep them on when, undoubtedly, she would have to sign some kind of a statement, perhaps even swear an oath about what had occurred the night before. Tomley didn't seem to notice how she rubbed her hands together, however, as he pored over a thin folder in his hands.

After about a moment, he seemed to find what he wanted. 'Ah, this will do,' he pulled out a photograph and paused.

Dulcie braced herself. This would be when he would warn her. When he would ask if she

41

needed a female officer to stand by. She wondered if she had done the right thing in not waking Chris. If she had to view the bloody remains of a slaughtered stranger, it would help to have someone she loved close by.

Instead, the portly cop simply laid the photo face up before her. 'Is this who you saw last night?'

She looked down at the photo. It was the man – the long-haired stranger – she had seen on the street last night. But this was not a crime-scene photo. Instead, it was a close-up, dramatically shot, with that thick mane lit so that it glowed. She nodded with relief as she picked it up to examine it more closely.

'Yes, that's him.' Until the words came out, she hadn't realized she was holding her breath. 'Thank you,' she added as she placed the photo gently back on the table. Poor man. He had been rather handsome. Looking up at the round-faced cop before her, she found herself comparing the two and silently rebuked herself. This officer might not be as good-looking as the stranger, but he had been kind. Asking her to identify the victim from a 'before' photo had been both considerate and professional, and she kicked herself for thinking that anybody here would have done otherwise. That smile must be how he dealt with the public, his way of making himself – and the crimes he must often have to help people with – seem a little less daunting.

'Has he...?' She wasn't sure how to ask her next question. 'Has he been found?'

'He has indeed.' If anything, Tomley's smile

grew broader. Shock, Dulcie figured. Of course, it was always possible the man was a sadist. She recoiled slightly, pulling her hands from the tabletop back into her lap. 'And, believe me, we aren't taking this lightly.'

'Excuse me?' Her voice came out as a croak, and she swallowed. 'He's – he's alive?'

The smile disappeared. 'For now.'

Dulcie heard herself gasp. Officer Tomley did, too. 'I'm sorry, Miss,' he said quickly, as he reached for her. 'It's okay.'

Dulcie shook her head, confused. She heard a buzzing and felt a strange chill running up her spine.

'It was a prank,' Tomley was saying. 'It wasn't real. This ... this "victim" you were so worried about? He's an actor. What you saw was part of some play they're doing. Only they're doing parts of it out on the street, trying to get audiences interested.'

The chill was almost physical – a brush, a soft touch – climbing to the base of her neck.

He was shaking his head now, his mouth set in a firm line. 'The most we can get them for is performing on the street without a license, but someone really ought to consider pressing charges. You're not the only one who was frightened, Miss. We had several complaints. Some people really thought they saw a man turning into a wolf.'

NINE

'You saw Heath Barstow?' Trista's smile looked positively lupine as she hovered. Dulcie had barely made it to the departmental offices before collapsing, and while Nancy plied her with coffee and donut holes, Trista did the same with questions. 'Up close?'

'Close enough.' Dulcie accepted another donut hole and a napkin from Nancy, and turned to her with a smile. 'Thanks.' The sugar was working; she felt a little less light-headed than she had. And angrier. 'What a jerk.'

'He's an artist,' Trista corrected her, a gleam in her eye. 'A genius of the stage.'

Dulcie rolled her eyes.

'Dulcie, are you sure you should be out of bed?' Lloyd was looking at her funny as he repeated the question Nancy had asked when she'd first shown up.

As she had before, she nodded in reply. 'I'll go get checked out later, I promise. It was just a shock, that's all.'

'I'd heard that they were staging scenes in the Square, but I couldn't find out when or where.' Trista was shaking her head. 'And it was realistic?'

'Too much so.' Dulcie took a sip of her coffee.

44

Nancy had put extra sugar in this, too. 'Trista, it was scary.'

'Scary good, I gather.'

'Scary.' Dulcie wanted to leave it at that, but honesty compelled her to continue. 'I've had a lot on my mind, I know, and that made me, well, it may have predisposed me to see things in the worst light, but still...'

'You don't have to explain,' Nancy interrupted, giving Trista a hard look. 'You thought someone had been hurt, and you ran to help. That speaks well of you.'

'Thanks, Nancy.' Dulcie felt herself warmed by the praise, as well as the sweet, hot drink.

'But...' Trista started to protest, as Nancy walked back to her desk.

'But nothing,' Lloyd cut her off. 'Seeing something on the street is very different from seeing it in a theater.'

'Yeah.' Trista nodded. 'That's true.'

'I'm thinking I don't even want to go.' Now that she was feeling better, Dulcie was getting angrier. 'Free or not, it's not like I don't have better ways to use my time.'

'Wait, what?' Trista voiced the question, but Lloyd was staring at her, too. 'You don't want to go in with us on tickets?'

'Sorry, no.' Dulcie drained her mug. 'They said they'd give me a pair. I think the police maybe pressured them into it. But, I don't know ... a disco version of *Metamorphosis*?'

'Dulcie...' Trista started to object, but Lloyd cut her off again.

'I know what you mean,' he said. 'From what

45

I've read, it is bringing in the crowds, but nobody...' He paused and glanced at Trista. 'Very few people are saying it's great art.'

'That's the knee-jerk reaction against what is perceived as popular culture...' Trista was off on a rant, but Dulcie jumped in.

'Would you want them?' Dulcie asked.

Trista looked so shocked that Dulcie wondered if her friend hadn't understood. 'I really can't take an evening off. Besides, I can't see Chris wanting to go after he hears the full story of what happened last night.'

'I...' Trista was not usually at a loss for words. Lloyd looked about to step in, but the pierced blonde recovered herself. 'No, thank you, Dulcie.' She swallowed. 'You were the one who was discomfited. You deserve those tickets.'

Dulcie couldn't help but smile, just a little, at Trista's choice of words. Her friend was trying. 'Well, do you want to come with me?'

Trista looked at her, about to ask.

'I've been told that Mr Barstow wants to meet me. He's going to apologize personally.'

At that, Trista was struck totally speechless.

'Come on.' Dulcie grabbed her friend's hand. 'You can come, too.' She looked at Lloyd.

'No, thanks!' He backed away. 'If I met Heath Barstow without taking Raleigh, I'd never hear the end of it.'

'Dulcie, are you sure?' Trista was almost whispering as the two left the building. 'I mean, he wants to meet you.'

'Tris, I don't care about this guy. You do.' To Dulcie it seemed obvious. What she didn't say out loud was that this would make it easier to palm the tickets off on her friend once she actually had them in her hand. 'But let's hurry. I've got a section in twenty minutes.'

Trista didn't need any more urging, and soon Dulcie found herself panting to keep up.

'Tris, wait!' she called, as they passed the corner of Bow Street. 'Let me just...' She stopped and turned, her eyes drawn to the opening of the alley.

Trista turned back. 'Is this where you saw them?'

Dulcie nodded, expecting her friend to object to the delay.

'Huh.' Instead, her friend looked around. 'Mind if I check it out?'

Dulcie felt a strange reluctance but followed along as her friend walked down the now well-lit sidewalk.

'Is that it?' Trista pointed down the alley, and Dulcie nodded. 'Cool.' Trista's voice had fallen to a reverential whisper, and Dulcie was just about to suggest they move on when Trista grabbed her hand. 'I think I see it.'

'What?' Dulcie heard her own voice growing sharp. 'There's nothing here, Tris. And I've got a section.'

'No, wait.' Taking Dulcie's hand, Trista led her into the alley. 'See?'

Dulcie didn't, not at first. She was staring at the pavement, looking for the blood that couldn't be there. For the tufts of hair or fur that she expected.

Then Trista pointed. 'Up here.'

47

It was a brick wall, like any other. Except –
yes, Trista was right – there was something
funny about it. The pattern didn't quite...

'There's a space here.' Dulcie stepped up to the
wall, which ran the length of the alley. Non-
descript red brick, the stuff of which Cambridge
was made. Except that the first part, near the
street, wasn't the solid barrier she had, at first,
taken it to be. Instead, part of it angled out, the
bricks growing smaller even as they extended
into the alley, so that her sense of perspective
didn't see it coming closer. And behind it, the
remainder of the wall – its bricks carefully sized
– or, no, painted – to match. Between the two
segments a small niche where a man could easily
hide. And, Dulcie saw as she approached, a door,
from which a pack of 'wolves' could emerge and
just as quickly escape.

'Well, I'll be...' Dulcie ran her hand along the
carefully painted *trompe l'oeil*. 'Did you know
this was here?'

Trista shook her head. 'I'm guessing it's a back
door to URT. I know they did a ton of renova-
tions when they took over the building.'

'It's pretty ingenious.' Up close, Dulcie could
see the level of detail involved. The 'bricks' were
individually speckled; the 'mortar' painted darker as the front section extended, to more closely
match the shadowed lines on the back wall. All
together, it was almost enough to make her
believe in the illusion. Except for one thing.

'Trista, the officer who told me about this?'
She turned to make sure she had her friend's
attention. 'He said other people saw something,

48

too.'

'Well, you weren't the only one caught out. And they were good.'

'No,' Dulcie objected. 'He didn't say that someone else thought a man was attacked. He said that someone saw a person – a man – turning into a wolf.'

'As I recall, in the Ovid...' Trista looked like she was readying a case. Just then, a church bell rang. It was ten o'clock. 'Come on.' Trista grabbed her hand. 'Do you want to be late for your section or not?'

Dulcie let herself be dragged out of the alley and around the corner to what indeed proved to be the front of the URT. Dulcie shook her head, momentarily unmoored by her memories. The University Repertory Theatre – URT – was as unlike the old revolutionary bookstore as a renovation could make it. In place of the familiar brick storefront, Dulcie saw chrome and glass, and where decades of flyers for sit-ins and lectures had left their scotch-tape smudges, now a large full-color poster advertised *Changes: The Metamorphosis Musical*. 'A Triumph!' ran one huzzah, above an illustration of a well-endowed nymph turning into a tree – or vice versa. 'See it now!' read another banner, over a set of glass doors that reflected the morning light in a way that made Dulcie's head ache again.

'So this is the Hurt,' Dulcie muttered. Trista shot her a look, and Dulcie bit her lip. At least she hadn't called the new theater by its other nickname: 'the Urp'. But to keep the peace, she reached for the doors – and found them locked.

49

Peering in showed nothing: the glass could have been painted black for all Dulcie could tell. But Trista found a small buzzer set into the frame and punched it, eagerly, twice.

'They're not here.' Dulcie took her hand to stop her from pressing it again. 'Come on, Tris.'

'Third time's the charm.' Trista twisted away and, as she did, she gasped. Dulcie turned, too, and saw why. A golden head had appeared inside the door and appeared to be floating toward them. She stepped back, but the head grew closer.

'It's him!' Trista sounded happy, rather than scared.

The door swung open, and Dulcie gasped – and started laughing. The floating 'head' was the stranger, his long hair shining like spun gold and his face lightened with a strange metallic powder of some sort. It was his black turtleneck and pants that had made his face appear to be suspended in the darkened interior. In the daylight, she could see a slim man, slight really, dressed for an illusion.

'Ladies?' He beckoned them in with one long white hand. The other, Dulcie was pleased to see, rested on a light switch, which the actor flicked on, revealing a small lobby, painted black. 'Please allow me to introduce myself. I am Heath Barstow, principal of the University Repertory Theater.' He paused – Dulcie suspected he usually got applause at this point. 'I assume one of you is Ms Dulcinea?'

'Dulcie,' she corrected him automatically. 'Dulcie Schwartz. And this is my friend Trista.'

'Charmed.' He took her hand and bent over it. Without thinking, she pulled it away, provoking a giggle from Trista.

'Don't mind her,' she said. 'She's still creeped out by your street theater from last night. Now she's talking werewolves.'

'Ah, the ultimate transformation,' said the stranger. 'Fascinating.' He looked up at that, and up close Dulcie saw that his eyes were oddly golden, too. 'We shall have to talk.'

'Um, I was told you had tickets for me?' Trista might be taken in by this theatrical stranger, but Dulcie wanted nothing more than to get to her section.

'Direct.' He smiled, his mouth shut. 'Please, follow me.'

'In for a penny, in for a pound,' Dulcie muttered, more to herself than to Trista, who had already begun to set off after the actor, who led them past a dark ticket window and down a hall through opened double doors into what had to be the main theater space. Dulcie saw a raised stage and what looked like low balconies. But instead of seats, cocktail tables and chairs littered the open floor.

'I was hoping to show you around, perhaps demystify our illusions for you.' He welcomed them into the open space with a gesture that seemed to encompass the bar, immediately to their left, as well as the leftover glitter that sparkled up from every surface. That smile again, over his shoulder, with his teeth and his own shimmer – it had to be powder – accompanying the gesture. It was, Dulcie decided, creepy. But not as strange as the faint impression she was getting. Someone else was here. Watching.

'Don't you think you should maintain some illusion?' Trista asked. 'Don't we all need a little?'

'Tris!' Dulcie whispered. She really didn't need her friend to begin flirting.

'Ah, a wise woman.' The actor turned. 'But, alas, your friend has more mundane concerns.' He had led them over to one of the cocktail tables, apparently empty of everything but a black cloth. 'And so – voila!' He fanned out his fingers and flicked his wrist, throwing a shadow that seemed to disappear into the corner of the room. Distracted by the movement, Dulcie turned. There was something familiar about that shadow. The way it moved...

'Voila,' Barstow repeated, more loudly. 'Miss Schwartz?'

'Sorry.' She turned back and caught him quickly tuck his glower back up into that smile. Once again, that stagey gesture, and this time Dulcie resisted the urge to look for a shadow. And before she could figure out how, he had an envelope in his hand. 'Dulcinea Schwartz' was inscribed on the front in an ornate script.

'For you, mademoiselle.' He bowed as he offered the envelope, and Dulcie reached forward to take it, noticing a line in the table cloth as she did so. Instead of taking the tickets, she reached over and touched what proved to be a fold in the cloth. The secret behind Barstow's little sleight of hand.

'I see you've already applied your scholar's

eye to our simple magic.'

She looked up. Barstow didn't seem annoyed, not now that he had her attention, and so she ventured a question.

'Not all of it.' How to phrase it? 'When you waggled your fingers just now,' she decided. 'You threw a shadow. I thought ... I was sure it moved on its own.'

'Oh, that.' He shook his head. 'That's not magic. That's Gus, the theater cat.'

'I thought it looked like a cat.' Dulcie fell silent, but after a moment realized that both Trista and their host were watching her. 'So, Gus,' she asked. 'For Asparagus, I assume?'

Barstow shook his head, uncomprehending. 'Our resident mouser. Management renovated, but these old buildings, you know...' He left the rest of his sentence unfinished, but seemed gratified as Trista wrinkled her nose in response.

Dulcie wasn't finished though. 'No, he's something else. I was sure, watching him move...' She let her own words trail off. Barstow was a stranger, and even Trista wasn't acting like her old friend these days.

'Our office manager, Roni, says he's a Russian blue.' Barstow's voice let his skepticism show. 'All I know is he showed up one day. But he does have his talents.'

'Oh?' Dulcie couldn't say why, but something about that shadow – the way it had moved, the way it had paused and seemed to catch her eye – made her think that vermin control was the least of them.

'You'll just have to come to our show and find

53

out.' Barstow again extended his hand. 'I hope you can make this evening's performance?'

'I...' Dulcie paused. Her plan had been to hand them off to Trista. She had no interest in the play. 'Gus is in the play?'

Barstow only smiled.

'Okay, thanks.' She reached for the envelope only to find that it had disappeared again.

'I'm afraid I will have to ask you to sign for them first.' Barstow sounded honestly disappointed as he reached under the table for a clipboard. It was an annoying trick, but Dulcie took the pen he had also pulled out from some invisible pocket, filled out the simple form, and signed it. The sooner she was out of here, the better.

The actor took the clipboard and the pen, surrendering, finally, the envelope with – Dulcie checked – two tickets for *Changes: The Metamorphosis Musical.*

'Will you be taking your enchanting friend?' Now that the business transaction was done, Barstow was again plying the charm.

'She'll be taking her boyfriend.' Trista's smile almost matched Barstow's. Great, she was flirting back.

'Well, then...' From another pocket, two more tickets emerged. Dulcie, handing back the form, couldn't help but notice how the actor held on to them for a moment too long, just as Trista took them.

Trista noticed too, for one pierced eyebrow arched up. 'Thanks,' she said.

'When shall we three meet again?' Barstow

intoned as Trista signed for her tickets. 'Tonight at eight, perhaps?'

Trista might be tickled, but Dulcie had had enough. 'Thanks, Mr Barstow.'

'Please, call me Heath.' He gave them a mischievous look. 'And are you sure about the tour?'

'Yes, thanks.' Dulcie grabbed Trista's sleeve. 'We're both late as it is.'

'Well, then.' Another wave of the hand, and he led them back into the lobby.

'Good goddess, can you believe that?' Dulcie hurried her friend out to the street. 'So affected.'

'Yes.' Trista seemed lost in thought, even as they emerged into the daylight. 'And yet effective. You may be right, Dulcie. I think that man is a wolf.'

TEN

To seem and yet not to seem. With brave heart, she faced the Night, holding still her quaking Hands lest they, too, betray her Heart. The very Dark held no Terrors, enveloping in its inky folds only absence – of light, of Friend, and Succor. 'Twas that which could not be viewed by merest Mortal which had turned her very Breath cold in her chest. Within the Shadows such a Creature as would do her harm, a demonic Beast as would steal away her very Soul, all while Seeming friend and acting Foe.

Dulcie made herself stop reading. All morning she'd been driving herself crazy looking for this passage, one paragraph buried deep in the surviving pages of a fragmentary masterpiece. Months before, she'd written about it, deconstructing its references as Thorpe had requested.

Some of that was easy. *To seem rather than to be.* The phrase was Machiavelli's, an inversion of Cicero. And although Dulcie hadn't read philosophy since her undergrad years, she found the source easily enough. In context, it made sense. The passage, from the misunderstood Gothic novel *The Ravages of Umbria*, referred to a supposed noble, one of the protagonist's suitors. He was what Trista would have called 'a handsome devil', and though Dulcie would have placed a different emphasis than her friend would, she knew the reading would be accurate.

In *The Ravages*, the work that formed the basis for Dulcie's thesis, the noble – like several other suitors for the heroine's hand – proves untrustworthy. Worse, in classic Gothic typing, he seems to have a demonic streak. Dulcie would never know for sure – less than two hundred pages of the book remained – but she believed he was true evil, an incubus sent to seduce and destroy the virtuous and independent Hermetria. He might, Dulcie suspected, have been based on a real character in the female author's life. At the very least, he served to send up the overinflated reverence with which the gentry were held in England as the rest of the world, Old and New, exploded into revolution.

Her reasons for looking up the passage now were far less worldly. That actor, Heath Barstow, had disconcerted her. It wasn't just his practiced flirtatiousness, although Trista's wholehearted response had been distressing. Nor even the sleight of hand that he used to make the simplest transactions showy. He was, after all, an actor, and at some level he was probably making a pitch for his show. No, there was something else about him – something Dulcie didn't trust. She had hoped that this passage, once she found it, would give her some kind of a handle – advice, even – on how to understand the mercurial man. Instead, it had just made her more wary. If it hadn't been for that cat, Dulcie would not even consider going back tonight. As it was, well, she wanted to be careful.

'Ms Schwartz?' Dulcie looked up. She'd gotten to her office early, to give herself time to dive into her notes before her posted hours began. But before she could warn off the wan-looking undergrad in her doorway, she caught sight of the clock. A half-hour had passed since then, and she was on duty.

'Please, come in.' She reached to take the pile of books off the one guest chair by her desk. 'Have you been waiting long?'

'I didn't want to bother you.' Tessa. That was it. From her English 10 section. 'But I did want to ask about the reading.'

Dulcie smiled to encourage her student to continue. Tessa Rayne, the bespectacled young woman before her, was a good student, if a bit shy. And English 10 – the year-long survey course of early American literature – could be daunting. At least they were finally past all those early Puritan sermons.

'I was wondering about the Hawthorne actually.' Tessa tossed one long braid over her shoulder to get it out of the way as she pulled a notebook from her bag and began leafing through it. 'About his moral stance.'

'Ah, yes.' Well, maybe they never did get past the Puritans, Dulcie thought. 'He can be a bit intense. That's one reason why we're reading from his papers and not just *The Scarlet Letter*.' Given her druthers, Dulcie decided, she'd have banned that short novel from the syllabus. For all its supposed moral complexity, she found it both dull and didactic.

'Well, that's just it.' Tessa, her brown eyes huge behind thick glasses, blinked down at the page. 'I was reading this bit here, and I couldn't help but wonder. Do you think he's having a bit of fun with us?'

Dulcie took the notebook and read. The passage wasn't from the author's best-known work, and it took her a moment to place it. '*The Blithedale Romance*, of course,' she said aloud. 'A work after my own heart.' It wasn't entirely true, but Hawthorne's dark romance at least had some of the characteristics of a true Gothic, complete with a good romance and some supernatural chills.

'Well, I was wondering about the narrator,' said Tessa. 'I mean, the point of view, of course.'

'Of course.' Poor girl, she was learning the lingo, but Dulcie couldn't help but regret the slow submergence of her more natural approach.

'Anyway, I couldn't help but wonder—'

Dulcie cut her off. 'I know,' she said, wanting to save the undergrad from struggling further. 'It changes halfway through. Some have cited this as an inconsistency and used it to disqualify the work, but the more widely accepted reading is—'

'No, it isn't that,' Tessa broke in, then bit her lip. 'I mean, I'm sorry. But what I was really wondering is, if it's real.'

Dulcie shook her head, not understanding what the girl in front of her meant.

'I mean, maybe it's a trick and this is, like, the reveal?' The big brown eyes blinked behind the thick lenses. 'Maybe the narrator doesn't change? Maybe, like, they're one and the same?'

Dulcie opened her mouth and closed it several times before she realized that the undergrad was staring. 'That's a reading I have not heard before,' she acknowledged finally. 'And it may have some merit to it.'

This was when Dulcie really hated her schedule. She should have reread the book, she knew that. But with so much of her own work pressing, she had trusted on memory to see her through.

'I found one paper from Yale that supports the theory.' Tessa seemed not to have noticed Dulcie's flustered state. 'And, anyway, I was wondering ... it's not in the reading, but do you think I could do my midterm paper on it? I mean, see if there's any way I can make the case?'

'Most certainly.' Dulcie could say this with confidence. She'd be the one grading the paper. 'I'd be interested in reading it,' she added, honestly. 'Do you have a title in mind?'

Tessa nodded enthusiastically, her braids bobbing. 'Seeming Otherwise,' she said.

ELEVEN

'Chris, please.' Dulcie nudged her boyfriend. 'They're starting.'

'How can you tell?' He didn't look up. Chris had, as she expected, protested against coming once she had told him about the stunt behind her accident. However, her insistence – and the free tickets – had won him over. To a point. Still, even with the music playing, she could hear Esmé's aggrieved mew as his phone powered down.

'Look.' He did, and she pointed. 'The waiters have all lost their trays.'

'So much for my beer.' He pocketed his phone just as a hand appeared between them, depositing a frosted pint on their table.

'How did you do that?' Chris turned to the waitress, a petite blonde whose bobbed curls caught the faint stage light. She only smiled and backed away.

'It's the lighting,' Dulcie explained, as she watched the server recede. 'They wear that matte black and these lights only pick up where they have powdered their hands and faces.'

'But...' Chris had turned, too, as the room went even darker. Whatever question he may have left was lost as the man at the next table turned and

61

angrily shushed him.

'Sheesh, you'd think we were at a real theater.' Chris leaned in to Dulcie's ear. She only dared smile back, but she took his hand – his real, unpowdered hand – as the show began.

'Ladies and gentleman, beasts and fowl...' It was the pretty blonde who had brought Chris's beer. Now speaking on the raised stage, she had donned a simple white gown over her black top and leggings. Behind her, Dulcie could make out movement – other black-clad actors, she guessed – and before she knew it, the actress was winding up what seemed to be both explanation and introduction. 'Let the transformation begin!'

'Well, this could be fun.' Chris leaned forward to whisper in her ear. 'But how are you feeling, Dulcie? Are you sure you don't want a drink, some water or a Diet Coke?'

A thunderclap cut off Dulcie's response, and before she could try again, the music kicked in.

'It's raining men...' That blonde had reappeared beside them, singing along with the recording. While her voice wasn't much – high and a little breathy – she threw herself into the performance, squeezing her eyes closed and throwing her head back. Dulcie was enjoying it until she stood up, those blue eyes sparkling, and wrapped her arms around Chris as the chorus ended. Before either of them could object, however, the performer had twirled off to the next table, the pleats in her white gown swinging behind her. *'Hallelujah, it's raining men!'*

Chris raised an eyebrow, but Dulcie just shook her head. It had to be something to do with the

Creation but to call this a loose interpretation was like, well, calling Esmé a scholar. Besides, she had no time to explain. Another thunderclap brought the number to an abrupt end – and served as the cue to summon all the dancers back to the stage. The beat kept on, though, segueing into a pulsing instrumental as Apollo – it had to be Apollo, Dulcie figured, from the golden beams emanating from his head – was lowered into the dancers' waiting arms.

'Oh no.' Chris's voice carried in the lull, and in a moment she saw why. The wires lowering the actor seemed to have caught, tipping his gilded 'chariot' at an awkward angle.

'Don't worry. That's got to be the next act.' Dulcie leaned over to reassure him. 'It's Apollo's son who crashes.'

'My son!' Dulcie sat upright. The actor – Heath Barstow – must have heard her. 'And where is the nymph who would bear me such a son...'

But, no. Apollo embraced one of the dancers – a nymph? – with more gusto than the role seemed to require. It was the blonde who had doubled as their waitress, and, despite her size, she pushed the long-haired actor off with enough force that he skipped back a step. She'd almost missed her cue, Dulcie saw, as the chorus began twirling again and she jumped to join them. The song had morphed into an amped-up version of 'Mad About the Boy', and despite the punishing volume, Dulcie found herself trying to make out the words.

She was distracted by Chris, who seemed to like the production even less than she did. 'Oh, hell,' she thought she heard him say, as he grabbed the fake candle off their table. 'I must have—'

Dulcie missed his next words as he shoved his chair out of the way and ducked under their table, earning a scowl from the couple to their right. Dulcie returned their stare and jumped off her chair to join her boyfriend. 'What is it?'

Boom-bah! Boom-bah! Boom-bah! The music was painfully loud, too loud for her voice to be audible under the table. She reached over to get his attention.

'Ow!' He looked up so quickly he hit his head. Dulcie saw feet turning in their direction. 'It's my wallet,' Chris yelled. 'It's gone.'

'What?' Dulcie sat back – and felt a hand on her shoulder as the pounding beat gave way to a synthesizer interlude.

'Never fear, mortals.' Their blonde dancer/waitress again, her face sticky with sweat and glitter. 'You rule here, while we divine are merely your fools.' With a smile, she bowed, offering her hand. In it, she held Chris's wallet.

'Chris Sorenson, please!' The quieter keyboard music was interrupted as a voice boomed from above, and they both looked up. Barstow, this time wearing an oversized crown, was back on stage. 'Dear mortal sir, your presence is requested. Please grace our stage, though I fear we may be bested.'

'Oh, man.' Chris let the waitress help him to his feet and, still holding on to her hand, followed her to the stage.

'It's all in fun.' Dulcie whirled around to find

64

herself face-to-face with a pair of glasses. 'It's part of the act,' said the woman attached. Seeing that she looked rather normal – brown hair, no glitter – Dulcie hesitated. 'I'm with the company.' The dark-haired woman must have seen Dulcie's scowl. 'Sorry if we scared you. Usually people don't notice, you see.'

'Huh.' Dulcie allowed the other woman to give her a hand up. For a moment, she found herself wondering why this woman, with her tied-back hair and oversized glasses, wasn't the one to take Chris's hand, rather than that pretty, glittery blonde.

'Please, let us comp your drinks for the night.' The brunette must have seen something on Dulcie's face. She nodded to the bar, before turning back to Dulcie. 'Champagne?'

'Uh, thank you.' A wave of self-consciousness washed over Dulcie. Of course, this woman was a manager of some kind. The blonde was just a performer, a pretty woman acting out a role. Another nod to the bar, and a second waitress/actress, this one in a green gown, came running over with a bottle and two flutes. The dark-haired woman took the bottle as if to open it as the waitress – a muse? another nymph? – skipped off. Dulcie put her hand on the brunette's forearm. 'Maybe we should wait until Chris comes back?'

'Chris?' Something about the brunette's grin made Dulcie turn toward the stage. Sure enough, her boyfriend was still there, seated in the throne. But before Dulcie could ask when he'd return a gasp went up from the audience.

'Look!' A woman pointed, and Dulcie looked up. There, above their heads, a tightrope appeared. It must have been there all along, Dulcie told herself, hidden in the shadows. And at one end, above the bar, a shadow appeared. No, not a shadow, a cat – a lithe and short-haired cat, almost invisible in the dark.

The music had started up again, a low, throbbing beat, and Dulcie waited for the cat to retreat. The noise, if not the crowd, would have sent Esmé scurrying. But this cat didn't seem to mind, even as other voices called out in surprise. Leaning out from his perch above the bar, he looked down at the crowd, turning back and forth as if to judge their reaction – or as if he were waiting. And then, when the murmurs had all but died down and every eye was on him, the silver cat reached out one delicate paw on to the narrow tightrope. Tentatively, as if to test it, he leaned forward, adjusting. And then he took a step, and another, until his entire body was on the tightrope, high above the audience.

The crowd gasped as one, but the cat didn't seem to notice. Putting one assured paw in front of the other, he made his way across the room, above their heads, to jump down on to the now vacant throne.

Chris had disappeared.

TWELVE

'That was a blast!' Chris had a sparkle in his eye, and not, Dulcie noted, because of the glitter that had rubbed off on to his cheek. 'That bit where she turned into a tree? And you didn't tell me they were doing magic.'

'I didn't know.' Dulcie looked at her boyfriend as if he, too, might turn into a tree. They were waiting outside the theater for their friends right after the performance, but Dulcie felt they might have come from two different shows. 'I guess I should have.'

Chris turned toward her expectantly, and Dulcie tried to explain. '*Changes* is a good title, actually. The original work, *Metamorphosis*, is all about things going topsy-turvy, the expected order being overturned,' she said. 'Like, people having more power than the gods, and, well, things changing.' She'd stopped herself before she started talking about love – the work's other theme. Things were too weird with Chris right now.

'At least we know why you thought that one guy was being attacked.' Chris didn't seem to notice her abrupt conclusion. 'I think I'd heard that one – the hunter who spies on the goddess, so she turns his own dogs on him.'

'Yeah, I guess.' Dulcie knew she was being silly. 'Here they are.'

Trista emerged, with Jerry in tow, Lloyd and Raleigh – who had used Jerry's discounted tickets – behind them. All of them were beaming, and Dulcie felt her heart sink. She had known that Trista would love the show, and Raleigh was a theater fan. But she had kind of counted on Jerry being resistant, if for no other reason than because his girlfriend seemed so smitten by the handsome lead actor.

'Tell!' Trista grabbed Chris's arm, nearly spinning him around. 'I want to hear all their secrets. Did you get to talk to Heath?'

'You were so lucky to get chosen,' added Jerry. More, Dulcie suspected, because of the blonde than because of Heath Barstow. 'Tell us everything.'

'It was crazy.' Chris looked so happy, Dulcie tried to put her own misgivings aside. She had no reason to be jealous, and if Chris wasn't upset about having his pocket picked, she should let it go. 'They said they had to,' Chris was explaining to Lloyd as they started to walk. Trista had started to steer them back to the bar they'd visited the night before. 'So I couldn't reveal anything, even if I wanted to. But when they took the hood off, I was behind the curtain.'

'Did you see the cat?' Dulcie asked. Chris might not have been a cat man originally, but he'd been won over to the breed by Esmé. 'It was pretty amazing up on that tightrope.'

'Classic misdirection.' Trista sounded sure of herself. 'We all watched it.'

68

Chris shook his head. 'There was a cat?'

'A Russian blue.' Dulcie heard herself repeating back what the actor had told her. 'At least, that's what those actors are claiming. Or, no, the office manager. Roni.'

'She's the one who sent over the Champagne.' Chris nodded in recognition. 'Roni Squires. She met me backstage and introduced herself.'

'But it was the blonde girl who led you away, right?' Jerry asked, his voice eager. Trista didn't flinch. Then again, she was blonde herself. 'Did you get to talk with her?'

'You mean Persephone?' Chris was smiling to himself at the memory.

Dulcie caught Trista's eye as her friend mimed gagging.

'Hey, that's what she said her name was.' Chris had seen her. 'She's an actress, so maybe it's a stage name or something. But that's what she said to call her.'

'Well, if that's what she said, I won't out her.' Jerry mimed zipping his lips shut.

'Come on, tell.' Chris leaned in, but Jerry only shook his head. Dulcie was beginning to get alarmed.

'Well, that's all she told me.' Chris glanced over at his girlfriend. 'Honest. She only introduced herself, really, and told me where to stand. Stuff like that.' He smiled at Dulcie. 'Which was totally fine. To be honest, I don't even think she was that into it. She seemed distracted.'

'Fight with her boyfriend.' Trista nodded, but when Chris turned toward her, she explained. 'Looked like she was mad at him, the way she pushed him off.'

'Don't you think that was because he came down awkwardly? I thought he was going to fall,' Dulcie said, trying to remember the scene. 'And she had to get into that line before they all snaked into the audience.'

'Maybe.' Trista shrugged.

'I think maybe Tris is right,' Chris chimed in. 'There was something going on between them. In fact, I was wondering if Roni was back there to keep things cool.'

'Huh.' Trista looked thoughtful. Jerry must have noticed, because he put his arm around his girlfriend. They had come to the corner where Dulcie had seen the performers on the street and as they crossed, she turned to look. A chill ran through her. Memory, she told herself. Memory or the frigid air. Here, in the crosswalk, the wind could run straight up the river. It was enough to make anyone shiver.

'So you didn't see the cat?' She asked again, taking Chris's arm. 'He was amazing. Very lithe and, well...'

'Un-Esmé-like?' He drew her close.

'I didn't want to say it.'

'She is a little butterball, isn't she?' With his arm around her, the night was neither too cold nor too scary, but she huddled closer, anyway. 'Sadly, though, no I didn't. Why don't you tell me about him?'

'What amazed me was his poise.' Dulcie didn't need a second prompt. She didn't even care that they were going back to that awful bar, or that Trista had once again commandeered their party.

'Especially considering how loud that music was. But he didn't seem to care. He was up on top of the bar and he looked down at us and then...' She was with Chris, and with her friends. It was a good night.

And then she heard the scream.

THIRTEEN

'What the...?' To his credit, Chris reacted by clutching Dulcie close, as if to protect her from whatever was out there.

'Chris! I can't breathe!' His gesture was sweet, but stifling, and Dulcie pushed away to listen. 'Oh, no – it's coming from down there.' She pointed, and they all turned. They'd gotten half a block past the crosswalk, but the sound – a woman wailing – was clear.

'Maybe it's another street theater thing?' Trista asked, the tightness in her voice belying the hope in her question.

'Maybe.' Jerry didn't sound any more convinced.

'Come on.' Dulcie had faced her own fears on that corner. If someone else was being needlessly scared ... She turned and started back the way they had come.

'Maybe we should call the police.' Chris caught up with her and was pulling the phone from his coat pocket.

'Let's see what it is first.' Trista, with Jerry in tow, caught up with them. 'Maybe it's nothing.'

'I don't know.' Dulcie had reached the corner where she had seen the attack – had been taken in, she mentally corrected herself. There had been no wolf pack. No real victim. No attack. It was deserted now, and so she turned down the street. There, ahead, lay the alley that she and Trista had explored only a few hours before. A small crowd had gathered, theatergoers like themselves, probably. Which made the chance that they would be fooled by stagecraft unlikely. Still, somewhere beyond them a woman was screaming. The cries were fainter now, and as she drew close, Dulcie could hear that each one cut off as the screamer drew in a ragged breath.

'Let me through. Let me through.' Dulcie pushed her way past a couple and stopped short, narrowly avoided stepping in a small puddle of vomit on the pavement. To her right, someone was sobbing. She heard it as if from a distance, just as she heard someone else, on her left, talking into a cellphone.

'Nine one one? I'd like to report—'

That scream again, a rising wail like the soul of the damned, forced Dulcie to focus.

There, in the alleyway, she could make out dark hair. A ponytail that was coming loose as a head bobbed up and down. A pale face, dark eyes wide and stricken behind large glasses. Roni Squires – the office manager – was on her knees, her mouth wide open as she drew in another gasping breath.

Before her, on the pavement, lay a silent, black-clad form. It was the woman who had waited on them, the nymph from the theater, her blonde curls matted down by the blood that must have come from the gaping wound in her throat.

73

FOURTEEN

'Amy!' As Dulcie stood there, frozen, another voice cried out. Heath Barstow, his hair wild, came crashing out of the back door and scooped the prone woman into his arms. 'Amy, no!'

'A lot you care!' Roni was on her feet, glaring. 'You brute.'

'No!' The blond mane lowered over the prone body. 'No.'

'Coming through.' Dulcie felt herself pushed aside by one navy blue arm, and then another, forcing her over behind one of the other on-lookers. 'Step aside, please. Sir? Sir?'

The officer was reaching down to Heath, pulling him up, away from the limp form of the actress. But the actor shook the cop off. 'No.' It was more of a moan this time. Dulcie could see his back heaving.

'Please, sir.' The cop's words were polite, but his words were clearly a command. 'You have to let us through.' He reached for the arm that now cradled the bloody body.

Another officer appeared on his far side and took his other arm. Dulcie looked away, but not so quickly that she didn't see his face. The hand-some features were distorted, the generous mouth open mid-wail. As the cops dragged him

74

to his feet, the crowd gasped. Although his black costume showed nothing amiss in the blue of the street lights, the actor's hands shone red and wet, covered in blood. Even his hair, Dulcie couldn't help but see, was tipped in it, the long blond mane darkened at its ends.

She wanted to turn away. This was a tragedy, but she had no role here. The police, the emergency personnel were on the scene, and she should let them work. She should turn away, she knew that. She should stop looking. Stop staring at the lone figure lying on the ground. At the blood, the dark stain that caught the light. The reflection was spreading. Spinning. She was falling.

Until a hand landed on her upper arm, gripping her firmly. Pulling her in.

'No!' The yell was instinctive. What happened next was not. She spun around, pulling away as she lashed out, her fist making contact with flesh.

'Ow!' Chris stepped back, dropping her arm. 'Dulcie, that hurt.'

'I'm sorry!' A space had opened around them. 'I felt someone grab me and ... I don't know.'

'Everything all right here, Miss?' Chris was eclipsed by blue: another cop, this one staring down at her.

'Yes, I'm sorry.' Dulcie shook her head to clear it. 'My boyfriend took my arm and, well, I guess I was jumpy.'

He eyed her, his forehead creasing.

'Really, Officer.' Chris appeared by his side – and stopped as the cop extended his arm in front

75

of him. 'I thought she was looking a little woozy, and I wanted to get her out of here.'

'Miss?' Brown eyes and a heavy brow.

'He's right.' Something about that glare made Dulcie feel like she was at fault. 'Really, we're fine. I was just startled.'

'Coming through.' This time it was two EMTs, both carrying large packs. Dulcie backed away from the large cop and wrapped her arm around Chris's waist. When the officer turned to look, she smiled and nodded. Chris, who had gingerly put his arm around her shoulder, seemed to be in shock.

'Let's get out of here,' Dulcie whispered up at him. To her amazement, the crowd around them seemed to have thickened. While that had the advantage of hiding the bloody scene down the alley, it made it harder to get through, and Dulcie took Chris's hand to lead him away from the carnage.

'Wait, is that a cat?' Chris had turned back toward the alley. Dulcie couldn't see over the heads around her, but he was pointing and she moved in front of him.

'There's a grey cat in the theater, but...' There, she saw him – a flash of silver-grey between the people in front of her. Behind them, the beeping of the ambulance as it pulled up to the mouth of the alley.

'Coming through, folks! Coming through.' Out the driver's side window, the driver called to move people aside. But the cat ... Dulcie pulled away from Chris and darted forward once again.

'Dulcie!' He called after her.

'Gus!' Ducking down, she pushed between the onlookers and under the arms of the large cop. The slim silver feline was frozen before her, his eyes wide and staring. Although logic told her Gus was staring at the crowd – searching, perhaps, for the source of that terrifying beep – Dulcie couldn't help but feel those green eyes were focused on her. In them, Dulcie could see the ambulance lights reflected and, well, something else. A spark of fear or recognition – or was it a message?

'Watch out, Miss.' She turned back as an EMT pushed by her, his heavy boots barely missing the stunned cat's tail.

'You watch out,' she yelled, shock turning to anger. 'Can't you see there's a cat here?'

He didn't even turn, and she found herself straining to keep her eyes on the cat. In the shadows, between the moonlight and the street lamps, his silvery-blue coat blended too well with the pavement.

She lost sight of Gus as another uniform jostled past her. The alley, already crowded, was getting packed.

'Everybody, back,' a male voice called. 'I want everybody to take a step back.' Behind them, on the street, a siren started. 'Make way.'

The cop was moving toward them, arms outstretched. Behind him, a gurney carried its covered load through to the ambulance. 'Back, everyone,' the cop kept repeating. 'Back.'

Dulcie stumbled as someone pushed, only catching herself on the rough brick wall. Somehow she'd moved to the far side of the alley.

From here, she could see down to where another officer, a black woman she hadn't noticed before, was talking to Roni. The office manager was also leaning up against the wall, staring at the ground with her hands jammed into her pockets as the officer jotted in a pad. At least she was no longer screaming.

'Dulcie?' Chris had gotten through to her. 'Can we go?'

'Just a second, Chris.' Dulcie raised her hand, motioning him to wait. 'I'm worried about Gus.'

In the far corner of the alley, she saw movement. The slim cat must have retreated as the EMTs came forward.

'Roni!' Dulcie called. 'The cat!'

The office manager looked up, her face pale behind the glasses.

'Gus!' Dulcie called again. 'He must have gotten out.'

'Miss, please.' The cop who was moving them back stood in front of her now. 'You have to go now.'

'You don't understand.' Dulcie peeked under his outstretched arm. 'Roni!'

Roni just stared at her, her face blank. 'She must be in shock,' Dulcie said to the cop. 'I've got to get the cat.'

He looked just as blank.

'He shouldn't be out. Not in this weather, not in the city.' Dulcie was at a loss. 'He must have gotten outdoors in all the fuss.'

'I'm sorry,' said the cop. But it was clear he didn't mean it as he started to push her back, his outstretched arms encompassing all the gawkers

78

who had now gathered.

'Roni!' Dulcie tried one more time. 'Gus!'

The woman with the glasses didn't hear her. But the cat did. As the cop's arm pressed against her, Dulcie saw a movement and then, out of the shadows, the delicate features of the Russian blue.

'Wait, Officer.' Dulcie reached over his arm and pointed. 'I just need to get the cat.'

As the cop turned to look over his shoulder, Gus stepped entirely out of the shadows and stood, staring up at Dulcie, his dark green eyes catching the street light's glow.

'He your cat?' The cop must have seen it too, the way those strange eyes looked up at her.

'What?' Dulcie didn't want to look up at him, didn't want to break the connection with the theater cat. 'Well, no, but he belongs inside, not out on the cold street.'

'Huh.' The cop turned slightly, clearly wavering. Dulcie bit her lip. 'Well, he's not your problem then,' the cop said. 'And I'm afraid I can't let you through.'

'But the cat...' Dulcie felt the tears rising.

'Don't worry, Miss.' The cop was moving them back, his arms barricades in the crowd. 'Looks like he's found one of his own.'

He shifted then, letting her peek over his meaty arm. The cat's advance, if not Dulcie's shouting, must have finally alerted Roni to the Russian blue's presence. Now she turned from the officer before her and knelt on the pavement. Taking her hands from her pockets, she reached for the cat before her. For a moment, they were frozen like that – Roni in black, her hands white under the blue light; the cat silver, almost glowing. And just then, the ambulance started up again, its siren beginning to wail. Gus, ears back, jumped.

'No!' Dulcie yelled. For a moment, she thought, the cat looked up at her again, those green eyes glowing in the light. Then he turned and darted away, his silver-grey form disappearing into the shadows.

FIFTEEN

'Okay, that's enough here.'

Even as Dulcie surged forward, she found herself blocked by an arm. A large arm, attached to a large man in the dark blue uniform of a city cop. 'Come on, Miss. Show's over.'

'I've got her, Officer.' Chris appeared by her side. 'She's upset. I'll take her home.'

'But...' She turned toward Chris, and he used the opportunity to throw an arm over her shoulder, pulling her around further. 'The cat...'

'Dulcie, this is a police matter.' He maneuvered her through the crowd. 'Besides, Trista and the others are waiting for us.'

'But ... Gus...'

'I'm sure the theater people will take care of him.' Chris looked around for their friends. 'You're in shock, Dulcie. Come on.'

So, apparently, was Jerry. They found their friends out on the street. Jerry was sitting on the curb, his head in his hands, Raleigh beside him. Trista, kneeling at his feet, glanced up at Chris and Dulcie.

'He knew her.' The expression on Trista's face said it all. 'He knew that girl.'

'Jerry?' Chris crouched down to talk to his friend, as Trista stood.

'No, it can't be.' Dulcie kept her voice low. 'It wasn't anyone we knew. It ... she was that actress. You know, the one who took Chris on stage.'

'Yeah, I know.' Trista bit her lip as she glanced down at her boyfriend. 'Turns out she was the "buddy" with the ticket deal. He didn't want me to know till after.' She shook her head sadly, looking positively pasty under the street lights. 'He wanted to preserve the illusion.'

Dulcie nodded, even as she wondered which illusion her friend's boyfriend had hoped to maintain. Not that it mattered now. 'It must have been quick,' Raleigh was saying. 'Her throat – she probably didn't know what was happening.'

Chris, meanwhile, was helping Jerry to his feet.

'I bet it was that actor.' Jerry bit into the words. 'Poor Amy. She didn't know this crowd. Didn't know what they were like.'

'You don't know...' Trista came to Heath Barstow's defense. 'You can't know what happened.'

'I heard what the other woman was saying, the one who found her.' He nodded knowingly. 'Barstow and Amy were a couple. And you know, most of the time when something like this happens...'

Dulcie breathed a small sigh of relief: at least Jerry and the actress hadn't been an item. Trista glowered, however, as if considering her own violent act. And Chris, ever the peacemaker, broke in.

'I think we should leave this one to the cops,

okay?' Dulcie leaned on him, grateful for his sane approach. 'I think we've all had enough excitement for one night.'

Jerry nodded, his face grim, and Trista took his arm in what Dulcie hoped was a conciliatory fashion. The friends walked silently up the street, each lost in private thoughts until the time came for them to part.

An hour later, Dulcie was still wondering if they had left too soon. Not even Esmé's attention could help. The little cat was always affectionate when the two came home after an evening out, but even repeated head butts – that soft insistent pressure, demanding to be held – couldn't calm Dulcie's shivers.

Dulcie knew she was upset over what they had witnessed. Even once Esmé was in her arms, if she closed her eyes, she could still see that dark, deep cut – the way Amy had lain there, limp, in Heath's arms. But Dulcie was also concerned about the living. Specifically, she was worried about Gus.

'The cops aren't going to look for him. They have their hands full.' She sniffed into the handkerchief Chris had given her, shifting Esmé's bulk to dab at her nose. 'I mean, they had ... they have...' She gave up, shaking her head as the tears came, and buried her face in her own pet's thick fur. At least she didn't have to explain her concern to Chris. He might know that she was reacting to everything that had come at them this evening – but he would also never ask her why she was so upset over 'a mere cat'.

'Maybe he ran back inside,' Chris suggested, following her lead. 'You know, went to hide in a favorite hiding space or something? That woman, Roni, was looking for him.'

'Maybe.' She sniffed. 'But it's more than that. He was trying to tell me something.' She could say this kind of thing to Chris.

'Sweetie?' She looked up. The doubt on his face made her worry that she had misjudged him. 'Your teeth are chattering.' He was definitely looking at her strangely. 'I don't like it.'

'It was cold out.' Dulcie hugged her own cat closer. 'And I can't help but worry.'

'Did you go to the health services?' His voice was low, but Dulcie could hear his concern. 'You were supposed to get checked out, you know.'

'I know, Chris.' She looked up. 'I'm sorry. I meant to all day – it's just, well, I feel fine.'

'Dulcie, I'm worried about you. You don't seem like yourself.'

You should talk. She bit back the words. He was speaking out of love; she knew that. Out loud, she worked to steady her voice. 'It was just a rough night. And I am worried about the cat.' She managed a smile. 'But really, Chris, I feel fine.'

'Well ... how about hot cocoa?' Chris's non-sequitur started Esmé purring. At least, something did.

'Thanks, sweetie.' As her boyfriend heated the milk, Dulcie stroked her pet, letting herself enjoy Esmé's warmth. Esmé seemed to know she need-ed comfort, and Dulcie wondered if the round feline was picking up some of her anxiety about the theater cat. 'What is it, girl? Do you want some cocoa, too?'

'I think she's glad you're giving her some attention.' Chris set her favorite mug on the place mat before her.

Dulcie was about to protest when Esmé jumped up on the table.

'No, kitty!' Dulcie grabbed for her. 'That's hot.'

Esmé jumped, in the process knocking over Dulcie's bag, which spilled its contents next to the mug.

'Dulcie!' Chris grabbed the mug, which had begun to wobble – and Esmé leaped from the table, sending her phone flying.

'Esmé!' Dulcie ducked down to retrieve the phone. Esmé glowered, tail twitching. 'I'm sorry, kitty.' Dulcie softened her tone. 'I guess I am still on edge.'

As she sat back up, Chris handed her the mug and went back to the counter to retrieve his own.

'Thanks, honey.' She sipped and found herself looking at her phone. 'Oh!'

'Too hot still?' Chris took a seat at the table and Esmé jumped to his lap. Dulcie didn't even notice.

'No, it's an email from the URT.' She clicked on it, holding her breath. 'It's probably about that poor girl.'

She paused, and Chris reached for her mug again.

'What is it, Dulcie?' he asked, his voice tensing up with concern. 'If you feel dizzy or anything...'

'No. It's not me. They – this is crazy.' She

85

looked up at him. 'It's a survey. They're asking people what they thought of the performance.' She was starting to get angry as she hit the button to respond. 'I'm going to give them a piece of my mind.'

He reached over and put his hand over hers. 'It's probably automatic, Dulce.' Esmé took the opportunity to jump back on to the table. 'You know, something that's been programmed to go out the night of a show.'

'Yeah, you're right.' She put the phone down. 'I guess I don't have any slack left.'

'Time for bed then.' He reached for her mug, and they both stood. 'And we'll see how you feel in the morning.'

'You coming?' Dulcie turned back toward Esmé. But the cat simply sat there, the light from the phone reflected in her green eyes.

SIXTEEN

The night grew wild, the Storm brew'd Clouds obscuring e'en the lambent Moon. Still, her nerve held Strong, supported in this by her helpmate in this endeavor, the faithful maid, upon whom tonight's Escape depended. For she would Flee, with the aid of this kind Lady, and ne'r more be made the Slave of one so invirtuous and so Cruel. Too long had she awaited her Release. This very night, though the heavens would scowl and glower, she would Dare, thanks be to the faithful Lady, her Demetria.

Demetria! Dulcie woke with a start. The night had indeed grown stormy. She could hear the windows rattling. But now that she was awake, any thoughts of 'fleeing' were banished. She looked over at Chris, who murmured and turned on to his side. He might be acting odd, and he certainly had been keeping a more watchful eye on her as she had gotten ready for bed. But he wasn't the focus of her dream.

No, the person she had been in her dream – a persona lifted from her reading – was in a much different kind of relationship. Thinking about it as she lay there, Dulcie wondered if she had somehow cast herself as Hermetria, the heroine of *The Ravages of Umbria*. After all, Hermetria had been betrayed, which you could sort of say was enslavement, first by her caregivers, who had stolen her family fortune, and then, more insidiously, by her companion, Demetria.

It was a theme, Dulcie was learning, that this author returned to. Some of that was the genre: Gothic novels were filled with betrayed maidens and duplicitous servants and suitors both. In the novel Dulcie was piecing together now, a second previously forgotten work by the author of *The Ravages*, the female narrator seemed to have been imprisoned, tricked into some kind of abusive relationship that must have acted like catnip on the readers of the time. Even today, it was thrilling, ever so much better than that soft-core best-seller she'd caught some of her students passing around, giggling.

In part, Dulcie suspected, that's because the protagonist in the older book had some spine. From the bits Dulcie had been able to reconstruct, it seemed she had managed to escape from her captor – at least as far as Dulcie could tell. It was frustrating to get so caught up in a book and not be able to finish it, but what she had read spurred her to work harder.

The bits she had managed to pull together told of a wild night-time chase in which the heroine found help from a stranger in grey. A still-unnamed heroine. Not, she shook her head to clear it, a woman named Demetria. That was *The Ravages*.

Dulcie slipped out of bed. Clearly, she had conflated the two works. Her dreams had been growing ever more jumbled, even before she had fallen and hit her head. Throw in her own growing suspicions that both these novels were in some way drawn from the author's life, and her confusion was almost total. What was real and what wasn't? Maybe Chris had reason to be worried about her.

'More likely it was the cocoa,' Dulcie muttered to herself as she slipped on her robe. Or maybe, she admitted silently to herself, it was Trista. More and more often these days, Dulcie found herself annoyed at her friend, and longing for the faithful buddy of old. What she didn't know was whether Trista had changed, or she had simply grown less tolerant. What she needed, she decided as she made her way into the kitchen, was some time with Suze.

Why hadn't her friend called her back? Unless she had, and Dulcie simply hadn't gotten her message. Her phone was still on the table, although Esmé had long gone, and she reached for it with a smattering of hope.

Hello Dulcie! The page that appeared at her touch wasn't what she expected, and for a moment the greeting unsettled her. Since when did her devices know her touch? As she blinked, she woke up enough to remember: she had clicked through to the URT survey, meaning to type in an angry response, before putting the phone down in disgust. That's what she was looking at now.

'Quit, please.' She knew it made no sense to talk to an inanimate object. It wasn't like the phone was a cat or something. Still, she couldn't help addressing it even as she scrolled to the bottom of the page, looking for an exit or an X to click on. 'Hello?'

Hello Dulcie! The salutation appeared again, the screen now glowing with life. *Won't you tell us about your evening with the University Rep?*

'You don't want to know,' she said, as she glided over the page. There was a 'submit' button, for after she had filled out the form. No 'quit' or 'exit'.

Hello Dulcie! This was getting annoying. To make matters worse, Esmé had woken, too, and while she had started off rubbing against Dulcie's ankles, she was now bouncing around her feet, jumping on her bare toes as if they were prey.

'Hang on, Esmé.' The little cat wanted to play, that much was clear. 'I just want to see if Suze has called. Ouch!' Not willing to be ignored, Esmé had bitten her hard. While this would usually be Dulcie's cue to pick her up, Dulcie had been trying very hard lately to follow her own advice: ignoring the cat when she misbehaved was better than rewarding the bad behavior with attention. And so she sat, tucking her bare feet beneath her, and turned her attention to the phone.

'All right, all right.' If Chris were awake, she could ask him for help. There had to be some way of getting out of this annoying program. As it was a little past two, Dulcie bowed to the inevitable. 'Seats were fine. Program was fine. Service was...' She stopped. The blonde – Heath had called her Amy – had been their waitress. Even though she'd only answered two questions, she hit submit.

Thank you for your feedback! The screen flashed, and then went blank.

The effort was worth it. When Dulcie flipped over to her voicemail, she saw that Suze had indeed called her back. The message, however, was not what she wanted to hear.

'Hey, Dulcie,' her friend had said. 'Yes, it's been too long. I'm sorry I've been out of touch. I'm caught up in this crazy credit-card fraud. Everybody thinks they can get something for free. I've got clients getting credit-card bills for thousands of dollars.' There was a pause, and Dulcie thought the message had ended. 'But call me. We'll talk. And don't give anyone your bank account info!'

Good old Suze. Dulcie should have known her long-time friend wouldn't desert her. Just the sound of her voice was cheering, and the fact that she was helping people with few other resources – her clients were the low-income patrons of a legal clinic – made her efforts seem even more worthwhile. Credit fraud. How despicable, especially when the crooks were preying on the poor and elderly. But how ... well, how peaceful, Dulcie had to admit to herself. Mean but, well, bloodless. Dulcie was beginning to feel like herself again. Esmé had calmed down, as well, and now lay curled at the base of her chair.

She listened to the message again, just to hear her friend's voice. There was no chance of calling her at this hour. Even when they had roomed together, Suze had tended to be a morning person. Dulcie had often come home from the library to find her asleep over her books. That didn't mean she couldn't respond, though.

Suze, she began the text. *Gd to hear your voice!* She paused at that point long enough for the screen to go black. This was the problem with texts, as with email. How could she tell her friend what had happened without alarming her? How could she reach out without giving her the whole picture?

Went to URT tonight. Terrible. No, that would not do. If Suze hadn't heard about that poor woman, she would think Dulcie was sharing her opinion of the play. If she had, well, she might still think Dulcie had turned particularly callous critic. She backed up over the last word.

There was a terrible ... She paused ... *incident.* That was the best word. *I saw her.* That didn't capture all of it, not by half, and she put the phone back on the table while she thought about what to say next.

This was the problem with all modern communication. People complained about the Gothics – about all pre-modern novelists, if truth be told. Said they were wordy, that they overwrote. But really, how could you explain the subtleties of a situation without giving the entire picture? Sometimes you needed to show the wind-tossed trees. Needed to feel the freezing night air and the way the dark night sky pressed in around one ill-lit area. Sometimes that was the only way to give an accurate picture, to show it all.

This wasn't writing. It wasn't telling, even. It

was typing. With a sigh, Dulcie picked up her phone again, waking it to her unfinished text.

There was a cat, she typed, and hit send.

SEVENTEEN

The next morning, everybody was talking about the murder.

'That poor girl.' Nancy was shaking her head as she poured Dulcie's coffee. 'I can't imagine what her parents are going through.'

Dulcie had ducked into the secretary's office hoping for a respite. Trista had been holding court in the student lounge, regaling their fellows with her first-hand account, and seemed to be relishing the attention. That, as well as the need-less – to Dulcie's mind – detail she was providing had driven Dulcie into the smaller room. The coffee was simply an excuse.

'I know.' It felt like poor form not to respond. Besides, the coffee was good and strong. 'Thanks.'

Dulcie took a sip and began reading the notices up on the board. Although she had managed to go back to sleep eventually, she hadn't slept well. The same dream, in various versions, kept recurring. Now as she tried to block out the sound of Trista's voice from the next room, she almost felt it had been prophetic. If only Trista would quit going on about the blood.

'And a student, too,' Nancy was saying. 'Just like you.'

Dulcie turned, about to disagree. Trista was, technically, no longer a student. As a postgraduate, she was a fellow of the college.

'And now she's gone.'

Nancy was still holding the pot. Dulcie rose to take it from her and replace it on the warming plate, when she caught herself. Nancy had not been reading her thoughts. Nor had she been talking about Trista.

'Wait, the woman who ... last night?' Dulcie wasn't sure how to ask. 'But she was an actress. A waitress and an actress.'

Nancy nodded, and Dulcie wondered if the older woman had heard her. Then with a sigh, the plump secretary leaned back against her desk and explained. 'I gather the acting was new for her. Or, well, doing it professionally was. That very nice commentator who handles the local news on NPR said this morning that she'd been working with the Tech drama department for years.'

'Wait, Tech?' Now it was Dulcie's turn to question whether she'd heard correctly. 'You mean the blonde actress – the one they found in the alley?'

Another nod. 'Yes, Amy Ralkov, that poor girl. She was a computer science major, but she was also quite taken by dramatics.'

Tech – of course. That was how Jerry knew the dead girl. The applied math concentrators here might joke about 'the vocational school down the road', but there was a ton of interaction between students, especially at the higher levels. The way Nancy said it, however, that poor girl had strayed too far from her chosen discipline.

'You make it sound like the theater is what killed her.' Blame the lack of sleep or the fact that she hadn't finished her coffee yet, but the words were out of Dulcie's mouth before she could think. As soon as she heard them, though, she stopped herself. 'Maybe it did.'

'Dulcie, what are you talking about?' She had Nancy's attention now, and Dulcie found herself scrambling to explain.

'I – we were there last night.' She'd been happy enough to be downplayed in Trista's account. Now it seemed important to explain. 'Chris and I, with Trista and Jerry and Lloyd and Raleigh. The blonde – Amy – she was our waitress, as well as an actor, a dancer, really, in the play.' With a twinge of guilt, Dulcie remembered her initial dislike of the girl – a resentment aggravated when it had become apparent that she had picked Chris's pocket. Skimming over that, she told Nancy about the seeming attraction between the pretty blonde and the lead actor.

'I think there was something going on between her and Heath Barstow,' she concluded. 'I wonder if he, well, you know...'

Nancy nodded. 'NPR also had a story on domestic abuse, though I don't think they were connected. They do say that when a woman is murdered, it makes sense to look at the boyfriend.'

Dulcie didn't know what to say to that and instead gulped down some coffee. It was still hot, and she sputtered.

'I'm sorry.' Nancy ran over with a napkin.

'I've been watching too many crime dramas, I guess. I'm sure Mr Barstow had nothing to do with it. It must have been random. A street crime...'

'The show was over.' Dulcie thought it through. 'And she was still in her costume – all black. But maybe she wore that outfit home?' An idea surfaced. 'I'm going to call Detective Rogovoy.'

'I'm glad you have time on your hands for snooping.' A male voice broke in on them: Martin Thorpe was standing in the doorway. 'I assume that means that you've finished those pages for me?'

Only then did Dulcie realize that the small crowd in the outer room had dispersed. Trista, standing behind Thorpe, shrugged in apology, and Dulcie knew she had no choice left but to get to work.

EIGHTEEN

'No.' Detective Rogovoy tended to be terse. This morning, he was being positively monosyllabic, despite Dulcie's repeated questions. 'No and no.'

'But, Detective...' It was nearly noon before Dulcie could get to the campus police headquarters. She'd rushed through her session with Mr Thorpe, in part by telling him that she had a lead on some new research. It wasn't exactly a lie. She did have some ideas – just not about her thesis.

When she'd found the portly detective at his desk, she'd been overjoyed. He, however, did not seem to reciprocate the feeling.

'But don't you think it's important?' Dulcie asked for the umpteenth time. 'I mean, Heath Barstow was clearly flirting with her, and she seemed to be rejecting him. I believe they were an item.'

'What part of "you're not involved in this" don't you understand, Ms Schwartz?' His voice betrayed his frustration. 'To be honest, neither are we.'

'But how can that be?' Dulcie stared at the craggy cop, trying to understand. 'You're the police.'

'University police.' He reached for a pile of

papers stacked on the corner of his desk. 'Now, if you don't mind...'

'But the girl ... it happened at the University Rep.' As she watched, he picked up a ballpoint. It looked like a matchstick in his grip.

'Technically, it happened in the alley behind the theater.' He clicked the pen. Dulcie half expected it to buckle. 'City property – and out of our jurisdiction.'

'Oh.' Dulcie paused, mulling over the complex relationship between town and gown. 'And it doesn't matter that the victim went to Tech?'

The slight rise of one eyebrow was encouraging. She knew something Rogovoy didn't. 'Amy Ralkov was a computer science concentrator – or major. Whatever they call them at Tech. Our friend Jerry knew her, kind of.' She paused. 'He got some friends tickets through her.'

'And did you or your friend Chris know her?' The question came out like a growl.

'No. That is, I don't think so.' She stopped again, considering this. Chris would have told her. Wouldn't he? The pretty actress had been awfully familiar with him. 'I don't know. I guess I should ask him.'

'I think you should go home.' He tapped the pen on those papers. It was going to break, Dulcie knew it would. 'This is a serious crime, Ms Schwartz. A woman was stabbed, her throat cut. We're not talking some scholarly wrangling here.'

He paused. That detail had done the trick – Dulcie had gone white. She leaned back in the visitor's chair and waited for the accompanying dizziness to pass.

'Look, Ms Schwartz.' He leaned forward, his bulk dwarfing the desk. 'I appreciate you wanting to help and that you know to come to me. But the city department is a good one, and if they need extra help, they'll call in the Staties. The Massachusetts forensics lab is one of the best in the country. I have no doubt they'll have taken statements from all of the principals at the scene, and that they'll be going over that alley and probably the entire theater with a fine-toothed comb. I do not think they will need anything from you, or they would have asked you to stay and give a statement. I think you should go back to the library or your office, or wherever it is you do your work. I think you should count your blessings that you're not involved, Ms Schwartz. For a change.'

He meant well. Still, she couldn't stop herself. 'But I *am* involved, Detective.' As he'd been talking, she'd recovered her equilibrium – as well as her memory of what she had seen and what she'd wanted to tell him. 'It wasn't just Heath or that other woman, Roni. There was...' Now that it came down to it, she felt a little embarrassed. 'There was a cat. A theater cat. Gus. And he, well, he got out.'

Dulcie paused. Most people, she knew, would think her a little odd. Detective Rogovoy wasn't most people, but still, she didn't think she could tell him what she suspected: that the silver-grey cat had been trying to tell her something. Instead, she fell back on her other concern. 'He got out of the theater, Detective. There was a crowd

100

and sirens, and with one thing and another, I'm afraid he might have panicked. It's cold out there.' She looked up at the craggy face. 'I'm worried about him.'

It was the right thing to say. With a sigh like the wind rolling down the mountain, the detective nodded. 'I'll see if they're still searching the theater.' He reached for the phone. 'If they're done and there's anyone working, you can go over and ask. Maybe he's home safe. If not, I don't think there will be any problems with you helping to look for him.'

He punched in some numbers and spoke briefly with whomever answered. 'This afternoon? After three? Okay, I'll tell her.'

'Thank you, Detective.' She waited until he had hung up.

'You're welcome.' His gruff voice was back, and he pulled the papers closer before looking up at her. 'Now, don't you have some teaching or something to do?'

NINETEEN

It was just as well, Dulcie decided, that she couldn't return immediately to the theater. Not only had she told her adviser that she was doing research, she had also reassured him that he would indeed have a draft of a chapter by Friday, which was only two days away.

'This spring, Ms Schwartz,' he'd said, as she had gathered her materials to leave. 'I wouldn't be doing my job if I let you malinger. That's not what the doctoral program is designed for.'

'It's just what the doctoral program is designed for,' Dulcie said to nobody in particular as she made her way over to the library. 'With this kind of class load, I'm amazed anyone gets a thesis written at all.'

As she crossed the Yard, church bells chimed, the sound clear and loud in the icy air. Noon – and she hadn't eaten all day. Ever since the spring semester had started, her days had been like this. Chris had even noticed that she was losing weight. To do him credit, he had mentioned it with concern. Just thinking about it made her stomach growl. But with office hours beginning at one, she figured she had just enough time to look up one document and then grab some lunch to eat at her desk. If she was lucky, none of her students would come by and then maybe she could get more reading done, too.

'Ms Schwartz!' Thomas Griddlehaus, the Mildon librarian, looked pleased to see her. Pleased or surprised, Dulcie decided. She'd been spending more time at home writing than in the rare documents library recently.

'Hi, Mr Griddlehaus.' No matter how well they knew each other, this formal mode of address felt right. Dulcie might privately refer to her adviser as simply 'Thorpe', but the diminutive librarian with the oversized glasses would always rate a 'Mister', even in her mind.

'May I assume you would like to pick up where you left off?' The librarian locked Dulcie's bag away and led her into the reading area, with its white table and boxes of gloves.

'Thank you.' She took a seat and reached for the gloves. 'Though, actually, Mr Griddlehaus?'

He had already ducked into the archives, but popped out again, eyebrows raised.

'Is there any Ovid in the Mildon?'

Those eyes, huge behind the lenses, turned quizzical. 'Were you looking for a specific translation? An early edition, perhaps?'

'Never mind.' Dulcie realized the pointlessness of her question. 'Truth is, I should just get a decent modern translation. I went to that show at the URT.'

Griddlehaus only shook his head, and Dulcie realized she was wasting both their time.

'I'm sorry.' If he hadn't heard about the murder, she wasn't going to bother him with it. 'I'm afraid I'm preoccupied. And, yes, please. Would you bring me the pages from the Philadelphia bequest?'

The first faint glimmers of Dawn gave shape to the mountainous terrain as the coach made its final descent. She let her grip on the leather bench relax as the furious pace abated, the throb and jangle of both wheels and harness quieting to a companionable rhythm. No longer must she cling as every rut and treacherous crevice threatened to disembowel the vehicle, to throw her and her Companion to their certain Death. Only now did she find herself considering that Companion, and felt herself once again appraised by those cool Green eyes.

It was good; Dulcie knew it. Worth the tortured minutes it had taken her to piece out the words, letter by letter, from the stained and darkened manuscript. Now that she allowed herself to pause and read what she had put together, she knew the painstaking work had been worth it.

The adventure of the runaway protagonist was nearing its next step. If she could locate and correctly place the next pages, she would probably find out how the heroine came to be in the first scene she had found: the one in which she discovered the young lord, dead from an apparent head wound in a library. She might even, she hoped, uncover whether the heroine had actually killed the man, or whether the mysterious 'companion', the green-eyed stranger who had offered her a lift on that stormy road, had somehow involved.

Still, she couldn't help but remember her

dream. Was the unnamed heroine another version of Hermetria from *The Ravages*? Was another deceitful Demetria going to appear? As far as Dulcie knew, there were no complete versions of this book in existence. That's what made the research exciting. But at moments like this, when she simply wanted to find out about a character and skim through the plot, it could be frustrating.

'*Once again appraised...*' Appraised or was it apprised? She needed to focus. Thorpe might be a tad unrealistic, but she knew he did have a point. After five years, she really should be winding up her thesis. One more year and the grants would start drying up. Before she knew it, journals would stop even entertaining her proposals. She'd become the dreaded 'ABD' – all but dissertation – and have to start thinking about what else to do with her life.

'*Those cool Green eyes...*' She should finish this chapter, get it off to Thorpe, and move on. If she applied herself, by the time she did finally get the edits on her paper, she could have most of her dissertation written. And if no other journal wanted her work, well, then she wouldn't have wasted time waiting.

But e'en as she settled back upon the leather seat, she perceived by some unnamed sense a shift in her Companion. As wistful Dawn approached, leavening the stormy Dark with shafts of light that threw the Shadows opposite into a novel disarray, concealing and revealing all anew as on the Road they turned and rumbled, her eyes found out a Change before her. The Stranger Yes.

No, that couldn't be right. Dulcie stopped her transcribing, putting down the pencil she had been gripping so tightly. *Eyes*, yes, that was it. *'The Stranger's Eyes...'*

The next bit was nearly indecipherable. A *G* or perhaps a *C*, and something with a tail – *y* or *g*, perhaps, but maybe simply an idiosyncrasy of the transcriber, or an outdated spelling. And then it was hopeless. A blot – water, blood, a centuries-old gravy stain – had obscured the rest of the word, turning the page as black as, if not darker than the aged ink, and Dulcie took it as a sign to rest her own eyes. The light in here was bright, purposefully so. And yet such close work was tiring, especially after a disturbed night's sleep.

She closed her eyes, rubbing them with her fingers. Maybe, she thought, she needed glasses. Were her eyes changing?

That was it! She sat back up with a start and grabbed her pencil. *The Stranger's eyes changing* ... And she could make out no more.

In her frustration, Dulcie nearly threw the pencil, but caught herself. She was, she reminded herself, a guest here. A scholar who had been given access to a treasure trove. Not some spoiled child, or an animal.

The eyes. The theater cat's eyes, darker than Esmé's and yet similar. Cat's eyes...

She flipped back through her notes. At times, before, she had wondered about the identity of the mysterious stranger. Even his name, Monsieur le Gris, recalled her own one-time pet, Mr Grey. But a cat couldn't become a human, could he?

Dulcie caught herself with a laugh. Of course he could – this was fiction. No matter how closely the plot may have drawn from the anonymous author's life, this was a novel. A Gothic, designed to titillate and thrill, and shape-shifters were hardly a modern invention. In fact, it was a wonder she hadn't run into one before. A night like the one the heroine had fled through, replete somehow with both storms and also, unbelievably, moonlight, was made for werewolves. Even Chris would have...

A low bark broke into Dulcie's thoughts and she started.

'I'm sorry, Ms Schwartz.' It was Griddlehaus, standing before her. 'I didn't mean to disturb you, but is everything all right?'

She looked up at him, at his kind eyes behind those glasses, and wondered how long he'd been standing there.

'Do you think people can, well...?' She wasn't sure how to phrase the question in her mind. 'That people can change, Mr Griddlehaus?'

He blinked as he considered the question and she felt briefly, unexpectedly hopeful. Here, with all these ancient manuscripts, he had access to knowledge the modern world would have forgotten. And as quiet and polite as he was, Griddlehaus was also a scholar. He wouldn't scoff at a theory, at something that sounded odd. He would research and weigh the results. He might even...

'I believe people can change, Ms Schwartz,' he said finally, his voice soft but firm. 'That is, if they really want to. Are you having an issue you'd like to discuss further?'

'I didn't...' She stopped herself. He was so sweet. 'Thank you, Mr Griddlehaus. Oh, is that the time?' She stood and began to peel off the gloves. 'If I don't head out, I'm going to change ... into a pumpkin.'

His look of alarm only dissipated when she added, reaching for her coat, that her comment was, in fact, a joke.

TWENTY

Stuck in her office for the next two hours, Dulcie found herself stymied by physics. Usually such a period would fly by. With no students, she should have enjoyed her freedom to work, in quiet, with all her books and papers around her. She'd even managed to grab a tuna roll-up on the way, and while she hadn't waited to have the pickles chopped into the sandwich, after her morning labors, it had been a welcome respite.

Granted, it had been messy. And as she'd found herself mopping up mayonnaise from yet another student paper, Dulcie wondered about the wisdom of her luncheon choice. True, the clean-up entailed did make her read three more of the papers than she had planned, diminishing the amount of work she'd have to take home that night. But all that did was remind her of why she hadn't caught up the night before. And when she opened a fourth and saw that the student – this was in her Early Feminist Literature seminar – had used the title 'Frankenstein: Making the Perfect Man', she nearly gagged, spitting tiny bits of chopped celery over several more papers and the blotter calendar that she had only minutes before unearthed.

Even when she'd finally stuffed the remaining

papers into her bag, Dulcie had not gotten any relief. As she tried to read through her notes again, all she could think was that she should be writing. And when she opened her laptop, her mind wandered back to the awful scene of the night before. That poor woman, Amy, a student like herself. Covered in blood, and so still.

Dulcie willed herself not to think of that. Pictured Detective Rogovoy's craggy face telling her to let it be. But that only led her to think about what had gotten her to the theater in the first place – the strange and troubling scene she had witnessed the night before. Granted, Heath Barstow had not been torn to shreds by a pack of ravaging wolves. But someone had reported a man in the process of becoming a wolf. Was such a transformation in fact possible? Could that awful wound – the ragged tear that Rogovoy had described as a stab to the throat – have been inflicted by such an animal? And could that creature have been Chris?

Or was her inability to focus on anything but the most morbid and depressing thoughts the result of the bump she'd gotten on the head two nights before?

This cycle of useless thought kept Dulcie busy until her office hours were nearly over. Quarter to – she looked at the clock with relief. Inquiring about the Russian blue wasn't going to help her thesis, or bring that poor girl back to life. But it would give Dulcie a sense of purpose, at least for a couple of hours.

It helped that the sun, low as it was, was still

shining when Dulcie finally got to the theater. The day was fading, along with any heat the pale sun might have generated, but the light, flat and cold as it was, at least made the building look different – just one more set of glass doors on another renovated building.

Those doors were locked when Dulcie tried them, and her first reaction was relief. Rogovoy was right: she should leave this be. But just then the breeze kicked up, delivering a blast of cold that hinted at the night to come and reminding her of why she was here. She wasn't going to get involved in ... in what had happened to that girl, Amy. She was here for Gus, and if the cat were lost, she would try to help find him. Winter in the city was not safe for a domestic feline, especially one with such a short, fine coat.

Steeling herself, she pressed the buzzer marked 'office' and was relieved when the bespectacled Roni appeared, blinking as the pale sun hit her face.

'Hello?' She didn't seem to recognize Dulcie. 'Oh, we're closed.'

'I'm sorry. I thought the police spoke with you?' The way the other woman started made Dulcie regret her words. It must have been a horrible night. 'I'm here about your cat?' She smiled, hoping to explain.

The dark-haired woman shook her head, confused.

'I was there last night. I'm Dulcie, Dulcie Schwartz.' She paused, unsure how much to explain. 'I was at the show last night. You came over to talk to us after my boyfriend was – ah –

chosen?'

'Oh, yes.' Roni pushed her glasses up her nose. 'Of course. Please, come in.'

Dulcie followed her inside, through that same darkened foyer and past the ticket window toward the auditorium. A door Dulcie hadn't noticed before stood open on to the hallway, spilling light from what appeared to be a small, windowless office. 'Excuse the mess,' Roni said, leading her in and clearing a chair of folders.

'You must be kind of overwhelmed right now.' Again, second thoughts plagued Dulcie. 'What with the police and all.'

The other woman didn't respond as she looked for a place to put the folders. Dulcie reached to pull a pile of papers, correspondence it seemed, over to one side of the desk, and ended up knocking three pens, a pair of scissors and a silver letter opener on to the floor. Dropping the folders in her own chair, the manager retrieved the letter opener and the scissors, shoving them into a drawer with a bunch of papers. Dulcie ducked down to get the pens, handing them over with an apologetic shrug. 'Maybe I shouldn't have bothered you.'

'No, no, I'm glad you did.' Roni looked up, and Dulcie saw that she was blinking. With one last shove, she closed the drawer, and collapsed on the pile of folders. 'There has been so much going on.'

'I understand.' Dulcie did, more than this other woman could know. For now, however, she just wanted to get out of the theater manager's hair. 'I really only wanted to check: is Gus okay?'

112

Dulcie heard her own words with dismay. They sounded so trivial. Who could care about a cat when a woman had been murdered? Roni seemed to be having the same reaction, and sat down, a blank look on her face.

'The cat?' Dulcie was regretting being here. But since she was, she might as well pursue her mission. 'The Russian blue? We saw him in the act last night and then I saw him ... afterward. Saw that he had gotten out. He seemed to be frightened by all the commotion. And, well, it's cold out.' She stopped. This was going nowhere. 'I have a cat,' she said. It sounded so lame.

'Gus.' The manager looked so blank that Dulcie wondered if she'd been drugged. Perhaps the shock had been so bad that a doctor had prescribed tranquilizers. 'The cat.'

Dulcie bit her own lip and waited, trying to figure out how she could make her own exit quickly and gracefully. 'Perhaps, I should—'

'The cat! Of course.' A light seemed to have switched on behind those glasses. 'Thank you, yes. Come to think of it, I haven't seen Gus all day. I guess I could use your help.'

'Good.' A sense of purpose helped. 'Now, have you checked Gus's usual hiding places?'

Another blank look, and Dulcie caught herself. 'Of course, you're busy. Would you like me to poke around?'

'What? No, I should...' Another hand to the glasses. Dulcie suspected the other woman was hiding tears. 'It's not just what happened. You know. Last night.' Roni paused for breath. 'Things have been difficult lately. The theater is,

113

well, even with the university support, we're not doing well. Ticket sales have never been strong, and we were hoping that with something fun that involved audience participation ... Bob, our director, has been frantic. And now ... this.'

Dulcie nodded in sympathy. She'd been so quick to judge that she hadn't considered the theater's side of it. *Changes* might not be great art, but it should have been popular.

'I'm sorry.' Dulcie glanced over at Roni's computer. 'Is there anything I can help with? My boyfriend – the one with the wallet? – he's a computer sciences guy. I'm sure he'd be happy to donate some time, if there's anything...'

'No! I mean, no thanks.' That hand to the glasses again. 'I don't think it's our programming. Or not that kind anyway.' She paused, a hint of a smile flickering around her mouth. 'Sorry, I'm new to all that. That's really Bob's department. It's just, well, tickets aren't selling like they should. And they brought me in because I used to be in marketing, if you can believe it.'

She fell silent. Dulcie thought about the survey. In retrospect, she couldn't blame them for trying to build a subscriber base, and it made perfect sense that the one time such a follow-up was most inappropriate was the one time nobody had a moment to cancel what must have been a regular email. 'But, hey, Gus is more important, right?' A wobbly smile. 'Let's go look for him.'

Roni stood to leave the office.

'Um, you don't think he might be here?' Dulcie looked over at the corners, where the big filing cabinets almost touched the wall. 'A scared cat can fit into some tiny places.'

'Oh, good idea.' In her eagerness, Roni pushed past Dulcie and dropped to her knees. 'No, no Gus. Besides, he usually hangs out in the theater itself. He loves being backstage.' Locking the door behind her, Roni led the way down the hall.

'How did you train Gus?' Dulcie caught up to the other woman as she opened a nearly invisible door, set flush in the black wall.

Roni turned, the question in her eyes.

'To walk the tightrope like that?'

'Oh, Gus? He just did that on his own.' With a flick of a switch, the mystery door revealed an ordinary-looking storeroom. Off to one side, a narrow set of stairs led up. 'We were doing some work on the sets and someone had a beam set out from the bar to the stage – same as the tightrope. It's funny.' She knelt to peer under a rack of white robes. 'He doesn't always want to do it.'

'Oh?' Dulcie checked behind the door and under a small metal desk. Obvious hiding places, it would seem, though Roni probably knew Gus's habits.

'Yeah.' Roni started up the stairs and motioned for Dulcie to follow. 'Sometimes, he's up here and we know we can do the stunt. Sometimes not. Last night, I thought we were going to skip it, but after the opening music, Gus ran up here, like he was afraid of missing his cue.'

The stairs led to a small balcony on top of the bar. To the left, a row of shelves held what look-ed like props – a large plastic jar of metallic confetti, some rope, and a stack of programs. To

the right, Dulcie saw a small platform that allowed access to a row of lights – as well as to the
edge of Gus's tightrope.

'Was someone up here?' Dulcie peered over
the platform to the seating area below. She
wouldn't have wanted to make that walk.

'I was.' Roni's voice made her turn. 'That's
how I knew Gus wanted to do the trick. I know,
I know.' She raised her hand before Dulcie could
ask. 'We're a small company, so, yeah, I'm the
office manager. But I also help out with the
stunts. Plus, I can keep an eye on the audience
from up here. That's how I knew to come down
when your guy started freaking.'

'He didn't...' Dulcie's defense was automatic.

'When he noticed,' Roni corrected herself.
'You'd be surprised how many people don't!'

'That's because we're good,' another voice
chimed in, and Dulcie saw Heath Barstow's
golden head popping up from the stairwell. 'It's
our job to amaze you. To take you away from
your daily cares, at least for a little while.' The
actor emerged with a dazzling smile directed at
her, or so Dulcie thought. Still, behind her, she
felt Roni shuffle and sigh.

'Not that we can forget.' Sorrow eclipsed the
smile, and Dulcie realized how different the star
appeared in real life, as compared to how he
looked on stage. Taller than Dulcie – everyone
was taller than she was – but smaller than he
appeared on stage. Everything but his head,
which seemed abnormally large. Handsome, but
no longer invulnerable. Dulcie struggled to find
the right words, but before she could Roni

116

squeezed by.

'Heath, I'm so, so...' Before she could finish, he had turned away, leaving Roni standing there, arms outstretched.

'Later,' he said, as he plodded back down the stairs.

'He must be devastated.' Dulcie stepped up to Roni. In the confined space, it was impossible to pretend she hadn't seen how dismissive Heath had been – or how hurt the bespectacled office manager now looked.

'Yeah.' Roni nodded. 'We all are, but...' She left the sentence hanging as she turned and ducked, the better to peer under the shelving. 'No, no Gus.'

Dulcie did the same, squinting into the dark corners in the hope of seeing those dark green eyes. 'I don't see him here, either.'

'Does he spend a lot of his time up here?' It seemed safer to talk about the missing cat than either Heath or the dead girl.

'Well, he did.' Roni was still on her knees. 'At least, once Amy joined the troupe.'

'I thought he was your responsibility?' Dulcie sat up, realizing her mistake. 'I'm sorry, I was talking about Gus.'

Roni sat up too, a sad smile playing across her pale face. 'No problem. I guess I was distracted. And, yeah, I'm the one who takes care of Gus.' She started to shake her head, then stopped as her ponytail began to come loose. 'He sort of fell into my lap cause I was the new girl,' she continued, as she reached back automatically to loop the elastic. It was the kind of gesture one did

117

without thinking when one was working. When one was used to being practical, to being businesslike. 'Like, well, so many things. Making sure he got fed. Setting him up with a litterbox.'

Dulcie waited, not wanting to say anything. Sympathy in such a situation would be unbearable, even though she certainly understood what the other woman must have gone through. It wasn't easy being a woman. Being a bespectacled brunette in the presence of a brilliant and beautiful blonde would have been worse. Especially if, as Dulcie suspected, you harbored a secret passion for the troupe's leading man.

Roni meanwhile seemed to be deriving some comfort by talking, and Dulcie was glad to be a sympathetic ear. 'Not that I mind, really,' the office manager was saying, leaning back against the shelf. 'He's such a smart cat, you know? Like, he knows when to stay out of the way, when the set builders are working. And when to show up, at least most of the time.'

'Wait, what did you say?' Dulcie felt she had missed something.

'That he showed up on time?' The way Roni looked at her, Dulcie wondered if she'd forgotten that she was here.

'No, before then.' Dulcie tried to play the words back in her mind. 'Where did you feed him? Where was his litterbox?' She could have kicked herself. This was so basic.

'Oh, his litterbox is in the basement.' Roni pulled herself to her feet. 'It had been in the ticket office, but some of the girls complained. He had a water dish in the dressing room. And,

118

really, everybody feeds him. We keep a stock of cat food down there, bought with petty cash, but everybody gives him treats. Especially before performances. I guess being able to pet a cat before a show is good luck?'

She looked at Dulcie for confirmation, but Dulcie only shrugged. 'Sorry, I don't know. Sounds nice though. And, hey, maybe we should check there next?'

Roni paused, pushing those glasses back up her nose, and prompting Dulcie to spell out the obvious. 'Because if that's where he gets fed, it makes sense that even if he got out, he'd try to get back there.'

'No, it's not that.' Roni walked to the edge of the lighting box to look down on the space below. 'I'm just wondering if we can.'

'You mean, because the police...' Dulcie didn't even want to say it. The tragedy was still too fresh.

'I think they're done,' the other girl said. 'But that means we might be open tonight. And the number one rule here is nobody who isn't in the show can go backstage.' She blinked up at Dulcie. 'I could get fired.'

It was a lot for Dulcie to take in. 'You're kidding.'

'No, really.' Roni nodded. 'Sometimes I think they're looking for any excuse to get rid of me.'

'Not that.' Dulcie felt for the other girl, she really did. But the brunette's feelings weren't her top concern right now. 'There's going to be a production tonight?' It seemed so wrong.

Roni nodded again, her mouth in a wry

grimace. 'You know what they say. The show must go on.' Before Dulcie could protest, another voice chimed in.

'The show *will* go on.' Dulcie turned, to find herself facing one of the more fanciful moustaches she had ever seen, as the stout man to whom it was attached emerged from the stairwell.

'Bob, Bob Gretna, artistic director.' Not much taller than she was, the hefty man held out a surprisingly delicate hand. 'Are you one of the ushers?'

'Pleased to meet you, but – ah – no.' Dulcie shook the outstretched hand and was about to explain when Roni saved her.

'She's worried about Gus,' the dark-haired girl explained. 'It looks like he got out last night, and it's so cold.'

'Ah, bad luck that.' The moustache, surely more wax than facial hair, twitched, the man's gaze straying to the back wall. 'Well, don't let me stop you. If you'll excuse me...' With an agility that defied his girth, the director ducked down to pull what looked like an oversized lunch box out from under the shelf. 'I've got a set to work on. Apollo's cart really can't get hung up like that again.'

With that, the director opened the box, revealing a multitude of tools in apparent disarray. Pulling out a screwdriver and pliers, plus what looked to Dulcie like some kind of vise, he looked up with a smile. 'This should do the trick,' he said. 'But just in case...' He slammed the box shut and tucked it under his arm.

'He's not as bad as he seems,' Roni said as they watched him retreat down the stairs. 'We're – well, we're really hurting, and most of our ticket sales are pre-orders. If we don't do a show, we have to reimburse those people. If we do, even if they don't show up...'

'You get paid, I get it.' Dulcie did. Barely. 'But the cast ... everyone must feel awful.'

'Everyone does.' Roni's face was grim. 'But they all know the bottom line. Besides, to be honest, Amy was new here. She showed up at an open casting call for this production. Only Heath was really close to her.'

'Poor guy.' Dulcie thought of the golden actor, of how his glamour seemed to suddenly shut off.

'Hey, let's go downstairs, anyway.' Roni roused herself. 'We can check the basement, and even if you can't go in, I can check the dressing room. Maybe we'll get lucky.'

As Dulcie followed the other woman down the narrow staircase, another thought hit her. Not that Roni had a crush on Heath Barstow. Probably half the cast did, and it was likely that proximity to the actor was one reason a business type would work for such a financially unstable company. Nor that he was into Amy Ralkov. Even if she hadn't seen his reaction last night, or the quick change in his mood today, such a pairing made sense. A golden god belonged with a golden goddess. It was that the director hadn't referred to the murdered girl at all. And that even after he had pulled out the tools he thought he needed, he had made a point of taking the toolbox with him when he left.

TWENTY-ONE

'I think the director is covering something up,' Dulcie tried to explain to Chris when she met him back at the apartment. 'He insisted on dragging this huge toolbox down the stairs with him, like there was something in it. And he had the weirdest moustache.'

It was after five and Chris was rooting around in the kitchen cabinets, but Dulcie wasn't thinking of dinner. 'I don't know if the police have the murder weapon yet, but I think they should know about that toolbox. Who knows what's in it?' she asked. 'Roni seemed pretty in awe of him. I mean, I know she's one of the newer hires, but still ... She pretty much just went on about how lucky she was to get out of sales and stuff, how happy she was to be doing something artsy, all the time we were going through that awful basement.'

Dulcie shuddered, remembering how unidentified creatures had scurried as she poked around the trunks and boxes. 'But she doesn't seem happy. I think she was trying to distract me. Or maybe distract herself.'

'Are we out of Fancy Feast?' Chris, taller by a good six inches, was craning to look. 'Didn't we just get some?'

'Next cabinet over. Bottom.' Dulcie couldn't help smiling. How could Chris think that she would put anything on a top shelf? Esmé, who was busy twining around Chris's ankles, turned toward her and chirped. 'Esmé's been trying to tell you that,' Dulcie translated.

'Sorry.' Chris reached over to the next cabinet, Esmé's attentions keeping him from stepping closer, and managed to extract a can. Dulcie, out of sympathy, handed him a clean dish. 'Thanks. But run that by me again? You think the director did it, and is hiding the murder weapon in a tool-box? And that the office manager knows something that she's not telling?'

'Well, knows or suspects.' Seeing that her boy-friend was still cornered, she took the dish and stepped over by Esmé's water bowl. 'There was something hinky going on with her. You think I should call Rogovoy?'

Esmé looked from one of her people to the other, momentarily thrown by the trade off of her food dish.

'And what would you say?' Chris gestured with the empty can. 'That the director might be a murderer because he was intent on fixing a broken prop? That maybe he hid the murder weapon in a tool box, in plain sight, but that they didn't think of looking there? And that the office manager knows and was covering up by helping you look for their cat?'

Dulcie opened her mouth but before she could clarify, Chris kept talking.

'I know how you feel, sweetie. Honest, I do. But don't you think you should let the police

123

handle this? You said you were going to help look for the cat, not—'

Esmé had had it. She'd leaped up, raking Chris's hand with her outstretched claws.

'Esmé!' Dulcie looked down and realized she was still holding the cat's dinner. 'Here, Esmé. Bad cat,' she added, belatedly. 'I'm sorry, honey. I'm afraid I caused that.' She followed him over to the sink, where he washed his hand.

'You weren't the one who scratched me.' He turned and looked over his shoulder at where the plump tuxedo was noisily licking at her dish. 'But really, Dulcie, I trust your instincts, I do. I just don't know about them this time. This is serious, and you've already been hurt. Which reminds me—'

'Do you think Roni knows what happened to Gus?' Dulcie broke in before Chris could ask her, yet again, if she'd consider going back to the health services for a check-up. 'Maybe it plays into what happened to Amy?' Dulcie tried out the scenario as she handed Chris a paper towel. 'Maybe the two crimes are related?'

'Dulcie, are you listening to yourself? Isn't one crime enough? Besides,' he paused as Dulcie handed him a paper towel, 'we don't even know that something has happened to that cat.'

'I know, Chris.' They both turned to watch their own pet eat. 'And I know I don't have any proof. It's just a feeling.'

'Maybe it's because you had a really long day – and we saw something terrible last night?' He put his uninjured arm around her and drew her close. 'And then you saw that poor scared animal

124

out in the alley and got worried about him? Maybe you've linked the two events, when there isn't a connection?'

His voice was gentle, and his words, Dulcie knew, contained sense. Still, she shook her head. 'I just don't know, Chris. I was with the office manager for a while. She's covering for someone, Chris. She knows something, and part of it is that Gus the cat is gone.'

Chris, wisely, declined to comment, and lost in their own thoughts, the pair managed their own dinner without further incident. Afterward, they both retired to the living room couch, Dulcie to work, Chris to tune into what seemed to be a sporting event in the middle of a snowstorm.

'It's football, Dulcie.' Chris responded to the question in her eyes. 'They play whatever the weather. Just as well; I think that storm is coming our way. See, that's the quarterback. We've got a first down and...'

'Bother.' Dulcie had been trying to listen. She really had, but it was just too easy to check email as Chris explained.

'What?' Luckily, he was used to her. 'Something from Thorpe?'

'No.' She made a few moves with the mouse. 'Well, yeah. Thorpe sent me some article he wants me to read. And incorporate into my new chapter.'

'By Friday?' Chris reached over to put a consoling hand on Dulcie's knee.

'Yeah, but that's not it.' Dulcie tapped away. 'Hey, maybe you can help me?'

125

'With your deadline, probably not.' He reached for the laptop anyway. 'Here, what is it?'

'I clicked on something, and now...' She leaned over and pointed out the window that had just opened on her screen.

'Dulcie, don't you know by now not to open everything that comes in?'

'I thought it was from Roni,' Dulcie cut him off. 'It said University Rep,' she explained. 'But it's just another ticket offer.'

'They must be hard up.' He closed the window, only to see another pop up. 'And they've got a bug in their software.' Another click, another window. 'Serves them right for spamming every-one.'

'It's not spam if I gave them my email.' Dulcie wasn't sure why she was defending the theater company. 'I don't think Roni is telling me every-thing, but still, they are hurting for funds.'

'Oh?' Chris muted the television and sat up, both hands working over the keyboard.

'I gather the university gives them a break on rent and access to some services, but it's not enough.' Dulcie had related what the office man-ager had told her earlier, but now she filled in the blanks. Or started to, until she realized Chris wasn't listening. 'It's like with all the arts, Chris. We should care.'

It was a last-ditch attempt to break through, but her boyfriend didn't even look up.

'You've got bigger problems, Dulcie.' With a mechanical sigh, her laptop shut down. 'Hang on.'

'What's wrong?' Dulcie looked over. Chris had

two fingers on the keyboard in what she suspected was an ominous sign. When he didn't answer, she felt the tension mount. But then with a happy chord the screen lit up and all her familiar icons began popping back into place. 'Chris?'

'It was that stupid survey.' Chris opened a window, then another and grunted what sounded like approval. 'Okay, all gone now.'

Dulcie simply shook her head. 'There's something wrong with their emailer,' Chris said. 'If you didn't buy tickets, it wouldn't close until you did the survey.'

'Well, I would've done the survey. They probably need the info.'

'Dulcie, you shouldn't.' Chris was looking at her and shaking his head.

'Why?'

'It's wrong—' He raised a hand to stop her protest. 'I don't mean morally. There's something wrong with a page you can't dismiss. Probably a bug of some sort.'

'Is my laptop okay?' Dulcie held her breath. She'd had the little machine for so long now that Chris and his buddies tended to laugh at it. And although he'd offered countless times to build her a new one – assemble, he would have said, from spare parts – she felt strangely loyal to it, its familiar bulk in her shoulder bag a companionable weight. Besides, she didn't want to learn the ins and outs of a new computer.

'Yes, I think so.' He tapped a few more keys. 'Yeah, everything seems to be working properly. Let me know if it freezes up again, though.'

'I will, Chris, and thanks.' Dulcie took the

machine from Chris and let her hands wander idly over the keys. 'I wonder if they know.'

'Seems like they should.' Chris reached for the remote. 'Sending a virus out to potential clients isn't going to endear them to anyone.'

'I'll call Roni in the morning.' Dulcie took the machine from Chris and closed it. 'It'll give me an excuse to follow up about Gus.'

'Maybe he's turned up by now.' He turned back to the television and hit the button.

'Maybe.' Anything else Dulcie would have said was drowned out by the cheers of a faraway crowd.

TWENTY-TWO

'Flee,' said the Stranger, his words as clear as a bell despite the turmoil of travel and the riotous Storm. 'Take that which grows within you and fly beyond the nefarious Reach of he whose claims upon you would give the arguments of lesser minds weight, he who would empower the ill-wishes of the very same who would have you broken.' Inside the coach, as if his voice were the very Dawn itself, the gloom was lifting. Light filtering in through the worn and tattered silken curtains, made dusky shadows on the cracked and stained leather of the bench behind him. 'Flee,' he pleaded, voice as soft as the Robe he had wrapped her in and yet rising, somehow, above the very Noise of the hard road they still followed. 'Flee,' he said, the fiery Spark of those green eyes flaring at the silken touch of dawn. 'Flee he who would do both you and yours harm.'

Dulcie's heart pounded as she woke. A woman in danger. A green-eyed stranger warning her. A...

Esmé, lying beside her, twisted around to scratch.

A flea?

'Esmé!' Dulcie sighed and fell back on the

pillow. 'Please don't let my dream be some kind of verbal pun,' she whispered. 'Please.'

It wasn't likely. Esmé was an indoor cat, and no other animal had come by. In fact, she realized as she lay there, it was much more likely that her dream had been spawned by her work, as well as the events of the last four days. The setting – a coach on a journey, complete with mysterious stranger – came straight from the manuscript she was reading. And the idea that the green-eyed stranger was trying to help the woman? Well, she might have been thinking of Gus, but Mr Grey had helped her out often enough. Unless, she thought, there was a message for her here, now.

'Mr Grey?' Chris, by her side, muttered and shifted, and she waited until his breathing was once more soft and even before she addressed the darkness again. 'Was my dream some kind of message for me?'

The sound of Esmé bathing, lapping at her fur, was the only reply.

'Was it a warning?' Images of Amy. Gus. Even Mr Thorpe swirled through her mind as she waited for a response from the one creature – a long-haired grey cat – who could comfort her.

She waited. There was a quiet 'mrup' as the cat by her side switched positions.

'Mr Grey, are you there at all?' A slight snore from Chris was her only answer. 'I guess it was just a dream, then.' Dulcie rolled on to her side, facing away from her cat and her boyfriend. Right now, they weren't much of a comfort to her, and she felt her hot tears rolling down on to

130

the pillow as she drifted back to sleep.

'*Right now?*' The voice, as soft as Esmé's fur, startled her back awake.

'I didn't mean...' Dulcie forced herself to stay still, afraid that the presence she now felt beside her would disappear or, worse, prove to be simply another dream. 'When I thought ... wait...'

'*Your thoughts are dear to me, Little One.*' Low and warm, the voice continued. '*Your dreams, as well. But you, too, must learn to listen—*'

'Dulcie, you awake?' Chris flipped on his back. 'I just thought of something.'

Dulcie sighed with frustration. 'I'm up now.' It wasn't the whole truth, and it certainly wasn't fair, but it was the best she could manage. Or, no, it wasn't. 'Sorry, Chris, what is it?'

'I had the strangest dream just now.' He propped himself up on one elbow to look at her, over Esmé who stretched out between them. 'Or maybe it wasn't a dream.'

'Mr Grey?' She didn't need to say more. Chris not only knew about her spectral pet, but he'd been visited by the feline spirit as well.

But he was shaking his head. 'No, I don't think so. This was, I don't know, the feeling of something eating its way through something. Like a worm in a flower or a piece of fruit.'

Dulcie wrinkled her nose in disgust, but tried to keep her voice even. 'Like something is bad at its core?'

'Like there's something wrong inside, anyway.' Chris began stroking Esmé in an absent-minded way. 'I kept thinking, "a sickness of the heart".' He shook his head. 'Sounds like one of your stories, Dulcie. But then it hit me – that email?'

'I don't follow.'

'What if it wasn't just a bug, but an actual worm in it?'

Now he had lost her. But even in the dark, he must have sensed her confusion. 'I mean, some kind of malware,' he continued. 'I'm thinking that either their email company is ripping them off – or it wasn't a real email. It was something that had hijacked their list to go phishing.'

'Chris?' Dulcie was beginning to wonder whether she was indeed awake. None of this was making sense.

'Phishing – with a "ph". Trolling for info. If they have the list, then they already have your email address and your name. Before you know it, they're getting your passwords, financial info. Whatever.'

'Well, I'm sure I know better than to give that stuff out.' Chris looked at her.

'What?' she asked. 'I know I buy stuff online, but I'm careful about...'

'But not everybody is, Dulce.' Even in the dark, she could make out his smile. 'And not everyone has someone who can clean their drive off when a program refuses to even force close.'

'And I didn't even thank you before.' She put her hand on his, when a thought struck her. 'Do you think that's why they're broke?' Dulcie looked up at her boyfriend, trying to make out his features in the dark. 'Hey, maybe it's not about the customer base. Maybe someone's stealing from them.'

She felt as much as saw him shake his head. 'I think there's probably a lot of reasons for a theater company to be losing money, Dulce. Even with subsidized rent, they've got to pay something. And can you imagine what it costs to heat that place? When it was a bookstore, it was always drafty and cold.'

'But it's got to survive.' She knew she was fading. The scene from her dream was coming back, almost like a scene from a play. 'We all still love drama. We all root for the hero.' She thought of the Stranger and then of Heath Barstow, dark and light. Shadow and gold. 'We all want the heroine to come out all right.'

'Good night to you, too, sweetie.' Chris looked over at his girlfriend, her lips still moving even as her eyes closed. Pulling the edge of the blanket out from under the sprawled cat, he tucked it around her, as her murmuring gave way to the even breath of sleep.

TWENTY-THREE

'Hey, stranger.' Slightly fuzzy from lack of sleep, Dulcie didn't immediately recognize the voice on the line.

'Suze!' Memory kicked in, as Dulcie poured her coffee. 'I've missed you!'

'I know, I'm sorry.' From the background noises, Dulcie figured her friend was already at her South End office. 'It's just been so crazy.'

'The credit fraud?' Just to hear her old friend's voice was comforting.

'Yeah, it's funny,' said Suze. 'The credit card companies don't seem to care. I guess it's just a write-off for them. They'll reimburse the false charges, which is good. But they won't prosecute.'

'Why not?' Dulcie wasn't sure she cared, but it felt good to talk about something other than her own work – or murder.

'I think it's a combination of things.' Suze, however, sounded tired. 'Partly, it just isn't worth their time. They've got insurance. And partly, it's really hard to prove – you can say that a charge was a mistake and you'll delete it. Unless you catch someone in the act, who's to say that you did it? Maybe your system was hacked or something.'

'Morning.' Chris walked in, reaching past Dulcie for the coffee and interrupting her thought.

'That's terrible,' Dulcie said into the phone. Chris barely raised his eyebrows. 'What were you saying about hacked?' Something was tickling her memory, if only she could place it.

'Oh, I doubt that happened here.' Suze sounded resigned. 'Usually these jerks just steal mail or receipts, if they have access. If they can get their hands on someone's check paying for a bill, they have the account number, the bank number – they can get a new card sent to their address and, voila, suddenly the client is buying high-end stereo equipment.'

'Free entertainment.' Dulcie caught herself. She didn't want Suze to think she admired thievery. 'For someone, that is.'

'Not even,' said Suze. 'Most of the time, they sell the stuff for cash. I guess someone gets a bargain out of it. Oh, hey, Dulcie, I've got to run. Call me later? I want to hear what's up with you.'

'Sure,' Dulcie said, warmed as much by the call as the coffee.

Dulcie was halfway through the metaphysical poets section when it came back to her.

'What do you mean by a conceit?' Adam, a particularly dense sophomore, was asking for the third or fourth time. 'You mean, like, it's an idea or something, right?'

'Close.' Dulcie had made herself smile. At least he hadn't asked if Donne had been bragging again. 'A conceit is more like a theme. A meta-

135

phor, like when Donne writes about the flea who bites both the speaker and his lover.'

'Ew.' Celia grimaced. 'Bugs.'

That was it: bugs. When Suze had mentioned hacking, she'd wondered if the University Rep bug might be what was draining the theater's finances, in some way. Chris had pooh-poohed the idea, but that didn't mean it wasn't possible. Maybe someone had hacked into the company's bank account. Maybe the email bug was a mistake. A clue...

'Ms Schwartz?' Celia's voice broke in. 'I'm sorry. That was out of line. It's just that I have a phobia, you know, like a really bad fear...'

'That's fine, Celia.' Dulcie broke in before her student could define the word for her. 'I was reminded of something. But you brought up an interesting point. Can any of you tell me why Donne might use something as, well, disgusting as a flea to make his point?'

It wasn't a bad question, and it got the students talking. It's primary advantage, however, was that it let Dulcie sit back and think about what might have happened.

For starters, who would want to steal from a theater company? It must be pretty obvious that a small venue wouldn't have much money. Then again, none of Suze's clients were rich, either. The legal clinic was open to all, but in reality it only took on cases for people who couldn't afford pricier (Dulcie was loath to say better) representation. Maybe aiming small was a way to stay off the radar. If a thief stole too much then maybe the credit card companies would bother

136

to pursue legal action. Or was it the university affiliation that had attracted the hacker?

'Ms Schwartz?' This time, eight sets of eyes were on her. 'What do you think?'

'It's a mystery, isn't it?' For this class, that usually worked, and from the nods around the table, she guessed that once again it had. And since the Memorial Church bell was ringing, Dulcie was content to leave it at that.

TWENTY-FOUR

Thoughts of Gus, as much as anything, determined her next move. Even if the city police were already looking for the murder weapon, surely, she reasoned, Detective Rogovoy would want to know about the hacking – well, the *suspected* hacking, she silently amended – especially if it involved someone getting into the university email system. And after the dressing down she had received, Dulcie wanted to prove herself useful again. But her concerns for the silver-grey cat urged her to visit the small theater first. Besides, she acknowledged, there might be a simpler reason for the faulty email, something that Roni could explain or had already fixed.

Still, she slowed as she made her way from the Emerson Hall classroom down to the theater. The police tape no longer fluttered, yellow and shiny, at the end of the alleyway where Amy Ralkov had been killed, but Dulcie found her eyes drawn to it anyway.

'What am I doing? Bothering those poor people when they've lost someone?' Dulcie only noticed that she was talking out loud when a black-clad woman turned to stare, her eyes made unnaturally large by thick eyeliner. 'Sorry,' she called after the woman's departing back, earning another stare. 'Wow, even the Goths think I'm weird.'

'You notice the eyes, don't you?' The voice, gentle and warm in her ear, nearly made her jump.

'Mr Grey?' Dulcie resisted the urge to turn around. She knew from long experience that when she heard the grey cat, she rarely saw him – and vice versa. To look for him almost guaranteed that he would stop speaking to her. 'What do you mean?'

'The eyes, so striking.' In her mind, she pictured not the woman's black-rimmed stare but the green eyes of her pet. Only for some reason she thought of them as a darker green, like a Russian blue's. Gus's eyes.

'Oh, no.' Dulcie gasped. Was she forgetting what Mr Grey looked like? The thought hit her like a punch in the gut, and she dug into her bag for her cell phone. She hadn't had this phone when Mr Grey had died, nearly two years before. But she'd transferred one of her favorite photos to it for easy access.

Before she could find the photo, however, she saw another familiar face. Lucy: her mother was calling.

'Dulcie?' Despite being the one who had placed the call, her mother sounded surprised when she answered.

'In the flesh.' Phone against her ear, Dulcie started walking again. The wind was getting vicious, which didn't help her temper. 'You expected maybe someone else?'

'I wasn't sure, dear. I've had another vision.'

Dulcie rolled her eyes but said nothing. Such 'visions', she was sure, were her mother's way of coping with loneliness now that her only child was gone. 'I saw you in it.'

'Mom, we're going to come visit this summer.' If she could address the underlying issue, Dulcie thought, maybe she could tone down her mother's wackiness. 'I promise.' She softened her voice. Lucy meant well.

'Dulcinea, don't you talk down to me.' Dulcie bit her lip. 'This is serious. I saw you in it – only I wasn't seeing you as myself.'

Dulcie had reached the theater and turned to face the glass wall. 'Did I look like someone else?' The wall was lined with posters, and she saw her reflection on top of one. Had there been a cat character?

'No, no.' Lucy sighed audibly. 'I wasn't myself. I was different. Shorter.'

Dulcie made what she intended to be an encouraging noise. It was getting colder by the second.

'And I was seeing you through a crowd of people.' Lucy kept talking as Dulcie tried to make out the image behind the reflection. Were those whiskers? 'You were standing at the mouth of an alley. And Dulcie, you looked like you were in shock.'

'Mom?' Surprised out of her reverie, Dulcie broke in. Too late, it turned out. The line was dead. Dulcie thought about calling back – it was certainly possible that Lucy, in her excitement, had accidentally hung up on her only child. It was also possible that she had done so for

140

dramatic effect. Or that the phone bill for the commune had once again been left too late. Plus, she was freezing.

Still, to hear that her mother had seen her as she had been two nights before – seen her as only someone in the alley could have – was too much. Dulcie was punching in the numbers when the door to her left opened.

'Ms Schwartz?' It was the dark-eyed woman who had turned to stare. 'Would you like to come in?'

'Um, sure.' She pocketed her phone for later and looked at the waifish figure in front of her. She was familiar, though Dulcie couldn't exactly place her. 'Have we met?'

'I'm Avila. I'm that cat-thing. You know, in the show?' The slim woman didn't seem to be asking for Dulcie's confirmation, but she found herself nodding anyway as she followed her into the lobby. This was the woman on the poster; she should have recognized those big dark eyes, the black body suit under the oversized charcoal sweater, even if the character – a woman who morphs into a cat and then back into a woman – wasn't anything she remembered from the original Ovid. 'Anyway, Roni saw you and sent me to bring you in.'

'Thanks.' Dulcie made her way to the theater's small office.

'Hi, Dulcie.' Roni looked up from her computer, the rings around her eyes accentuated by those large glasses. 'I saw you were on the phone, and I had to get these payments in by noon...' She gestured to the envelopes piled by the computer, all ripped open, and then to the screen in front of her. 'Anyway, thought you'd want to come in out of the cold.'

'I did, thanks.' Dulcie pulled up the same chair she'd sat in yesterday. 'Any sign of—?' She stopped herself. 'How are you doing?'

A wan smile gave her the answer. 'I'm better, thanks.' Roni was clearly pushing the truth. 'And no, no sign of Gus. But we're all keeping our eyes out for him. It's just – well, there's been so much going on, you know?'

'I can imagine.' Dulcie could, although she didn't see how that would interfere with the search for a missing animal. Still, it didn't seem right to press that particular point just now. 'I may have some news that will be helpful, though.'

'What?' Roni's question was broken by a crash from the lobby. A crash – and could it be laughter? 'Oh, lord.' Roni stood and started around her desk. 'Not again.'

'I've got it.' Dulcie stood and reached for the door. The office manager probably wanted some quiet to work. As she closed it, she couldn't help pausing. Heath Barstow had apparently stumbled in – and nearly fallen on the dark-eyed girl. What was her name, Avila? The two were laughing as the blond actor righted himself.

'He doesn't take long, does he?' Roni had reached Dulcie's side by then and, reaching around her, closed the office door. 'You were saying?'

'I have a friend who does legal work.' That sounded odd and out of date. 'That is, she's a lawyer. She does public interest law.'

Roni was staring, her eyes enlarged by the glasses, and Dulcie realized she was repeating herself. 'Anyway, Suze was telling me about all these cases of credit card fraud she's getting. And, well, I think there's something wrong with your email.'

Dulcie paused. She'd gotten up to the speculative part and wasn't sure how to continue.

'Oh my god.' Roni had gone even more pale. 'You think we...'

'I think you may have been hacked.' Dulcie had to say it. There was no way around it. But as Roni groaned and ducked her head into her hands, she felt guilty. She should have couched the news more gently.

'You can't...' The voice seeping out from behind the hands was strained. 'You can't let this get out.' The face that peeked up showed that desperation. 'If our client base heard about this—'

'I won't tell anyone,' Dulcie rushed to reassure her. 'Only my boyfriend knows. You know Chris? From the other night?'

Roni nodded, color coming back into her cheeks. 'Thanks. This has been a nightmare. If our customers found out—'

'Found out what?' Heath's golden head appeared in the doorway.

Roni shook her head once, quickly, motioning for Dulcie to stay silent. 'Computer problems,' she answered.

'Amy would have been all over that.' Those startling blue eyes turned to Dulcie, pinning her to the spot. 'She was a whizz,' he said. 'Another reason to miss her. Hey, Roni, you got a minute?' The actor turned his attention to the office manager, allowing Dulcie to breathe. 'We've got another call.'

'I'll take it.' Roni reached for her phone. 'Do you mind?'

She was talking to Heath, but Dulcie figured this was her cue, too. 'I'll step out too.' She rose and started toward the door. 'Maybe someone's seen Gus.'

Roni nodded as she punched a blinking button. 'University Rep, please hold.' One hand over the receiver, she looked up at Dulcie. 'You know, she wasn't that great,' she said. 'He just thought she was.'

Dulcie nodded in what she hoped was a noncommittal fashion and stepped out, nearly smacking into the dark-eyed girl, Avila. From the close-lipped smile on her face, Dulcie figured she'd heard the exchange. The fact that Heath was now slumped over, near tears, wouldn't have helped.

'Don't you mind?' Dulcie asked. The dark girl had seemed like she was enjoying the actor's attention before his sudden mood swing. She only shook her head, the heavy bangs of her short pixie cut bobbing. 'That's Heath. He's an actor, you know? And, well, he's blond, at least for now?'

Dulcie hadn't realized that the stereotype carried through to men. Then again, she wasn't part of the theater world. 'I guess,' she said with a shrug. 'Are they all like him?'

'Aren't they all?' Avila smiled for real this time. 'I mean, men?'

'Maybe.' Dulcie didn't want to correct her – or to sound smug. 'Or maybe it's a Cambridge thing. You know, the university?' The brunette's habit of turning every statement into a question was contagious.

'I wouldn't know about that,' Avila countered with a declaration. 'I'm one of the newbies here. Decided to give up the circus when I saw the casting call.'

'Oh?' Dulcie tried to think of a way to turn the conversation toward the cat. 'I guess Heath was here before?'

'Heath and Roni, yeah.' She rolled those dark-rimmed eyes. 'Guys like him? They always talk about moving on. In reality?' She shrugged, and Dulcie noticed how broad her shoulders were, given her size. 'Well, he's a draw.'

'My friend has a huge crush on him.' There, it felt good to say.

'Join the club?' For a moment, Dulcie thought Avila really was asking a question, but before she could decline, the other woman continued. 'Not just audiences. He's, like, the troupe's best recruiting tool?'

'You mean ... Amy?' The other girl just shrugged again, as Roni opened her door.

'Dulcie? Sorry about that.'

With a smile for Avila, Dulcie walked back into Roni's tiny office.

'I'm so grateful you warned me.' She sat down heavily behind her desk. 'Between this and Gus...' She shook her head, and Dulcie noticed that her ponytail was coming loose. Already a strand of thick, dark hair hung by her face. 'Heath didn't help the situation, picking up the phone and rambling on to a customer.'

'He must be a handful.'

'He's a child.' As she talked, she grabbed her hair, pulling it back as if it were the thick locks she was angry at instead of the handsome actor. 'He thought Amy was all that, but it was just book learning. Poor girl,' she added as an after-thought. 'He's an angry, selfish child who likes his pretty toys.'

'Did Amy know that?' The pretty girl had seemed equally smitten.

'She would have learned.' A shrug. Roni didn't seem to notice what else her words could mean, but Dulcie did. Maybe Roni was right. Maybe Amy had learned.

TWENTY-FIVE

'I've got to admit, I'm not a cat person, you know?' Avila had the grace to look embarrassed by her admission. At least, Dulcie thought that's what the shrug had meant as she hiked up her shoulders under that flowing charcoal sweater.

'Not everyone is.' It was as diplomatic as Dulcie could be. The woman had agreed to take her around and introduce her, and now she was leading Dulcie down the entrance hallway. 'But I would have thought, considering the part you play...'

Another smile and nervous shrug before she turned and continued walking. It was a tick, Dulcie figured. And although she found herself wondering just what exactly the slim actress had to be nervous about, she stopped herself. The woman was an actress, and from all Dulcie had heard, that was reason enough. Besides, one of her colleagues had just been murdered. And the company that employed her was teetering on the brink of financial ruin.

'Anyway, thanks for helping.' Dulcie backed down. 'I know, it's minor in the scheme of things, but, well, it's so cold out.'

'No, no.' Avila waved her off, showing Dulcie her silver-painted nails. 'I get it. He's a pretty

147

little thing. I mean, most of the company considered him like some kind of good-luck symbol or something?'

They were in the theater proper now. With the house lights on, it looked smaller than Dulcie remembered. Smaller and dingier.

'Doug?' A sandy head popped up from behind the raised stage. Dulcie recognized him as one of the gods. 'Did you see Gus? You know, the cat?' Avila's querulous tone was finally appropriate, but the freckled face just looked at her, before reaching up to his ears.

'Sorry, what?' He was wearing earbuds, Dulcie noticed. 'Hi. I saw you here yesterday, didn't I?' This was to Dulcie, but Avila jumped in.

'Doug, this is Dulcie. She's looking for Gus who, I guess, got out?'

'Hang on.' Propping himself up on the edge of the stage, the sandy-haired man stood. He was taller than Dulcie remembered. Taller than Heath, and dressed in jeans and a flannel shirt. The hand he extended was calloused. 'Doug Melrose,' he said. 'Set builder, at least today.'

'Hi. Dulcie Schwartz.' She felt her hand dwarfed in his. 'I thought I saw you in the show.'

He laughed. 'Yeah, actor by night. But I do contracting to pay the bills, so when the company needs something nailed tight...' He gestured to the edge of the platform, where a hole gaped under the stage.

'I thought the director did the set repair.' Dulcie looked around, but the portly man was nowhere in sight.

'Bob?' Doug's tone said it all. 'You're kidding,

148

right?'

She shrugged. 'I saw him take the toolbox down the other day.'

'Well, that explains why I couldn't find it.' Doug hefted the hammer. 'Luckily, I keep my own tools in my truck.'

'What happened?' Dulcie ducked down to look. By the hole, a splintered board – its raw edges showing tan under the black paint – lay on the floor. Its replacement waited nearby.

'Someone had a tantrum.' He shook his head as he reached into his pocket. 'Heath says he tripped over it making his entrance. Caught his foot and nearly went flying.' Pulling out a handful of nails, he knelt too. 'That's what he says, anyway.' He placed a nail and drove it in with two hard whacks. 'Do you know anything about it?'

'Maybe he really did trip?' Avila shrugged again. 'I mean, with the chariot malfunctioning and everything?'

'Maybe.' Doug eyed the board, adjusted it slightly and nailed the other end. 'Anyway, no, I haven't seen Gus since the night that Amy ... well, you know.'

They all did, and the room fell silent.

'What about under the stage?' Dulcie kicked herself. She should have thought of this before Doug had nailed the opening shut. 'Do you think Gus might have gotten under there?'

'You said he's been missing two nights now?' Doug asked.

Dulcie nodded, and Doug paused before responding. 'Well, it could be, but Heath just told

149

me about this hole this morning. Now, granted, we've all had a lot on our minds, but I don't know that I would've missed a hole this big. This is what I do.'

'You do a lot more,' Avila cooed and turned to Dulcie. 'He's a great Minos and when he gets to do Hercules, you can really believe in him, you know?'

'I believe it.' Dulcie had had trouble seeing the slender Heath as the muscular hero. Then again, the Village People song blasting during his feats of strength hadn't helped.

'Thanks, hon.' Turning back to Dulcie, he elaborated. 'I just don't think it happened during a performance. For all of Heath's issues, when he's on, he's on. I think he kicked it.'

'He was in a mood yesterday, wasn't he?' Avila looked thoughtful. 'The police kept him for most of the day,' she explained.

'Really.' Dulcie wasn't sure how to respond. Detective Rogovoy would want her to stay out of it. Clearly, the city police – or was it the state? – must have known about Heath's relationship with the dead girl. But had they spoken with his colleagues? 'Do you know what they asked him?'

Avila gave a most unladylike snort, and Doug grinned. 'Heath had a reputation,' he said. 'And in this case, I'm afraid it landed him in the hot seat.'

'So, he was a lady's man?' Dulcie tried not to look at Avila as she asked, but the two actors nodded.

'That's how he cast himself anyway,' said the

Goth girl. 'And, hey, we're all here because we want to play a different part, aren't we?'

'But you were asking about Gus,' Doug broke in before Dulcie could follow up on that provocative statement. 'No, I don't think he's under here. But why not be sure?'

Before she could stop him, he'd pulled the two nails out and was lying on his belly. 'Hang on.' He popped up again and extracted a flashlight from his toolbox. 'No, I don't see anything. Want to check?'

'Sure.' Dulcie felt a little silly getting down on the floor. If she didn't, though, she knew she'd feel worse. 'Thanks.'

Taking the flashlight from the big carpenter, who knelt beside her, she reached into the hole and slowly panned over the space. The beam reflected off nail heads and some kind of metal brace, only to be softened by myriad dust balls. The black paint, she could see, had been haphazardly applied. While most of the boards had some paint, at least two were raw wood on the inside. Clearly, this wasn't the first patch job Doug had done.

'Nothing.' She sat up, brushing dust from her sweater. 'Sorry to make you go to all that trouble.'

'No trouble at all.' As if to illustrate, he re-attached the board with four quick taps. 'Better safe than sorry, and I'd hate to be responsible for trapping the little guy in there.' Four more taps, and the board was secure. 'Hey, maybe he just went back to where he came from?'

'Where he came from?' Dulcie looked at Avila,

who shrugged again.

'He was new here, too.' Doug stood and began putting his tools back in the box. 'Showed up around the same time you all came in.' This was to Avila. 'We joked about it, the cat who came for casting.'

'Did someone bring him?'

'That was it, we thought Roni did at first. He took to following her around. He settled into her office like it was his new home. She said she'd never seen him before, though. Said that he was as new to the job as she was.'

'That's why I was afraid of him,' said Avila. 'I mean, he really got poor Amy good.' Doug nodded, remembering. 'All she did was go into Roni's office, but I guess she scared him or something, because he jumped her. I'll never forget it. He must have been on top of one of those cabinets or something? He came out hissing – totally freaked me out. And she had a scratch like, well, it was bad. Really bleeding a lot, right across her throat.'

TWENTY-SIX

At first, Dulcie didn't believe Avila. That a cat would scratch someone, sure. Even, she knew from Esmé's rough-housing, to the point where blood was drawn. But to swipe a woman across her throat? The description was too over the top, not to mention too close to the wound that had actually killed the young actress. And since Avila was on the stage herself, Dulcie simply assumed that the dark-eyed woman was indulging a flair for the dramatic. Only Doug's quiet assent had convinced her.

'It was bad,' he said, nodding. 'Amy almost quit then and there.'

'Maybe if she had...' Dulcie started to put her thoughts into words when she saw the look on Doug's face. 'I'm sorry.' She backtracked and looked for an excuse to move on. It would have been wrong to ask the big contractor to help her look for the cat after that.

'Dulcie, why don't we try the dressing rooms?' Avila came to her rescue, reaching for her hand and spiriting her away. 'Don't mind Doug,' she said, as soon as they were out of earshot. 'He feels like he should have protected Amy from Heath.'

Dulcie looked up at that, but Avila, flushed,

153

was already explaining. 'Not like that,' she said as they passed from the open stage area into a backstage corridor. 'Gosh, I've got to start watching what I say. I mean, just that Heath always went for the new girls.'

'So there were others?' Dulcie couldn't reconcile this cavalier attitude with the dark-eyed girl's obvious pleasure in the actor's company.

'We were all new girls at some point.' A shrug as Avila's tan cheeks took on a rosy hue. 'And, hey, it's part of the deal.'

'The deal?' Dulcie was definitely in over her head.

Avila nodded. 'Heath knows people. He's worked down in New York, supposedly. If he likes you...' The expression on Dulcie's face must have stopped her, and she shrugged again. 'Anyway, here's where we change.'

'Am I allowed in here?' Dulcie paused. She didn't want to get the actress in trouble.

Avila rolled her eyes, and taking Dulcie's hand led the way into a long and narrow room. Dulcie would have taken it for another utility closet, were it not for the rack of white dresses hanging along one wall and the mirror opposite. At the far end, a pile of what appeared to be costumes, many streaked with greasepaint or glitter, covered a threadbare couch. Dulcie got down on her knees to peer beneath it, while Avila picked through the pile. Without any windows, the room was close and smelled frankly of sweat.

'Glamorous, isn't it?' Avila once again read Dulcie's face. 'But this is it.'

'It's tiny.' Dulcie didn't mean to be insulting,

154

but the words just came out.

'It's actually not bad,' Avila corrected her as she shook out a sequinned top. 'When I was on the road, we worked in some real dives.' She leaned in, still holding the glittery piece. 'At least we don't have rats.'

'Maybe you have Gus to thank for that.' It was an honest reaction, but Dulcie was also grateful to have an excuse to talk about the cat again.

'I guess.' Avila seemed to have abandoned the search for Gus as she pulled off her sweater and a torn tank top to reveal a ripple of muscle down her slender back. Dulcie turned away, although the actress didn't seem to have any issues with being topless. 'Damn.' Dulcie turned back to see the actress struggling. The top wasn't fitting over her shoulders. 'Hand me those?'

She pointed to a pair of pinking shears, which Dulcie fetched.

'Thanks.' Two snips and the neckline was customized. 'All that trapeze work,' she said as she shimmied into the top.

'Is that from the show?' Dulcie watched as Avila turned back and forth in front of the mirror on the opposite wall.

'It's from *some* show, anyway.' With a sigh, she pulled it off, throwing it back on the pile. 'Do you mind?'

Dulcie shook her head. It would be too much trouble to explain the commune. 'I can't imagine you have much privacy here.'

A sputtered laugh. 'Much? Try none,' she said. 'Believe me, we all know each other's business. That's why you can't bother getting jealous,

155

especially of someone like Heath. It's bad luck.'

With that, she batted those large, dark eyes. 'He's just another spangly bit of flash, really. All peroxide and banter.'

Dulcie smiled back, enjoying the implied sisterhood. It had been a while since Dulcie had had this kind of girl talk. Not that Trista didn't welcome it, but this woman's flirtatiousness felt somehow less aggressive than her blonde colleague's.

Then again, Dulcie thought, a pang of disloyalty biting in, she might feel different if she had to work with Avila, day in and day out. In fact, she thought, as the other woman pulled what looked like a gold lamé sock down over her head, that might be the point. Was this woman downplaying the rivalries that might have heated this small room? Had someone resented the pretty newcomer for claiming Heath's attention, even briefly?

Avila talked about Heath in an almost disparaging tone. He was 'just' an actor, but so was she. And while she dismissed his affections as so much froth, she had clearly been enjoying them, back in the hotel lobby. Plus, if the handsome star really could help an aspiring actress's career, well, Dulcie had to wonder. Could Avila have been the one to stab Amy?

The other woman had started singing to herself, and Dulcie found herself staring at her bare back as she sorted through the clothes. Thinking about how those pinking shears had cut right through the sequins.

'What is it?' Avila was standing before her in

purple satin. 'You look like you've seen Hamlet's father.'

'I was wondering about Gus. About the time he lashed out at Amy.' Dulcie was covering, but it made sense. 'Cats can be very territorial. Do you think he felt Amy was invading his space? Threatening in some way?'

She was fishing for a reaction, but Avila took it with another shrug. 'I don't know. Maybe? But it wasn't like he was shy, you know? He liked to sleep right on Roni's desk. He had a thing for paper, and she was always pulling papers out from under him to enter them into the computer. I mean, she had to, and he didn't care.'

'So maybe it was Amy he had a thing against.' Dulcie didn't want to think that of a cat. However, it seemed like the only logical conclusion.

'Cats.' Avila gave up the satin with a sigh and reached for her sweater. 'Who knows?'

The visit hadn't turned up Gus, and Dulcie was beginning to think the cat was indeed gone. Still, she decided to stop by the theater office one more time, if only to confirm what Avila had said. But Roni was out, and the office was locked shut when she came by. After a bit of thought, she opted to leave a note. Dulcie didn't want to push, but it would help her clarify things. She didn't think that Roni would forget to check on their email list program. In fact, that might be where the other woman had gone, but she did want to make sure. Besides, she assured herself, it was in the theater's best interest to deal with something that could potentially alienate the customer base.

Pulling her yellow legal pad from her bag, she leaned against the door to write. *Roni*, she jotted, *sorry to have missed you.* Her students, Dulcie knew, would find such an opening as dated as, well, carrying a yellow legal pad. But it was just such occasions that made her glad to keep some old habits alive.

Wanted to follow up ... She paused, wondering how to phrase it. After all, Roni was understandably nervous about anyone else finding out. *About that computer thing*, she wrote finally. There, now she could ask about Gus – in a friendly way. *And someone else we both care about.*

'And who could that be?' Heath had come up, quiet as a cat, and was reading over her shoulder.

'Do you mind?' she snapped, pulling the pad toward her.

'Whoa, sorry.' He backed off, hands up in surrender. 'It's just that Roni's a friend.'

'A friend?' Somehow, Dulcie didn't think Heath had women friends.

'A good friend.' Heath nodded vigorously, shaking that blond mane. 'I know she's been shaken up by all of this. I want to protect her, you know?'

'Well, I'm not attacking her.' Dulcie looked at the man, wondering. Was it possible that he didn't know that the office manager had a crush on him? Maybe he could be friends with a woman – provided he wasn't attracted to her. 'In fact, I'm trying to help. I'm a friend, too.'

He stopped then, taking her in with one long, appraising glance before nodding. 'I'll see she gets your note, then,' he said finally, holding out his hand.

'Don't worry about it.' Dulcie ripped the page free and, folding it in half, slid it under the door. 'Roni knows how to reach me.'

TWENTY-SEVEN

'Why would a cat attack somebody?' Dulcie couldn't help but voice the question out loud. Lloyd, sitting across from her, looked up. 'Somebody who hadn't done anything to him?'

Dulcie didn't mean to obsess about Gus. She'd tried to distract herself by calling Detective Rogovoy. He needed to know about the possible hacking of her email, and she was determined to bring up all the possible murder weapons she was finding, no matter what Chris had said. But the detective had been out, and leaving a message had been unsatisfying. So she had tried to take heart from Doug's words – that the silver-grey cat had simply returned to a former home – but that just raised more questions about the theater's feline mascot.

'You also mean a healthy, normally well-behaved cat?' Lloyd added quietly. 'Because, Dulcie, some cats are simply mean.'

'Lloyd! Gus wasn't—' Dulcie stopped herself, reminding herself that her office mate's allergies had undoubtedly prevented him from under-standing the finer nature of felines. And, in truth, she didn't know what Gus was like. All she knew of him was what she had seen in those brief moments in the theater and then, later, in the

alley. 'I don't think a cat who performed voluntarily would have been so badly socialized. After
all, the company was quite happy to have him
there.'

'Some of them were.' Lloyd put down his pen,
all semblance of trying to work discarded. 'But
how much contact did they really have with
him?'

Dulcie shook her head. From all she'd gathered, Roni was the most involved with the mysterious cat. 'Maybe I should try Roni again,' she
said, as much to herself as to Lloyd. She picked
up her phone and began to dial.

'Maybe,' her office mate said, his voice low,
'you should be focusing on your own work?'

She paused. Lloyd was right. He was watching
her now, concern clouding his round face. It was
funny, she thought, how different people looked,
once you knew them. Heath Barstow, for in-
stance, had lost his golden aura rather quickly.
Whereas Lloyd – pale, balding, pudgy Lloyd –
could not be more dear to her. Besides, he was
trying to work, and the unspoken rule in the tiny
basement room was that when both were present,
phone conversations should be taken outside.

Closing her phone, she pulled her latest pages
from her bag. At the very least, she could go over
Thorpe's notes.

*What you need to address is the question of
Authorship.* That was what her adviser had
written on top of the first page, the word 'authorship' underlined twice. No wonder she preferred
to focus her attention elsewhere. This was
Thorpe at his most dense. As far as Dulcie was

concerned, she had answered the question of authorship. No, she didn't yet have a name to put on the mysterious genius who had penned both *The Ravages of Umbria* and the fragmented work in the Mildon. What she did have was a strong sense that they were one and the same, an unheralded 'she-author' who had begun her career, and presumably her life, in England and then moved to the fledgling United States some time in the early 1800s.

What was most annoying was that Dulcie felt sure she had proof of this, too. Skimming down that first page, she saw what Thorpe had clearly chosen to ignore. Textual comparisons, repeated phrases and motifs that carried through from work to work. Evidence, hard evidence, repeated here and elaborated on from the earlier parts of her thesis in progress. Had Thorpe even read this chapter? Had he looked at her previous work at all?

With a sigh of frustration, Dulcie pushed the pages back into her bag. What was the point in writing more when her adviser wouldn't even read what she had done? Some of the problem, Dulcie knew, was because of her latest paper. The piece that was waiting on publication had been done under the auspices of Professor Showalter. Thorpe's response had been to ignore the work – almost to pretend it didn't exist. Once it was published, however, it would be different. If it ever got published...

'Lloyd?' Her long-suffering office mate looked up at her. 'Do you ever think, maybe, the whole process is broken?'

162

'Constantly.' He bent back over his book.

'Sometimes, I think I'm never going to finish my thesis.' Dulcie kept talking anyway. She needed to get this out. 'That I'm never going to get another thing published at all.'

'Oh, bother.' Lloyd ducked down, his head disappearing behind his desk. For a moment, Dulcie thought she had finally gone too far: she had forced her friend to hide from her. Before she could apologize, however, he popped back up – a smile on his face and an envelope in his hand.

'I meant to give this to you as soon as you came in,' he said, reaching over his desk to glide it on to hers. 'It came into the departmental offices right after you left this morning, and Nancy thought you'd want to have it as soon as possible.'

'Is it...?' Dulcie grabbed the missive and tore open the envelope. *Dear Ms Schwartz, We were quite interested to read* ... 'Yes! They're taking it.' She quickly skimmed through the rest. 'Pursuant to revisions, yeah, yeah, yeah...' She looked up. 'Lloyd, it's Chicago. They're interested in my new proposal.'

'Still feel hopeless?' He was beaming broadly, all bother at her interruptions seemingly forgiven. 'Still want to quit?'

'I never wanted to *quit*.' She was tempted to throw something at him, but this letter was too precious to ball up into projectile. Instead, she lay it flat on her desk – as flat as she could, considering the piles of paper underneath – and read it through once more. For a letter from one group of English language scholars to another, it was

163

amazingly opaque. 'There's something here about coordinating with my departmental chair, but that's fine. I need Thorpe to be a little impressed with me, and if this doesn't prove the validity of my authorship argument, I don't know what will.'

'Authorship, huh?' Lloyd sounded amused, and Dulcie realized that she hadn't voiced her latest problem out loud. 'Is Thorpe still going on about that?'

'Yeah.' It didn't bother her quite so much any more. 'You have any ideas?'

'I'm wondering if you might circumvent the entire issue. Reject the very idea of authorship.'

'Uh-oh.' Dulcie sat back. 'Are you getting all postmodern on me, Lloyd? Because my entire thesis is based on identifying *The Ravages* author.'

He chuckled, shaking his head. 'No, actually it's not, Dulcie,' he said, his voice gentle. 'It's based on a body of work. Who wrote it might not even matter, except as a construct. Take *The Metamorphosis*, for example—'

'Oh, please, not more of that.' Dulcie didn't think she could deal with this kind of analysis right now. 'Look, Lloyd, I know you're trying to be helpful. But you might as well say that, I don't know, that *The Ravages* wrote themselves. Or that my cat really writes my work when I'm asleep each night.' She paused. That was an intriguing idea. Only Esmé, she was sure, would demand credit. 'Or that Gus was behind what happened over at the URT...'

'Dulcie.' Lloyd's tone let her know she was

164

going too far. 'I know things are topsy-turvy there, but—'

The ringing of her phone interrupted them.

'Sorry.' Dulcie reached for it. Had Roni gotten her message? 'I'll call her right back.'

'No, Miss Schwartz.' The voice was gruff and decidedly male. 'You will not. At least if you are talking about who I think you're talking about.'

'Detective Rogovoy?' With one hand over the receiver, Dulcie looked up at Lloyd. 'Um, I'm in my office. May I call you back?'

'There's really no need, Miss Schwartz.' The deep voice was so low and grumbly today that Dulcie wondered if the university detective had a cold.

'But I have some new—' She didn't get to finish.

'In fact, I'd rather we didn't hear from you for a while.' Rogovoy kept talking, his voice rolling over hers. 'Except for one thing. Would you answer one question for me, Ms Schwartz?'

'Sure.' She had so much to tell him. Lloyd, meanwhile, was quite openly staring. At least she wasn't disturbing his work. 'What is it?'

'Do you know what "leave it alone" means?' It wasn't a cold that she heard in his voice. It was more like a bark. 'As in, leave the solving of a major crime to the professionals, Ms Schwartz.'

'But I didn't...'

'You've been calling the theater, Ms Schwartz.' The detective didn't let her finish. 'You've gone by. Asked questions.'

'I was asking about their cat, Detective Rogovoy.' She had to make him see. 'Their cat, Gus.

165

He's a Russian blue. A short hair, though even a long-haired cat in this weather—'

'Enough, Ms Schwartz.' The voice on the phone had gotten quieter. 'I, well, I believe you. Not that anyone else would.' Dulcie had the distinct impression that this last bit was to himself. 'But it doesn't matter.'

'How can it not...?'

'It doesn't matter because you're interfering in what is still an active investigation. Yes, even if you're only asking about the cat. People are talking about you, Dulcie. We've had complaints.' A sigh like an ocean wave broke over the line. 'Please, Dulcie – Ms Schwartz. Leave this one alone. I'm sure the cat will be fine without you. Okay?'

'But I've managed to find out some—'

'Okay?' There was thunder in that voice.

'Okay, Detective.' She felt the weight of her assent. 'I will.'

'Thanks, kid.' And he was gone.

'The police?' Lloyd asked as soon as she'd hung up.

Dulcie nodded, too disheartened to answer. 'I guess I better get to work. Appropriate revisions and all that.'

'At least you know it's been accepted.' Lloyd was trying, she had to give him that.

'Yeah, I think so anyway.' She didn't have the heart to wade back into all that bureaucratese. 'All I have to do is rewrite it, figure out the authorship – and not think about one poor cat who may be lost in the Cambridge winter.'

TWENTY-EIGHT

'Wait, Rogovoy was asking about authorship?' Dulcie climbed the steps from her office, the reception getting better as she surfaced.

'No, no, that was the letter. And Thorpe.' Dulcie had been hoping they could meet for lunch, but the downside of Chris not working nights was that his days were busier. She had reached him on his way to a tutorial in the Quad, less than a quarter of a mile – but an unbridgeable distance – away. Well, the plus side was that she could go back to the Mildon. 'Rogovoy was warning me off going back to the theater.'

'But you told them about the email virus, right?' Yelling – possibly about some sporting event – was audible over the line.

'I did. Chris, are they playing Frisbee?' Dulcie remembered her own undergraduate years as being full of books and late-night talks. 'Aren't they freezing?'

'Last game before the big storm.' Chris, who clearly had different memories, was laughing, but Dulcie gasped. 'What is it, Dulce?'

'We're getting a storm?'

'Nor'easter.' Chris sounded resigned. 'It is January, Dulcie.'

'I know, but...' She swallowed the lump that

had risen into her throat. 'Gus, Chris. A cat, out in a storm.'

There was quiet on the line. Dulcie waited. She didn't have to spell this out, not to Chris.

'Look, honey. Why don't I meet up with you after my students take off? We can do a search – not in the theater, but outside. If he's still inside, he'll be fine. And if we are just searching the alleys, then we're not bothering anyone. Okay?'

'Chris Sorenson, I love you.' She could feel tears springing into her eyes. 'Yes, that would be great. In fact, I think I'll call Roni and tell her. Gus is her cat, basically, so I'm sure she'll want to help. Maybe she can get more of the URT folk to join us.'

'I don't know about that, Dulce.' Her boyfriend's voice had become cautious. 'Maybe we should stick to just us.'

'But it gets dark so early these days.' Dulcie's mind was racing. 'And if we can get more people – especially people who Gus knows, so maybe if we call to him, even if he's scared...'

'Dulcie, think about it.' Chris sounded serious. 'You were just warned to stay away from the theater.'

'But you just said it, Chris. We won't be looking in the theater. We'll be outside...'

'Don't you see, Dulcie? You didn't talk to the police. You only talked to people in the theater.'

'Yeah, so?'

'So one of them dropped a dime on you, Dulcie.' Chris's voice was clear now, and his words sent a chill down Dulcie's spine. 'One of them told the police that you were out of line.'

TWENTY-NINE

'Does it even matter who said what?' Dulcie collapsed into her seat. 'I may never know.'

'The Philadelphia bequest?' The little man gently placed a page in front of her, as if offering solace.

'That, too.' With an overly dramatic sigh, Dulcie reached for the page in its protective coating. 'And, that's what I should be focusing on, Mr Griddlehaus. Thank you.'

Instead of returning to his post, he stayed, blinking at her through those large lenses. It was as much an invitation as he would give.

'It's the whole thing with that theater group, Mr Griddlehaus.' She hadn't come here to confide, but it would be easier to concentrate if she could get this off her chest. 'I was over there yesterday and, well, earlier today.' The more she talked about it, the more she felt that maybe she did seem a tad obsessed. 'I was only trying to help out, you understand. But, well, it seems that somebody has complained about me.'

'I am sorry.' He clasped his hands together. 'Is there anything I might do?'

'Thank you, no.' His concern warmed her – and gave her a second thought. 'Unless, do you know anything about trapping cats?'

Griddlehaus stepped back, his eyes widening in surprise.

'I mean, a lost cat. Not...' Dulcie shook her head. 'Never mind, but thank you.'

'Someone has lost a cat?' He stepped closer again, imagined sins dismissed. And so Dulcie explained. Everything. The quiet clerk made a good listener, not interrupting and nodding sympathetically whenever she looked up for confirmation. Somehow it felt better to get it all out: from that first misleading sighting to the email that led her back to the theater and finally to Gus.

'Chris said we're going to have snow,' she wound up, several minutes later. 'And, well, I'm worried.'

Griddlehaus nodded, as if sharing her concern. 'Plus, there's that question of authorship.'

'Excuse me?' Not that her thesis wasn't important, but hadn't he been listening to her?

'Authorship,' he repeated, pronouncing the word carefully, as if she might have misunderstood. 'The question of who created that ... that virus you spoke of,' he said. 'Surely, somebody was responsible for writing that as well.'

'I guess so.' Dulcie toyed with the idea. 'But that could have been a glitch.'

Griddlehaus's eyebrows went up again.

'Mr Griddlehaus, I do believe you are seeing a conspiracy at work here.' Dulcie couldn't help but smile. Life probably wasn't very exciting for a librarian, even a librarian in the renowned Mildon Collection.

'I don't know, Ms Schwartz.' He shook his

head slowly. 'It seems to me that when such nefarious deeds as murder are afoot, the analytical mind would be wrong to dismiss any event that appears to be out of the normal scheme of things.'

'Are you saying it's a clue?' Dulcie wasn't sure whether to take the little man seriously.

He nodded. 'Perhaps,' he said, 'it was done by the cat.'

'Oh, Mr Griddlehaus.' Dulcie shook her head. 'You think I'm wasting my time, too.'

She waited, expecting a quick answer, but the clerk only shook his head.

'What?' she asked.

'I've seen something similar with other grad students, Ms Schwartz,' he said, finally. 'It is perhaps rather too easy to become derailed. Especially in the final stages...' He was actually biting his lower lip.

'Point taken, Mr Griddlehaus.' Dulcie summoned a smile, to show that she harbored no hard feelings. 'So now, let me look at this page.'

Whether because of the librarian's gentle admonishment or because she had finally unburdened herself, Dulcie found that she was in fact able to concentrate on the page before her.

'Flee,' cried the Stranger, his verdurous Eyes near Sparking in the Night. 'For to Save the very Soul, you must abandon all Propriety. Take passage, fair Lady, lest He who Claims your fortune by unjust Law also comes to lay his wrongful and unmerited title upon that which dearer still remains yet to you.'

* * *

171

It wasn't much, Dulcie had to admit, but it was gratifying. This passage, following hard on the segment she had already deciphered, seemed to confirm her dream of the other night. And, while verbose, it did serve to move the story forward. And now she knew for sure that the protagonist was fleeing a man, she could begin to theorize how the confrontation would take place. Except, of course, that she shouldn't theorize – not until she had more of the fragments in order. And, of course, she shouldn't be focusing on the story at all. What mattered, as everybody seemed to be reminding her, was the authorship.

Well, there were clues to that here, too. Several of the phrases were reminiscent of lines in *The Ravages*. Those eyes, for example, that 'sparked'. For a moment, Dulcie thought of Mr Grey. He, like this book's mysterious stranger, seemed to have some crucial role. But, no, she had to focus. Better to look at the repeated use of 'wrongful and unmerited'. Not only was that a direct echo of the earlier work, it also had the ring of a legal suit. Had the author been involved in legal proceedings? Perhaps attempting to obtain a divorce? It would fit with what Dulcie suspected ... But no, that was reason enough not to pursue it. Not for now, anyway. If she was to make any progress, she had to stick to the facts: Decipher more of the text. Note the repeated phrases and recurrent images that would allow her to make her case. She wasn't, she told herself for the hundredth time, interested in the story. What mattered was the question of authorship.

By the time Griddlehaus came for the box,

Dulcie had made a satisfying number of notes. Tonight, she told herself, she'd write up her newest findings. With a little effort, she would finish this chapter.

'And then I'll have time to start on the new paper,' she said, reaching for her coat.

'Excuse me?' Griddlehaus poked his head out.

'Nothing.' She smiled back. 'Only I've had a proposal accepted. Chicago is interested in it, once the department signs off.'

'Congratulations.' He looked honestly pleased. 'That will buy you time to focus on your dissertation.'

She didn't dare correct him, and instead headed toward the exit, where she and Chris had planned to meet. On the way up the elevator, she turned her phone on. While she wouldn't be caught dead talking on it in the confines of the library, she thought she could dare a text. And with a winter storm coming, time was of the essence.

Clicking on Lloyd and Raleigh's names, she quickly typed: *Help look for a lost cat? Meet behind URT?* With a moment's thought, she added Trista and Jerry. The pierced blonde was a friend and part of their crew. Besides, she deserved a chance to redeem herself.

'Miss?' She looked up to see a plump young man staring at her. She'd been so preoccupied, she hadn't noticed that the door had opened on the B level. Dulcie quickly shoved her phone into her pocket.

'Uh, can you move over?' The plump man looked down. Following his eyes, Dulcie saw a

173

full cart of books before him. 'Please?'

'Oh, yeah. Sorry.' Resisting the urge to correct him (she not only *could*, but she *would*) Dulcie stepped to the side.

The large clerk pushed his cart in with a dramatic sigh, and as the elevator rose, Dulcie slipped her phone out of her pocket again to hit send. As the car opened on the main floor, she added Suze to the chain. Her old friend was a long shot, but nobody would understand the plight of a lost kitty more.

'You know that's against the rules, don't you?' The plump clerk was looking back at her.

'It's an emergency.' Dulcie pocketed her phone and walked past him, head held high. 'A feline emergency.'

'Grad students,' she heard him mutter as she strode toward the exit. In the greater scheme of things, she decided, it could have been worse.

THIRTY

Chris was waiting on the corner when she got there, ten minutes later, wool cap pulled low over his ears and a flashlight in his gloved hand.

'I thought we might need this,' he said, as they turned off Mass Ave. 'Especially if we find any small spaces.'

'Thanks, sweetie.' Dulcie looked up at him. 'I wonder if anyone else is coming?'

'Jerry was here a few minutes ago.' He nodded back toward the Square. 'Trista sent him off to get some chicken fingers from the Hong Kong.'

'What?' This was too much. 'He went out for food?'

'For the trap.' Jerry appeared, jogging around the corner, a white take-out container in hand.

'What trap?' Dulcie was at a loss. Jerry, pausing to catch his breath, only nodded.

'This trap.' Trista appeared, holding up a boxy wire cage. 'Sorry I'm late. Chris filled us in on what was happening with that cat – Gus – and I remembered that they use these in the bio labs. Don't worry.' She saw Dulcie's look. 'It's humane. See?' With one hand she pushed the catch, so that the wire gate fell. 'If we can't find him, we bait this with the chicken. If he's out here, he'll be hungry.'

Dulcie opened her mouth, but Trista wasn't done. 'We'll put it someplace sheltered – don't worry, Dulce. Storm or no, we'll get him.'

'Thanks.' Dulcie looked at her take-charge friend. 'Really.'

'No problemo, kid.' Trista reached over with her free hand and hugged Dulcie. 'We're all in this together.'

For a while, it didn't seem to matter. Working their way down the street in pairs, they looked under every loose bit of paper and into any crevice they could find where a scared feline might be hiding. The first alley, by the ice-cream shop, had been a mess, and with the late afternoon shadows already blanketing the narrow space, Dulcie had been particularly grateful for Chris's flashlight. A slight vibration – the scurry of something fleeing – had briefly gotten her hopes up, but Chris had stepped ahead, pulling the vibrating sheet of soggy cardboard that had moved in such a promising way away from the brick wall. The tiny black eyes that stared back were nothing like a cat's, and Dulcie had had to swallow her revulsion to keep looking.

'Would a rat be here if Gus were here?' she asked her friends.

'I don't think they're afraid of anything,' Jerry responded, a conclusion Chris supported with a nod.

Gritting her teeth, Dulcie moved down to the end of the alley. The large dumpster there had a closely fitted lid, but Dulcie lifted it anyway.

'I don't think a cat could do that.' Trista, coming up behind her, nearly startled her into

176

dropping it.

'No, but people can be mean.' Dulcie didn't need to explain more. Trista, who'd also brought a flashlight, was shining it down into the corners of the cavernous metal bin. It was, Dulcie was happy to see, empty, and she let the lid back down with a bang.

'Well, that should've woken anybody up.' Trista was already on her knees, peering under the bin. 'Nothing here.'

'Maybe this is hopeless.' Dulcie looked back to the street, where the boys were waiting. Although the wind had died down, she shivered in the damp air. Out west, Dulcie could often smell snow coming – a certain kind of moisture, the air actually rising a few degrees right before a storm started. Here, she just felt the pervasive nastiness. If Chris were right, this might be a nor'easter to remember.

'Come on, Dulcie.' Trista flung one arm over her friend. 'I'm not ready to call it quits.'

For once grateful for her friend's bravado, Dulcie heard herself agreeing, and together they walked up to the street.

'Where to next?' Chris looked at Dulcie for guidance.

'Well, they say that lost cats don't go very far. What they tend to do is hide.' Dulcie had already said as much. Now she was stalling for time, looking around. The street they were on ran down to the river. But before the next intersection were only these four alleys. Would Gus, perhaps panicking, have crossed Mount Auburn? Would he have gone the other direction, up

177

toward Mass Ave? No. No animal with any sense would try to cross such a busy thoroughfare. Unless...

'Dulcie, what is it?' Chris was by her side.

'I was just wondering.' Dulcie looked up, her boyfriend's face full of concern. 'I didn't think to call animal control or any of the local vets. I'm wondering if maybe Gus tried to cross...' The words wouldn't come.

'No, from what we saw, that was a smart cat.' Chris was shaking his head, shaking off the possibility of a fatal accident. 'And besides, those theater people would have heard.'

'Would they?' She wondered out loud. 'Not all of them liked having a cat around.'

'Come on, Dulcie.' He held her tighter. 'You can't think that way. Besides...' His voice lightened as a new idea hit him. 'They all know you're looking for Gus. Even if they don't care, they would have told you.'

'If they knew.' Dulcie kept her voice low. She had gotten her friends out here. There was no point in being defeatist about the search when it had barely started.

But forty minutes later, even Chris was ready to give up. The four had searched every alley down the small street and through the church-yard down on the corner. On the chance that Gus had found a way over the theater building – or had doubled back at some point – they had even gone down Mass Ave a block on either side, prompting some queries from passers-by.

'How'd he get out?' one woman asked, a note of censure in her voice. 'Who was responsible

for him?'

'Ah, friends,' Dulcie had replied. The the company was in enough trouble without alienating animal lovers.

'Hm, better hurry,' said the woman's escort. 'It's going to snow, you know.'

'Thanks.' Dulcie made herself stick to the monosyllable.

A few people did offer to help, and to them Dulcie explained further: a silver-grey shorthair with striking green eyes, last seen in the alley behind the theater. Most of them had been distracted by the timing. 'Oh, is this connected to the murder?' asked one woman, who seemed a bit excited by the concept. 'Is he a witness?' Only one young woman, a local teen, had stuck around long enough to really lend a hand, and when she had left, she had taken Dulcie's contact info, promising to send word if she heard of a Gus sighting.

'Thanks, Greta.' Dulcie had been sorry to see her go, but with both dark and the storm closing in, she couldn't blame the girl.

'Maybe we should check by the theater again.' Jerry had been quiet for a while by this point. Dulcie suspected that it was only loyalty to Trista that had kept him here this long. 'You know, in case the cat has shown up?'

'I don't think I can,' Dulcie said. 'I'm not supposed to bother them.' She looked from Jerry to Trista to Chris, seeing the same expression on all their faces. 'But maybe one of you could?'

'That's it.' In this situation, Trista's take-charge attitude served a purpose. 'We'll go check the

ehind the theater one more time.
on't find anything, I'll go ring their
hey've got to be preparing for to-
w anyway, so someone will be there.'
e group seemed heartened by the
exist... of a plan, and with renewed energy
they walked back down the street. Even Dulcie,
who knew the odds of finding Gus in that same
alley were small, felt lighter somehow, but she
made herself lag behind for a moment of privacy
in the growing dusk.

'Mr Grey, is this a sign?' She addressed the
dark grey clouds that seemed to grow lower by
the moment. 'We're doing the right thing, aren't
we?'

Her answer came in a low rumble that roiled
from the clouds. A rumble that could have been
a purr or a growl of warning, when Chris called
back to her. 'Thunder. Did you hear that,
Dulcie?'

She didn't have to answer. As they passed the
copy place, she could already see. The bright
light shining out on to the street highlighted the
first few flakes of snow.

'Great.' She ran to catch up with her friends.
'It's starting.'

The alley behind the theater was only about ten
meters away, but the brick sidewalk was already
slick by the time they reached it, a fact Dulcie
noticed as her friends took longer and quicker
strides through the deepening dusk. It wasn't just
wet: although the falling flakes were melting on
the asphalt of the alley, Dulcie could see a thin
film of frost forming on the cars parked on the

street. With each passing second, the flakes that landed on her sleeve took longer to dissolve.

'We'll take this side.' Trista had her flashlight out as she reached for Dulcie's arm.

'Hang on.' Dulcie felt herself slipping and righted herself. 'We should start out here.' Trista looked at her, puzzled. 'If Gus has been hiding in the back, we don't want to chase him out to the street,' Dulcie explained.

A thud and a muttered curse caused them both to turn. 'What?' Trista asked.

'Just another rat.' Chris reached for his flashlight, which had fallen to the pavement. 'It startled me, that's all.'

'Be careful,' Dulcie called out. 'I wouldn't want you to get bitten.'

'Don't worry,' her boyfriend replied. 'I wouldn't either.' It was an honest answer, but in it Dulcie could hear the beginning of testiness. Her friends were really putting themselves out for her, and there was a limit to how much more she could ask.

'Damn.' Chris was shaking his head as Dulcie turned back. It seemed, she thought, that the limit had been reached.

'Chris?' She wouldn't beg. She might, however, stay on after he had gone home.

'It's the flashlight, Dulcie.' He turned and held the light out toward her. 'I think it's broken.'

'We still have mine,' Trista chimed in. 'Though I think my battery may be going.'

'Maybe that's a sign,' Dulcie said, trying to resign herself to giving up.

'Hey, can we help?' A woman's voice came

from the depths of the alley.

'Hello?' Dulcie called out.

'Dulcie!' A pale face appeared as if by magic out of the wall. Roni, followed by Avila, emerged out of the hidden door from the back of the theater. 'We heard you out here and thought we should see what was up.'

'We didn't want to bother you.' Dulcie had rarely felt more relieved. 'We were looking for Gus again. With the snow starting and all, we thought we'd poke around.' She turned to her friends. 'Do you guys all know each other?'

'I think we've met.' This from Jerry, but Trista was nodding.

'The other night...' Roni looked away, blinking.

'Of course.' Dulcie stepped in, before Jerry could say any more. 'Anyway, thanks for coming.'

Just then another figure emerged: Doug, holding an industrial-size flashlight. 'Here,' he said. 'It's getting dark out. Maybe you could use this.'

'Awesome.' Trista stepped forward to take the light, and Dulcie followed. 'Is Heath here, too?'

'I thought he was.' Roni was looking around, as if the golden-haired star would appear suddenly out of the gloom.

'Nah, he took off about an hour ago.' Avila said. 'Why didn't you tell us you were doing a search?'

'Well, we knew you were getting ready for a performance,' Dulcie hedged, but Avila was shaking her head.

'Bob canceled,' she said. 'Didn't even come in

– just called. That's why Heath split. The weather forecast is dire and, well, the house was less than half sold anyway. Right, Roni?'

'It's pretty bad,' the other woman agreed. Only then did Dulcie notice that the office manager wasn't wearing a coat. Leaning against the wall, her arms wrapped around her, she was visibly shivering.

'You must be freezing.' As Dulcie walked toward her, she could see the other woman's lips turning blue. 'You shouldn't be out here.'

'Neither should you.' Dulcie turned as the alley lit up, bright as day. But the glaring light that shone down into the alley kept her from seeing where the voice – male, deep – came from. 'One of you is a Ms Schwartz?'

'Yes, that's me.' One hand over her eyes, she took a step forward. Up ahead, she could see two figures, both of whom appeared to be holding large lights.

'Ms Dulcinea Schwartz?' said the one on the right. For a moment the light bobbed, and Dulcie could make out a dark blue parka with a badge on it. 'The rest of you should leave before this storm gets any worse. But you, Ms Schwartz,' the voice said, as the other figure, also male, stepped toward her. 'You're going to have to come with us.'

THIRTY-ONE

'What? Why?' Chris stepped forward, as if he were going to challenge the man Dulcie could now see was a Cambridge police officer. 'What are you talking about?'

'Chris, wait.' Dulcie turned back to stop him. As much as she appreciated his coming to her defense, she didn't think that confronting a cop was the way to do it. As she reached for her boyfriend, however, she saw a flash – a movement back beyond him. 'Wait—'

She took another step – just to make sure – and felt a hand land on her shoulder.

'Dulcie!'

She whipped around, ignoring her own counsel and ready to argue with the officer. 'This is important—' She began, but the rest of the sentence never came. 'Suze!'

Instead of the uniformed officer she expected, Dulcie found herself face to face with her old friend.

'Sorry.' Suze pulled down the scarf that had covered the lower half of her face. 'Didn't mean to startle you, but this weather...'

She didn't have to elaborate. The snow was coming down fast and thick, falling in clumps that filled the angled street light and then seemed to disappear. Except that it wasn't: even on the black pavement, the snow was no longer melting, and white ridges had begun to accumulate between the shrinking puddles of slush.

'No, I'm glad you're here.' Dulcie took her friend's hand. 'But I thought I—'

'Ms Schwartz?' The cop was waiting. 'Would you come with us, please?'

'No, she won't.' This time, Suze turned to confront them. 'What is this about, anyway?'

'It's Gus!' Dulcie pointed. 'Gus – the missing cat!'

It was hard to look up. The snow might look gentle, but it was cold and wet. Keeping her eye on the roofline, Dulcie blinked it away. 'There!' Gus, perched on the gutter, blinked down at them and then stretched. Dulcie was struck by the thought that the commotion below had woken him from a nap. The stretch turned into a step as one outstretched paw came down on the snow-slick roofing, to be followed by another. Tail high, as calmly as if he were on level ground, the silver-grey cat made his way from the back of the alley to just above the door.

'Is that him?' Chris had turned. They all had, to watch the graceful creature who now stood, poised as if to jump.

All except the cops. 'Ms Schwartz?' The closer one stepped in, and Gus gathered himself for a jump.

'Please, Miss.' Dulcie shook off his arm as the grey cat leaped into the alley. 'Don't let him run into the street,' she called.

Behind her, she could sense movement. Trista

185

and Jerry, she hoped. But she didn't have time to turn. Instead, she crouched down on the wet pavement, hoping against hope she wouldn't startle the cat.

'Gus? Are you okay?'

The cat had landed neatly, without even a skid, between Dulcie and the door. As he turned to face her she was struck, again, by his dark green eyes. If only she could tell what they were trying to say.

'May I pick you up, Gus?' It seemed only right to ask permission. He tilted his head, as if considering – or listening to something. And just then the door opened, and Heath Barstow's oversized head peeked out, blinking in the glare of the cop's flashlight.

'Heath.' Roni called out.

'I thought you had left.' Avila beside her sounded quizzical and, Dulcie thought, somewhat hurt. Clearly, the actor had lied to avoid her.

'Watch it!' The personal dramas of the acting troupe didn't concern Dulcie, though. As Heath had stepped into the alley, he nearly trod on the cat. Gus's shadowy coloring was easy to miss in the stormy dusk, but the actor seemed to be distracted by more than the policeman's lights. 'It's Gus.'

'I know.' Heath's words didn't make sense, and he took another step into the alley, one booted foot narrowly missing a slim tail. 'I wanted to tell Roni.'

'You knew?' The question on Dulcie's lips in fact came from behind her. Roni, the office

186

manager, stepped forward.

'What? Oh.' Heath looked down, as if seeing the slender creature at last. 'There you are.'

He reached for the cat, but Gus was too fast for him. Dashing around his ankles, the Russian blue darted toward the door and disappeared inside the theater.

'Well, that settles that.' Chris came up to Dulcie and put his arm around her. 'I'd say our work here is done.'

'Now, just a moment.' The cop was clearly not going to let Chris hustle his girlfriend out of here.

'Yeah, really.' Chris's eyebrows shot up in surprise at Dulcie's protest. But she had questions. 'What just happened? Heath, did you see Gus inside the theater?'

The actor nodded. 'Yeah, it was the strangest thing. I was just passing by Roni's office, and I saw him. At least, I thought I did, underneath her desk.'

'What were you doing in my office?' Roni's question seemed off point to Dulcie. Before Heath could answer, Avila stepped forward again.

'You said you were leaving, Heath. What's up?' This time, the hurt in her voice was obvious.

'Look, we found the cat.' Chris raised his hand to get everyone's attention. 'That's what we were here for. That's what was important. What say we all get out of the snow?'

'I'm afraid Ms Schwartz is going to have to come with us.' The officer wasn't going to be so easily mollified. 'There have been complaints

187

that she has interfered with an ongoing investigation, repeatedly intruding into the theater, and that's a serious charge.'

'I don't see any tape cordoning off the theater.' Thank goddess for Suze, Dulcie thought. Her friend had slipped into defense mode. 'Nor do I see any here, in what is a public alley.' Her friend waved her hand, to indicate the now crowded space. 'If there was a specific complaint, I'd like to hear it.'

'And who made it,' Dulcie added. Only Heath had still been in the building. Could he have called the cops?

'We're not at liberty to discuss that.' The cop was looking tired. Tired and cold.

'Then we're not going with you.' Suze wasn't as tall as the cop, but she was close. Pulling herself up to her full height, and fleshed out by her parka, she made an imposing bodyguard. Dulcie was warmed by the sight of her, but also a little worried. Suze was a lawyer now; Dulcie really didn't want to get her in trouble with the police.

'Maybe I can help resolve things.' A familiar voice broke in as a familiar shape hulked into the alley. 'Rogovoy,' the large man introduced himself to the Cambridge cop. 'University police. I'm hoping that as a courtesy, and since Ms Schwartz is a member of the university community, you might let me handle this one?'

'I'll go with Detective Rogovoy.' Dulcie made the offer to keep the peace and looked hopefully at the Cambridge cop.

'Sure.' He sounded resigned. 'It was a nuisance call anyway. Anonymous complaint.' He nodded

188

to his colleague and the two walked back to the cruiser.

'Ms Schwartz?' Rogovoy, hands on hips, was almost wide enough to block the alley. That was fine: Dulcie wasn't planning on ducking by him.

'Thank you.' She paused, wondering how far she could push him. 'I just need to clear something up.' He didn't say anything, and so she turned toward Heath. 'I'd love to see where you saw Gus. He must be going in and out of the theater.'

'I think you've done enough for one day,' Rogovoy broke in before the actor could answer.

'The cat is safe,' Chris pointed out. 'And it is pretty foul out.'

'But there's got to be a hole. A broken window or something.' She turned toward Roni. 'Is there a vent or something in your office? Maybe I could help you look?'

The office manager was shaking her head. 'I don't think so. I'm sure Heath was wrong.'

'Come on, Ms Schwartz.' Rogovoy waved them toward the street. 'I can give you and your friends a ride home, but you can't stay here.'

'I'm kind of cold,' Jerry said quietly.

'And we did find Gus,' added Trista.

'Okay, you're right.' Dulcie turned one last time toward the office manager. 'May I call you tomorrow? Just to follow up?'

Roni was nodding, as Chris pulled Dulcie away. 'Maybe you should let them be, Dulce,' he whispered into her ear as they walked. Now that the idling cop car had left, the sound of the snow had become audible, a soft padding as the heavy

189

clusters built up. It didn't entirely dampen the sounds of the city. In the distance, Dulcie could hear a siren and, back in the Square, somebody yelled. But it amplified small sounds, like Chris's voice, so close to her ear. And as they walked away, she heard another voice, pained and angry. Avila, she thought, speaking to the blond actor who she claimed not to take that seriously.

'What were you doing?' A whisper, rather than a spoken voice, and when Dulcie turned, she realized the alley had emptied. The actors, behind that *trompe l'oeil* doorway, unaware of the sonic tricks played by the snow. 'What are you playing at, Heath? Tell me.'

THIRTY-TWO

'So, he's a cad.' Chris was making cocoa as Dulcie sat with Esmé on her lap, an empty mug on the kitchen table before her. Detective Rogovoy had given them both a lift home, but Dulcie had been shivering by the time they climbed up to the apartment and now sat, wrapped in a comforter in the kitchen, as Chris fussed with the stove. 'He consoled himself with that whippet-looking girl, and he doesn't have the courage to break up with her. Maybe he's going for the office manager now.'

Dulcie looked at her boyfriend in wonder as she tucked her toes into the fluffy down. To men, things seemed so simple.

'Roni is not his type, Chris.' She liked the bespectacled office manager with the too-tight ponytail. If it were up to Dulcie, women like that would be considered as desirable as the pretty blonde had been – or the dark-eyed gymnast. But, well, she wasn't. Surely, Chris could see the difference. 'And he didn't just move on. He charmed Avila. Lied to her. Maybe because he needed something from her. Like, I don't know, an alibi?'

'An alibi would be the least of it,' Chris muttered, more to himself than to her, as he poured

191

the hot cocoa into her mug.

'Chris Sorenson!' Dulcie couldn't get too angry. She knew her boyfriend wasn't the type to lose it over an actress. Besides, he was making her cocoa. 'You're not listening to me.'

'Oh?' His voice came back, muffled, from inside the cabinet. 'Did we use all the marshmallows?'

'Hang on.' Dulcie unwrapped herself enough to walk to the adjoining cabinet, where she found the opened – and nearly empty – bag. 'I'm not sure how fresh these are. And I bet you want something, too.' This was addressed to Esmé, who had begun twining around her ankles.

'She already had a can.' Chris took the bag from her and squeezed the remaining contents. Seemingly satisfied by what he felt, he then pulled three conjoined white puffs out and dropped them in his mug. When he saw the expression on Dulcie's face, he shrugged. 'Hey, it's a celebration.'

'How so?' Dulcie shook some kibble out on a plate, placing it on the ground before resuming her seat.

'Are you kidding?' Chris offered her the open bag. 'You found Gus.'

'Yeah, but, I don't know.' Dulcie reached for the marshmallows. They were definitely stale. She dropped one in her cocoa anyway.

'Dulcie?' If she had been more alert, Dulcie would have noticed the warning tone in her boyfriend's voice. As it was, she ignored the implicit question. Esmé's claws, reaching up her leg, were less easy to dismiss.

'Stop it, kitty.' She detached the claws to an annoyed mew. 'Why? What is it?'

'Naow!' Esmé pulled back even as Dulcie held her forepaws. *'You don't listen!'* The voice, as clear as the cat's mew, came to her ears.

'I guess someone didn't like being left alone.' She smiled up at Chris. 'Ow! Esmé!' The cat had nipped her.

'Or she means what she says.' Chris nodded over the table. 'You aren't hearing yourself, Dulcie. And you sure aren't listening to what others are telling you. For starters, wasn't the plan to find the cat? You've done that.'

'Yes, but don't you think it's odd—'

'Dulcie!' Chris didn't yell. He did raise his voice enough so that both his girlfriend and their cat stopped to stare at him. 'You wanted to help find a lost cat. You did. Well, he showed up – and went inside. You've told that woman, Roni, about the spam problem. And that's enough. They've lost one of their members and the police are involved. Now you've got to leave them alone.' He paused, seemingly as startled by his unaccustomed outburst as they were. 'Okay?'

'But...' Dulcie paused, unsure how to continue.

'But what?' Chris, to his credit, looked resigned.

'What if all those things are connected?' Chris just shook his head, so Dulcie continued as she pulled the comforter back around her. 'Well, on one level, obviously Gus got out the night Amy was ... The night Amy died.' Dulcie stopped to take a sip of her cocoa and to think through what she was going to say next. 'But what if Gus saw

193

something? What if he had something to tell us about who killed her?'

She paused to pull Esmé on to her lap. 'Even Esmé has been telling me I don't listen.'

'Dulcie, this wasn't a game. This was murder. Let the cops handle it.'

'But maybe the cops don't know everything. Do you think they even know that Heath was seeing Amy?'

'I'm sure they do, sweetie. That's their job.'

'Do they know about Bob – or about Avila?'

'Wait a minute, Dulce.' He was smiling, as if he had her now. 'You were just saying that he wasn't serious about her – so now she's a suspect?'

'No.' Dulcie shook her head. Those pinking shears had been sharp. 'At least, I don't think so. But I don't like that he lied to her.'

'She didn't like it either, Dulcie. Now do you want the last of these marshmallows?'

There wasn't much more to say after that, and the three sat in companionable silence. The storm outside had gotten bad, but somehow the wind only made their cocoa that much sweeter. Out the window, Dulcie could see one poor, bare tree, its branches whipping back and forth in the wind. The snow on the ledge had already formed a frame to the scene, and between the cocoa and their breath, the inside began to fog up as well.

'It's almost as if...' The sound of her own voice startled her. She hadn't been aware that she was speaking out loud.

'As if what, Dulcie?' Chris, also staring at the

window, seemed equally mesmerized by the storm.

'Nothing.' One hand automatically went to the cat on her lap, stroking the smooth black fur as she purred. It was almost as if Gus had appeared in time to send her home, knowing that he, too, was safe. Was that what Esmé had meant? Or was it something else: 'What are you playing at?' She repeated the question softly.

'I'm not playing at anything, Dulcie.' Chris had obviously heard her.

'No.' She turned from the window to smile at him. 'Not you. I heard Avila – at least I think it was Avila – saying that to Heath.'

He just shook his head.

'You're making drama where there isn't any, Dulce.'

Before she could comment, she heard a ping. 'Hang on.' Carefully, so as not to disturb the cat, she reached for her phone. 'Maybe Suze is taking a break.'

Her friend had left as soon as Rogovoy had cleared Dulcie, explaining that only the apparent emergency of a lost cat had dragged her away from work. She had promised to schedule a good catch-up coffee break as soon as the latest crisis ebbed. Dulcie hadn't expected it to be so soon.

'What? Bother.' It wasn't Suze, and Dulcie slammed the phone down on the table. 'It's another email blast.'

'From the URT?' Chris reached for her phone. 'I guess she didn't have a chance to cancel these yet. Or maybe they don't consider them spam. Want me to opt out of it for you?'

195

'Oh, I can do that.' Dulcie scrolled down, but her mind was still on the scene by the theater. 'Did you hear how Roni talked to Heath about going into her office?' She went over the scene in her head. 'Do you think he broke in? He wouldn't rob the company, would he? He's its star.'

'Would seem a little short-sighted.' Chris up-ended his mug. 'But stranger things—'

'Oh, bother.' Dulcie sat up so fast that Esmé protested.

'What?' Chris put his mug down.

'I think I just did something wrong.' She held the phone close, ignoring Esmé's aggrieved mew.

'Give it here.' She handed him the phone. 'Dulcie, what's your password?'

'Um, Mr Grey.' She heard her voice sink. Chris was always on her case to change her passwords regularly. But not only was it a bother, it also meant giving up one of the last remaining ties she had to her late pet. 'Or maybe Mr Grey One,' she offered.

Chris didn't seem about to lecture her. Instead, he was busily punching buttons on the phone, a crease forming on his brow. 'Shoot.'

'Chris, what is it?' She must have let her hand rest too long on the cat. Esmé stirred and pulled herself up to a seated position.

'Hang on.' While she watched, Chris peeled the phone's case off and opened its battery compartment, shaking out the battery into his palm. 'Well, that should work.'

'Chris?'

196

'Dulcie, that email wasn't just spam. By acknowledging it at all – I know, you didn't know – you activated it. It was downloading a worm. If I hadn't stopped it, it would have gotten all your security codes and who knows what else off your phone. If you had opened that email on your computer, your thesis might be gone.'

THIRTY-THREE

The first manifestation fell upon her like a Shadow with the darkness of the Moon. Deep her chamber sat, set among the ancient Stones of his close, protected it would seem by the mold of Honour and of Name, beneath the very watchful eyes of Ancestors both venerable and fierce. This chamber, to which she had been accompanied, would seem the very Heart of Soundness, and with grateful tears she had fallen upon the thick-furred rugs laid out for both Comfort and for Warmth. Such had been the stress of her o'er long winter Journey that she ne'er questioned the Lord who gave her succor, not yet till like a creeping thing, he did...

Dulcie sat up, gasping. She was not alone.

'*Of course not, silly.*' Esmé, beside her, yawned and stretched. Chris, facing the wall, snored gently. The room was dark, as in her dream. Outside, the storm still raged. But the room was their regular old comfy bedroom. No stone walls, no blazing fire. No luxurious furs, unless you counted the cat, who had sat up to knead the pillow to her satisfaction.

'Sorry, Esmé.' She settled back down to watch the cat at work. 'Bad dream.'

The cat lay down, her black back to Dulcie's face. Dulcie decided not to take it personally and instead stared up at where the ceiling probably was. The room wasn't quiet: Esmé's soft vocalizations now joined Chris's snorts, and the windows rattled with each gust. But it was cozy. So very unlike the scene in her dreams that Dulcie was at a loss to figure out from where she had conjured that.

A traveler, a room – a midnight manifestation. It seemed taken right from the book, only this scene had no precedent. More troubling, to Dulcie's mind, was the nature of the manifestation. So far, she had only seen her heroine with the green-eyed stranger, and while she considered him quite catlike, something about this midnight visitor did not seem feline. Nor friendly, for that matter. It was silly, she knew that, but she had come to associate him with Mr Grey. To find out that she was wrong would be disheartening. Though, of course, that would be all it would mean. It wouldn't – it couldn't – mean that Mr Grey was bad in any way, an evil spirit insinuating himself into her life...

Another gust sent a volley of snow against the panes, the window rattling as if a malignant spirit did indeed want in. It was the wind, it had to be, that had sparked the dream. Or maybe, she realized with relief, that stupid spam. What had Chris called it? A worm, slinking into the heart of her phone.

Ick. She almost giggled at the mashed-up metaphor, and with that she felt better. Yes, it was the wind, combined with the nasty virus that

199

had tried to attack her phone. But their apartment house was solid, and she had Chris to protect her from a cyber attack. On top of it all, Gus was safe, and she had done Roni a favor, warning her about the hacking.

Dulcie turned toward Esmé and felt the luxuriousness of fur on her face. She should call Roni in the morning, she decided, to tell her about this latest attack. The little troupe might be blamed if this happened to more people. And she should ask about how Gus managed to get in and out.

Maybe, she thought, her eyes growing heavy, Gus himself would tell her. What was it Esmé had said to her? She needed to learn to listen. To listen to learn. To learn...

Outside, the wind was dying down, replaced by the patter of falling snow. Inside, the soft breathing of the cat was soon joined by another, as Dulcie joined her companions in sleep.

THIRTY-FOUR

'I'm checking on the weather.' Chris was looking at his cellphone when Dulcie entered the
kitchen.

'Why not just look outside?' Dulcie was glad
for her fuzzy slippers and heavy robe. As she
walked over to the window, she could feel the
draft that leaked in, and the sight of the white
world outside only made her feel colder. 'Wow,'
she said, her voice hushed. 'It is beautiful,
though.'

'You won't think so when you have to walk
through two-foot drifts.' Chris put his phone
down. 'But I guess the university doesn't care
that the T and most of the city is calling for a
snow day. They never do.'

'Most of the students just have to make it from
the houses.' Turning her back on the sparkly
white world, Dulcie went for the coffee. 'Of
course, I've got to go meet Thorpe this morning.'

'Ugh, I'm sorry, Dulce.' He looked up. 'Can
you wait till noon? I'll be going in then.'

She shook her head. 'Ten a.m. And I've got the
English Ten section at eleven. In fact.' She paused to look up at the clock. 'I should get dressed.'

'Here.' He took her mug and poked around the
cabinet until he found her travel mug. 'I don't

want you running out of gas out there.'

'Thanks, sweetie.' She looked back out the window. 'I don't think I can count on Nancy being there to make coffee today.'

Ten minutes later, she was pulling her boots on while Chris waited, holding her scarf. 'My phone?' She asked, wrapping the long muffler around her neck.

'Sorry.' He shook his head. 'I don't think it's safe to start it back up yet. I want to take a look at where that worm went.'

She nodded, as if she understood what he meant, and wrapped the wool around her mouth.

'I should have it back to you by the end of the day.' Chris leaned forward, looking for some face to kiss. 'But you've got your laptop.' She nodded. 'I've updated the virus protection on that pretty recently. Dulcie? I know you're a trusting soul. It's one of the things I love most about you. But, please, don't open any emails from anyone you don't know.'

It was, Dulcie decided as she turned for the door, a good thing that her scarf kept her from replying.

Ten minutes later, Dulcie nearly lost her coffee. Dulcie had thanked Chris for filling her travel mug for her, never realizing that one small canister would be a problem. But as she clambered over the second waist-high pile of snow, she found she couldn't hold on to it and keep herself upright at the same time. It simply wasn't possible.

'Bother.' Dulcie screwed the mug into the top

202

of the pile – a compact, icy wall that stood between her and the other side of the street. 'This is crazy.'

Using both mittened hands to steady herself, she managed to find a toehold. Clearly, someone else – someone also of diminutive height – had passed this way before. With a grunt of exertion, she pulled herself to the top and jumped down, only remembering to reach back for the beached mug as she turned to survey the peak she had scaled.

'Damn plows.' Another pedestrian, head down to watch for the icy patches, looked up and smiled. No other words were necessary. Winter in New England could be a beautiful thing, and snow should be its frosting. Except that the plows that must have been working all through the night to clear the streets had no place to deposit the snow they scooped up, apparently, except the sides of the roads. Which may have meant that cars – of which Dulcie saw precious few – were able to get around and about in the first hours after the storm. But any pedestrian who had the temerity to actually cross one of those cleared roadways had first to climb over the hard-packed wall of what had been pushed aside.

The next block was worse. Dulcie once again anchored her travel mug in the man-made drift, made sure her bag was secure on her shoulder, and pulled herself up over the barrier. Only this time, instead of dropping down to a nicely shoveled walk, she found herself in calf-deep snow. Clearly, someone had shoveled at some point, but hadn't kept up with the overnight storm. Pausing just long enough for some snow to drip, melting, inside her boot, Dulcie decided to turn back. It would be easier to walk in the street, and with the lack of cars on the road, probably safer. Another plow was heading toward her, but its progress was slow and steady as it scraped up the last of the storm.

Unlike at the corner, the frozen barrier here had no pre-made footholds. On the sidewalk side, however, the waist-high pile was still rough and uneven – churned up from where it had fallen. Grabbing the top, she was able to step into a crevice and pull herself up, before swinging a leg over and feeling for a place to dig her toe in.

'Hey, did you forget something?' A man called out as she eyed the street side of the pile. 'Miss?'

Dulcie looked up as she pulled her second boot over the curbside pile. 'Are you—?'

Too late, she realized that turning would change her balance. Her foothold on the street side slipped, and she scrambled, unable to gain purchase on the snow that had been compressed into ice by the plow.

'Watch it!' A horn sounded, deep and loud, and she turned to see the snowplow. Up high, the driver, eyes wide with horror, leaned frantically on the wheel. It was too little, too late. Dulcie felt herself slipping down the ice, into the street.

'Got you.' A hand latched on to her forearm and pulled, and Dulcie looked up in surprise.

'Heath?' With her free hand, she grabbed the top of the snow pile and swung her leg over it. Sitting up here, she found herself eye to eye with

204

the handsome actor, his blond mane peeking out from a wool cap.

'Dulcie.' His smile, as he helped her down the other side of the snow wall, looked intensely bright in the reflected light. And, Dulcie thought, a tad inappropriate considering that she had nearly slipped under what was essentially a truck. 'I saw you start to climb, and you'd forgotten your mug.'

He turned from her now and took the few steps back to the corner, where her silver travel mug was still standing at hip height in the snow.

'Thanks.' Dulcie, waiting for him to return with it, realized her legs were shaking. 'For the mug and for – well – everything.'

'Not a problem.' He tilted that overlarge head toward her and dropped his voice. 'Those of us who aren't giants have to help each other.'

Dulcie could only nod. Heath might not be a big man, but he was taller than she was. And stronger, too. Dulcie thought of the strength of his grip. If he hadn't been so strong ... No, she didn't want to think of it.

'Are you heading into the Square?' He didn't seem to notice how flustered she still was. Or, she realized, he might be used to women reacting with shaken silence.

'Yeah. You too?' The thought that he might mistake the cause of her agitation did her more good than the now-cold coffee she swigged. 'Is the theater open today?'

He shrugged. 'Don't know. Nobody answered the phone this morning, but I figured I'd better go in.'

'That's dedication.' She took his outstretched hand as she clambered through the snow. 'Wouldn't Roni usually be in by now?'

'You'd think.' He shuffled his feet to clear a path. 'Maybe you should walk behind me?'

'Thanks.' With anyone else, Dulcie would turn it into a joke. Right now, she was too grateful. Besides, the system worked. The two were making progress.

'Hey, if she's in, would you bring her a message for me?' Dulcie was getting her breath back, despite the difficulty of the walk. 'Or I can stop in, with you, if that's okay.' Dulcie didn't know what her status was at the little theater. But surely this man knew her motives were good.

'Is this about Gus?' Heath glanced over his shoulder at her, before plowing ahead. 'Cause I promise you, we're going to try to keep him inside from now on.'

'Did you find out how he got out?' Even with Heath clearing a path, Dulcie needed both her hands out for balance. 'That would be the best way to keep him safe.'

'No, not yet.' Even he seemed to be having trouble with the snow. 'That's one of the reasons I want to go in. Poke around, see what I can find.'

It could have been a trick of the snow, or maybe because the actor was looking down as he spoke. Dulcie found his voice strangely muffled.

'Heath, I know about what's happening.' It could also, she realized, have another source. 'About the money. In fact, that's what I want to talk to Roni about. I found something...'

206

She stopped short, because he had. But the Heath that turned to face her was not kind or smiling. At that moment, he wasn't even handsome.

'Don't you dare.' The blue eyes were wild, the handsome lips drawn back in a grimace. 'You keep away from Roni. Do you hear me?'

'Sheesh.' Dulcie stepped back, and felt herself stopped by the snow piled behind her. 'I'm not ... I didn't mean anything.'

'Sorry.' He wiped one gloved hand over his face. 'It's been a bad week. People are...' He shook his head, and Dulcie thought she saw tears in his eyes. 'People are saying crazy things about her. About us.'

'I was just trying to be helpful.' Dulcie's own voice had dropped to a whisper. 'Roni had shared some things with me, and I thought I could help.'

He nodded, and suddenly he looked older. Tired. 'I'll tell her,' he said. 'I will. Just ... let me, okay?'

'Okay.'

Nodding once more, he turned and trudged on. Dulcie followed in silence, trying to make sense of what had just happened. She didn't know enough about the troupe – about the theater world in general – but it seemed that what she had witnessed might be more than the bonding of a theatrical company.

As they reached the end of the block, she found herself stuck on one question: Was there more going on between Roni and the handsome lead than she had thought? With a grunt and heave, Heath broke through the piled-up snow blocking them from the intersection and started crossing the street. Dulcie began to follow, but as she stepped through the barrier, she hesitated.

The plow had long gone by, but if she closed her eyes she could still see it, remembering that moment when it had loomed right before her, bearing down. And remembered, too, the strength of the slight actor as he gripped her arm and pulled.

THIRTY-FIVE

Nancy was seated in the front room of the departmental offices, struggling with her boots when Dulcie arrived.

'Here, let me.' Dulcie knelt in front of the plump secretary and pulled.

'Thank you, Dulcie.' The second boot off, Nancy stood in her stocking feet and turned toward her own office. She emerged with an old-fashioned boot jack, which she placed by the door. 'Here we go,' she said. 'Not that I expect many visitors today.'

'They still haven't cancelled classes, have they?' Dulcie pulled her own boots off.

'The world's greatest university? Of course not.' The normally soft-spoken secretary's voice took on a bit of an edge. 'I'm sorry, Dulcie,' she immediately recanted. 'My bus was late, and the walk from the Square was simply treacherous.'

'You could have taken the day off, you know.' Following Nancy's example, Dulcie left her boots to dry on the mat by the door.

'Thank you, dear, but I felt somebody should open the office.'

Dulcie must have made a sound, because the secretary looked up from the coffee maker. 'You didn't hear? I'm so sorry, Dulcie. Mr Thorpe said he was going to call you.'

'My phone's broken.' Dulcie sat down with a thud. 'He's going to be late?'

She knew what Nancy was going to say even before she answered. 'I'm so sorry. He's not coming in at all. But now you have all this extra time!'

Dulcie forced a smile. 'I confess, the pages I was going to give him aren't in the best shape.'

'Well, there you go then.' Nancy's good cheer never seemed forced. 'Coffee?'

It was, Dulcie had to admit, a perfect way to work – the departmental offices had never been quieter and her first section wasn't until noon. Hunkered down in the upstairs conference room, away from the distractions of home or her own office, Dulcie opened her laptop. Today, she would finally get some writing done.

Picking up from the rough pages she had been going to present to Thorpe, she began right away with her main argument:

'Considering the pages from the Philadelphia bequest in light of new discoveries, certain phrasings, last seen in the works of a London-based author, call out for further study.' It wasn't how she'd chosen to say it, but it was close enough. After all, wasn't all scholarship a question of interpretation?

She typed a little more, copying passages from her notes that most closely echoed those she had already discussed in both *The Ravages* and the political writings of the anonymous author. *'Call out...'* She stopped. Yes, she'd be revising later, but still, if she could avoid repeating phrases, she should. 'Call,' she said out loud. 'Point out, cry out, yell.'

Why hadn't Amy called out when she was attacked? Had it been so sudden that she hadn't had a chance to yell?

'In both these newly uncovered pages and the anonymous political tracts recently identified, recurring phrases may be seen that mirror those used in The Ravages of Umbria. *Such anomalous phrases may indicate...'* She stopped. Was that too forceful? No, she decided, shaking her head. It wasn't forceful enough. *'Such unique phrasings indicate a singular authorship.'* No, not indicate. That sounded too wishy-washy, like someone was pointing in the general direction. *'Signify a singular authorship...'* That was better.

Or was it? Lots of things could be signifiers. Like the fact that Amy hadn't called for help. Or that Heath didn't want Dulcie to talk to Roni. Or that Heath was stronger than he might appear. Of course, so was Avila.

Dulcie shook her head to clear it. She had done what she meant to do when she had assured herself that Gus, the theater cat, was safe. What had happened to Amy was a tragedy, but it was not her concern. Everyone, from Chris to Detective Rogovoy, had made that point. She'd been lucky not to get in trouble for poking about, as it was. Though she had to wonder, who had called the cops on her? The director probably had the most to lose, but he hadn't even come into the theater last night. That left...

No, this wasn't her problem. Better to stick with her own area of expertise. *'As centuries of*

211

readers of The Ravages of Umbria *may reasonably infer...*' Of course, one couldn't help what one thought, as well as what one might reasonably infer. That Amy had not cried out because she had known the attacker, and had not feared any violence until it was too late. That someone within the theater community had not wanted Dulcie to inquire further. That a particular actor, who had been linked with Amy, was actively dissuading Dulcie from inquiring further.

'A close analysis of these pages, therefore, reveals a textual similarity from which identification may reasonably be inferred.'

That was the crux of the argument, and she sat there, watching her cursor blink silently. All the papers she had been deciphering, all the letters and fragments of a story led to this. What she hoped to prove in her dissertation was that one woman, one great mind, had been behind both *The Ravages of Umbria* and this as yet unnamed novel, the one Dulcie was just piecing together out of found fragments. And in between were the political writings – funny, smart texts written under a variety of pseudonyms for various Philadelphia newspapers that laid out, more nakedly than in the novels, a strikingly modern argument for universal suffrage, focusing on women's rights within marriage.

What Dulcie sensed, but might never be able to prove, was that these novels – especially this more daring, later work – echoed real-life events from the author's life. Not the ghouls and winged demons, perhaps. And probably not the apparently supernatural wolves. But the oppressive

212

lord, a lover – or a husband? – who had forced the author to flee from London to Philadelphia, and maybe beyond.

This she would probably never be able to prove. Not unless, somehow, she could find out whom the author had been. Locate her in time and place. Finally put a name to her anonymous genius.

The cursor blinked, but Dulcie no longer saw it. All the scholarship in the university might as well not have mattered in that moment. Her deductive reasoning had been on overdrive, working away while she typed. Dulcie might not have a name for the author of *The Ravages*, but she had something else. She had the name of Amy's murderer. And if she was right about this, she just might have the proof of his crime, too.

THIRTY-SIX

Not having a phone was a major pain. Dulcie's first instinct was to run downstairs to Nancy's office. Surely, in such a case, the secretary would allow Dulcie to make a personal call from the departmental land line.

But as she rose from her seat, Dulcie caught herself. Who to call? She didn't know anyone in the city police department. She surely didn't know any of the state police officers. And her one contact in the university police had expressly forbidden her from any involvement.

Standing there, drumming her fingers on the conference table, she weighed the options. Odds were, anyone who didn't know her would ignore her – or worse, dismiss her as a crackpot theorist and, just maybe, be even less likely to look into the blond actor's motivation as a result. No, she couldn't risk that. Rogovoy might get angry, but at least he would listen. And really, her own standing wasn't important in this case. What mattered was starting an investigation.

Though, in truth, it would be better if the idea came from someone else. Someone who ... well, not Chris. Rogovoy might not be a scholar, but he'd see through that one. Trista? No. Her flirtatious friend had come through in the crunch, but she was too partial to the handsome actor to be trusted to pass along a tip that might implicate him. What would be best would be someone who was intimately involved.

Roni. It came to her in a flash. She meant to contact the office manager to tell her about the latest bug, anyway. And – she shivered as she thought of it – if Heath's strange behavior had meant anything, the mousy brunette might be in danger.

Dulcie sat back down, opening her laptop as she did. The easiest thing would be to email Roni. That way she could explain in detail what had happened – make her case before the smitten girl could dismiss her concerns as some kind of strange rant.

She found the email from the URT ticket office and hit 'reply'. *Roni*, she typed. *We have to talk. It's urgent. Call me?* And just as she was about to hit 'send', she stopped herself. What was she doing? This was the same email system that had let a worm into her phone. Granted, this time she hadn't opened any attachments or started any surveys, but still, she didn't know the risk. All she knew for sure was that there *was* a risk, and one that she had been expressly warned against.

Erasing her message, she closed the program. Before she opened it again, she'd confess all to Chris. Whatever she had done, he'd be able to fix it. At least, she hoped. At any rate, she resolved, no more email until she got home tonight. Which left the phone – and again she stood, thinking to use Nancy's office extension. Only the thought of someone else – of Heath – picking up was a bit unnerving. She should have a story ready. An excuse for why she was calling.

'Dulcie?' Nancy's voice reached up the stairs. 'Do you think you'll be up there for a while?'

'Actually, I was just finishing up.' Dulcie leaned out of the office to yell down. 'Do you need the conference room?'

'Not at all.' Nancy, she could see, had her coat on. 'Only I just got a call from my dentist. What with the weather and all, she's had a cancellation and she could see me now. So I thought, well, if you didn't mind covering...'

Dulcie hesitated for a moment too long before answering.

'Or I could lock up, put a note on the door.' Nancy was buttoning up her long blue overcoat as she spoke.

'If you wouldn't mind.' Dulcie felt a bit like a heel. 'I know nobody will show up, but I do have a section at noon.'

'Not at all.' Nancy ducked out of sight and came back with a scarf. 'You can put the alarm on when you leave. You do have the new code, I'm sure.'

'Yes, it's on my—' Dulcie caught herself. At what point had she stopped writing things down? 'Sorry, Nancy. It's on my phone, and I don't have it...'

The other woman was knotting her scarf in a rather dashing fashion, but her knitted brow ruined the effect.

'I'll just head out with you now. Let me grab my stuff.' It was simply easier, and besides, she didn't want to use her laptop again until Chris had looked at it anyway.

'Were you able to get some work done?' Nancy stood by the door as Dulcie pulled her boots on. The secretary was, as always, too kind to fidget.

'I think so.' Dulcie jammed her hat on and stepped out into the cold, as Nancy turned to lock the door. 'In fact, I think I made a very important discovery.'

'Good for you, dear.' The departmental secretary picked her way slowly down the packed snow on the stairs. 'Now step carefully, Dulcie. Remember, this kind of weather can be treacherous.'

THIRTY-SEVEN

It really had been a happy accident, Dulcie decided as she made her own way down the sidewalk. Left to her own devices, she would have called and she wouldn't have known what to say if Heath had answered. But if she dropped by, well, she could be inquiring about the cat.

As Dulcie shuffled down the icy sidewalk, she tried not to think of the down sides of this argument. That nobody would believe her. That somebody would call the cops. That she'd be labeled as the local crazy cat lady.

Actually that last possibility wasn't a bad one, she decided. It might even have some upside, if it allowed her to become more involved in Gus's welfare. This thought cheered her enough to add a skip to her step – which was *not* a good idea. The university buildings and grounds crew had done a decent job of clearing the snow, but the bright sun had melted just enough of it for the run-off to freeze, coating the bricks with a treacherous sheet of ice. Someone had thrown some salt down, but not enough, and Dulcie found herself skating along on one foot, arms akimbo, as she struggled to maintain balance.

'This is ridiculous,' she complained out loud, catching hold of a sad-looking street tree. A

218

squirrel looked down in alarm, chittering his complaint as Dulcie kicked a clump of snow and began to make her way more carefully along. 'I can't email, I can't call, and I can't drop by, either?'

It would help if she knew who had complained about her. While she doubted that she would have gotten into serious trouble last night, it had been unpleasant, at least until Detective Rogovoy had shown up. Suze had been on her side, too – and it hit her. If she could call her former room-mate, she would know what to do. The question was, once again, how to reach out to her legal eagle friend.

Suze's law firm was in the South End, clear across town. And while Dulcie was sure that no mere snowstorm would keep her friend out of the office, she didn't have time for the combination of T lines that would get her there. Not to get there and be back in time for her section. And time, if what she feared was true, was of the essence here.

'Dulcie!' She looked up to see herself being hailed by a slim polar bear. Or, no, a petite figure in a white fur cap with what looked like ears. 'Hang on!'

Never before had Dulcie been so glad to see Trista. 'Hey, Tris, can I use your phone?'

Her friend raised one pierced eyebrow, but dug into her pocket for the device.

'Thanks.' Luckily, Dulcie had committed some numbers to memory. But whether because of the weather or – more likely – a client in the office, the call went straight to voicemail. 'Hey, Suze, it's Dulcie.' She pondered briefly how to phrase her question. 'I need to get a message to someone at the theater group, only I'm afraid I'll get in trouble if I go down there. Thought maybe you might be able to help.' She paused, realizing the impossibility of her situation. 'I don't have my phone on me, but I'll try you back later.' That was it; the line cut off. She handed the phone back to Trista.

'You going to tell?' Her friend looked deceptively innocent in the big fake-fur hat, but Dulcie recognized the glint in her eye.

'I ended up running into Heath this morning,' Dulcie started to explain, then stopped. Trista was not the person she could confide in.

'Oh, so that's why you want to go over to the theater.' What Trista's smile didn't imply, her tone did. 'Dulcie, you're a better liar than I thought.'

'No.' Dulcie was firm. 'No, I'm not. I really do have to talk to Roni, the office manager, about something.'

Trista looked at her quizzically, and Dulcie realized she needed to tell her friend something.

'Their email system has been hacked. They're sending out some kind of corrupted file with their ticket offers,' she said. 'Roni knows, but she thinks she's caught it. But last night, I got another one. That's why I don't have my own phone. Chris is working on it.'

Trista nodded. 'Jerry's always trying to get his hands on my phone.'

'No, I mean he's fixing it.' Why was everything so difficult with Trista these days?

220

'Of course he is.' Something about Trista's tone made Dulcie think she wasn't telling the truth. Her next words confirmed it. 'Not every guy is like Chris, Dulcie.'

Dulcie looked up, afraid to ask, but Trista shook off the question in her eyes.

'Hey, I couldn't help hearing you, and I've got a better idea,' she said. 'Let's just go over there. Nobody's said anything to me about not showing up. And you could just be tagging along, right?'

Dulcie opened her mouth – and shut it again. 'You know, that just might work.'

It wasn't easy walking back down to Mass Ave. More of the walks had been shoveled since Dulcie first came in, and the dull roar of snow-blowers heralded the university grounds crew at work. But still she found herself walking behind her friend as the shoveled or blown up snow made narrow canyons of the walkways. In a way, not being face to face made it easier, though, and Dulcie found herself voicing a long-considered question.

'Trista?' she called up to the bulbous white bear head in front of her. 'Do you ... are you and Jerry good?'

The bear head turned, revealing a pink, pierced face. 'You mean, are we breaking up?'

Dulcie shrugged. That wasn't it exactly. 'Well, the way you talk about other guys...'

Trista's smile grew into a big grin. 'Like Heath?'

Something must have shown on Dulcie's face.

'Wait – Dulcie. What is it?' Trista had stopped walking and turned to face her friend. 'Did

221

something happen?'

'No, not really.' Dulcie shook her head, unsure about what to say – or how much.

'Dulcie.' Trista was holding her shoulders in her big white puffy mittens. 'Talk to me.'

'I started to tell him about the email, that I needed to talk to Roni, and he turned on me,' Dulcie said finally. 'He scared me, Tris. I think, maybe, he's not who he seems.'

To her surprise, Trista nodded. 'I think you're right. I heard something...' Her voice trailed off.

'Trista, tell me.' Her friend appeared lost in thought. 'You've got to.'

A nod. 'It was something one of the other players said. Something about how Heath can't leave, can't get any better gigs. There's some kind of history there.'

'You think Amy found out?' Dulcie's voice had fallen to a whisper.

'Wait – you don't think...' Trista's face had gone pale. 'You can't...'

Dulcie only shrugged. 'I don't know. I just know that he's hiding something. And maybe someone found out what it was.'

THIRTY-EIGHT

The two friends continued on in grim silence. At least, Dulcie thought it was grim. In truth, all she knew was that Trista's white hood kept bobbing in front of her along the narrow walkway. The one time her friend turned to offer her a hand, as they came upon a lone unshoveled stretch, she did look thoughtful, at least, her usually smooth brow appeared furrowed beneath the shaggy white fur.

A half block from the theater, though, Trista stopped and turned toward her friend. 'I was thinking,' she said.

'We've got to do this, Tris.' Dulcie didn't mean to cut her off. The words simply spilled out. 'I know you like him and all, but we've got to.'

'I know, I know.' Trista waved Dulcie down. 'But how, that's the question. And in my experience, a little bit of gamesmanship – or gameswomanship – might be the answer.'

Trista had leaned in conspiratorially with this, but Dulcie only shook her head, confused.

'You were asking before, about me and Jerry?' Dulcie hadn't exactly, but clearly Trista had seen what she was getting at. 'Let's just say, I've spent some time thinking about male psychology.'

'Okay...' This was beginning to sound too much like flirting, but Dulcie wasn't sure she had a choice. Up ahead, they could see the theater – and the heftier actor, Doug, shoveling.

'Hi!' Before Dulcie could stop her – or even ask what the plan was – Trista had started waving, catching the eye of the muscular actor.

'Hello.' He put down his shovel and smiled at Trista, who waded through the remaining snow.

'Hang on.' Dulcie was used to this. Trista had that effect on men, but she wanted to be around to hear what her friend said.

By the time she had trundled through the remaining half block, Trista and Doug seemed to be best friends. Dulcie was still brushing snow off her jeans – the last drift had reached above her knees – as Trista filled her in.

'Doug says they are going to have a show tonight.' Her broad smile seemed real, but that could have been because of the proximity of the muscular actor. 'So we came by just in time.'

'We did?' Dulcie was trying to follow Trista's lead. Only she didn't see what it was.

Trista wasn't standing close enough to nudge her. The briefest of nods served the same purpose.

'Yeah, we did.' Her friend sounded confident. 'We were thinking, maybe some of your regulars couldn't make it in, what with the snow and all. We want to be ushers for tonight's performance.'

Dulcie was struck dumb by Trista's gambit. Doug, however, seemed to take it in stride. 'That's great.' He leaned on his shovel, thinking.

'I know we had some of our volunteers give up after ... well, after what happened. And I bet, with the roads still slick, we will get some cancellations for tonight. You know the drill?'

Trista nodded even as Dulcie shook her head. 'I don't,' she managed to squeak out.

'Well, I think you're supposed to be here like a half-hour early, and you have to dress in black, like the cast. But you get to watch the show from the back of the room.' He paused. 'You should get the official version from Roni, though. She's the one who keeps all the lists in order.'

'Is she in?' Dulcie didn't want to appear too eager.

'Yeah, I believe so.' Doug looked down at his snow shovel – and at the snow still covering half the sidewalk.

'We know where her office is.' Trista grabbed Dulcie's arm and pulled her toward the front door. 'Catch you on the way out,' she called over her shoulder as they slipped inside.

'Trista! What were you thinking?' Once they were inside the empty lobby, Dulcie turned on her friend.

'Perfect excuse, don't you think?' Trista looked around. 'Nobody can complain about two people coming to volunteer, can they? And on top of that, you get to talk to Roni without anyone wondering why. Plus, if we actually usher, we can ask questions about Heath. Find out what he's up to. And we get to see the show again.'

'I can't take another night off work.' Dulcie rubbed her forehead, having forgotten that her mittens were full of snow. 'I just can't.'

225

'Oh, come on.' Trista leaned over to knock a stray bit of ice off Dulcie's hair. 'It's a Friday. What's a few hours going to matter? And besides, this *is* work. It's a classic, only under a different name.'

'It's not just the name.' Dulcie pulled her cap off. The inside was dry and she used that to wipe her face. 'It's not the same thing at all.'

'What do you mean?'

Dulcie looked up as Trista turned around. Behind her, at the back of the lobby, stood Heath Barstow, a blank look on his face.

'She didn't mean anything,' Trista jumped in.

'Yes, she did.' Heath took a step closer, his face turning grim. 'What did you mean by that?'

'Hey, I'm an English major, not Classics.' Dulcie couldn't help but remember how strong the actor's grip had been. She and Trista outnumbered him, and they were right by the front door. But the look in his eye was so intense. 'In fact, I want to see the play again, see if it really does hew to the original.'

'The play, right.' Heath paused. 'So, you came by to ask for more tickets or something?'

Dulcie couldn't help herself. She shot a glance at Trista, but her friend was staring at the blond actor.

'We're hoping to usher tonight,' Dulcie filled in after a moment's awkward silence. So much for not committing, she told herself. 'Doug said we should check in with Roni? He's right outside, you know.' She couldn't resist adding that last bit.

It didn't seem to have an effect. Whatever

mood had been on Heath, it had passed. 'Yeah,' he said, nodding. 'I was heading over to talk to her myself when I heard you two come in.'

'We can come back.' Dulcie knew she wasn't making sense. Still, she didn't want to talk to Roni with Heath there.

'Nonsense.' Trista took her arm. 'We're here, right?'

Too late, Dulcie realized that she hadn't shared the full extent of her concerns with Trista. 'No.' She mouthed the word as Heath turned to lead them to the tiny office.

'What?' Trista mouthed back. 'Maybe she knows something,' she whispered as the two fell in line.

'Hey, Heath.' Avila was coming out of the darkened theater area. 'I didn't hear you come in.'

'Avila!' Dulcie turned to greet the dark-eyed actress, but Trista grabbed her.

'You wanted to get Roni alone?' Her stage whisper must have been audible, but Avila had taken Heath's arm by then, spinning the actor around to face her.

Dulcie paused, out of concern for Avila, but agreed with a nod. 'Come on.' She led the rest of the way to the tiny office.

'Knock, knock?' The door to Roni's office was closed, but not latched.

'Tris—' Dulcie grabbed for her friend, but Trista had already pushed the door open.

'Hope we're not interrupting.' Trista stepped into the office, and so Dulcie followed.

'No, no.' The smile that turned up to meet them

couldn't have been more fake, and Dulcie cringed inwardly. 'Just let me save.' Roni's fingers pattered over the keys. 'There.'

'Roni, I'm so glad we caught you.' Dulcie pushed past Trista. Since they were there, she might as well relay her message – both her messages. 'I think I found something.'

She looked over her shoulder. The door was still open. 'Trista?' With a nod, Trista turned toward it.

'Look, I don't want to alarm you or anything.' Keeping her voice low, she leaned over Roni's desk. What she was going to say next was risky. 'And I know – well, I think I know how you feel about Heath, but—'

'There you are.' Trista had almost latched the door when it burst open. Heath, a broad grin on his face, came striding in. 'Roni. Sorry, meant to bring these two by to see you, but I got detained.'

'Heath?' Behind him, Dulcie could hear Avila. She sounded confused. 'What's going on?'

He ignored her, focusing that big smile on the office manager, who seemed to shrink back from all the attention. 'They want to be ushers, Roni.' His voice, overloud, sounded as false as his smile. 'They want to see the show again.'

'Ushers.' Roni sounded as stunned as she looked. 'Of course.'

'I was hoping to get a chance to chat, too.' Dulcie glanced over at the actor. She didn't know what he knew about the company's precarious financial situation, but if it gave her an opportunity to speak privately with the office manager, so much the better. 'Something new

228

came up with, you know, the thing that we'd started talking about?'

'The thing?' Roni was pale, to the point that Dulcie began to worry that the other woman might faint.

'It's not that bad,' she added quickly. 'Probably nothing. My boyfriend's working on it. He's a computer guy. I don't know if you remember his name.'

A heavy hand fell on her shoulder. 'I don't think we should take up any more of our Roni's time.' Heath. She could feel his breath, hot on her cold ear. 'Roni can put you down for ushering tonight, and we can let her get back to work, okay?'

As if in response, Roni started scrambling among the papers on her desk. 'Two for tonight. Dulcie Schwartz and – ah?'

'Trista Dunlop.'

'Great.' The hand slid to the middle of her back, turning Dulcie as neatly as if they had been dancing. 'We'll see you at seven twenty tonight, then.'

'Roni?' Dulcie tried to turn. She had to give it one more shot. But all she saw was Roni shaking her head, as Heath propelled her out the door.

'Wow, that was odd.' Trista, who had been herded ahead of Dulcie, pulled her aside as soon as they were out of the theater. 'Since when does Heath Barstow greet visitors? He said he heard us and that's why he came over, but I don't know.'

'I don't think it's that either, Tris.' It was time, Dulcie decided, to tell her friend all that she

229

suspected. 'Did you notice how he hung around while we spoke with Roni? The way he kept interrupting, and the way he wanted us out of there? He's stalking her, Tris. Roni might be his next victim.'

THIRTY-NINE

'On top of everything, we forgot to ask about Gus.' Dulcie paused, tempted to turn back.

'You mean the cat?' Trista looked confused. 'But he's okay. Isn't he?'

'He was last night. Well, he went inside before the storm got too bad,' Dulcie explained. 'But I don't like that he can go in and out like that. This is a big city, and it's not safe. Someone should take responsibility for him.'

'It sounds like everyone at the URT has their hands full,' her friend responded. They had reached the edge of the area in front of the theater that Doug had cleared, but the muscular actor was nowhere in sight. 'You want me to go ahead again?'

'Yeah, thanks.' As her friend stepped up and over a small wall of snow, Dulcie turned around. 'Maybe I could ask Doug if he could ... Wait!'

Trista turned toward her. 'What?'

Dulcie pointed to the corner of the building, where a narrow path had been partially cleared between the theater and the fence that marked the edge of the property. 'I saw something move back there – something grey.'

'Oh, please. It's probably a rat.'

But Dulcie was already there, wading into the

231

knee-deep snow by the path's edge. 'Gus! Gus?'

'Dulcie.' Trista's tone was not amused. 'People are going to think you're losing it.'

'Hang on.' A movement, a bit further back, had caught her eye. 'Gus?' Yes, the apple-shaped grey head popped up, those green eyes blinking. 'Gus, come here.' Dulcie clambered through the snow, but the cat, lighter and swifter, leaped from his perch and was gone.

'Oh, hell.' Behind her, Dulcie heard Trista curse as she started to follow her friend.

'Wait, Tris.' She held up a hand behind her. 'I don't want to scare him.'

The path wasn't, as Dulcie had originally thought, shoveled. Instead it looked as if some-one – probably Doug – had forced a way through the snow. Probably to a back entrance, Dulcie thought. Perhaps to a storage or service area, where the snow shovel had been stored. Could that have been Gus's means of egress from the building?

'Dulcie...' Trista's voice might as well have been a growl, but Dulcie ignored her, pushing on. Sure enough, the path ended at a door, set into the brick building's wall. And sitting by the door, tail neatly wrapped around his front paws, was Gus, the Russian blue.

'Come here, boy.' Dulcie scooped the cat up. 'You must be freezing.' She turned back toward Trista. 'You see? I didn't imagine him.'

'Fair enough.' Trista nodded. 'But he must have his own way in and out.'

'I don't know.' Arms full of cat, Dulcie nodded toward the closed door. 'Maybe he snuck out

232

when Doug came out to shovel. I'm going to bring him in.'

Trista opened her mouth, but it was several moments before she started to speak. 'Dulcie,' she said finally. 'I don't think they really want us in there. We're going back later, but...'

'No "buts" about it.' Dulcie started walking and motioned for Trista to turn around and lead the way back to the street. 'I am not leaving this little guy out in the cold.'

In her arms, Gus began to purr.

Back in front of the theater, Trista held the door open for Dulcie and the cat. But Dulcie felt a strange reluctance to enter. Or maybe, she decided, it was that she didn't want to relinquish the cat.

'Do *you* want to go back in there?' She murmured into the grey fur. Although Gus's coat was shorter than Esmé's, it had a silky quality that made it feel almost as lush, and Dulcie buried her face in its warmth. 'You don't want to, do you?'

'Dulce.' Trista was standing by the door. 'Why don't you drop the cat, and we can get going. Don't you have a section?'

Maybe it was Trista's voice; there was an edge to her tone that couldn't be explained away as simply due to the cold. Maybe it was that Dulcie had turned, twisting at the waist as she held the cat close. Gus used that moment to squirm, pushing his powerful hind legs against Dulcie and jumping free of her arms.

'Well, that's that.' Trista reached for her arm. 'Let's go.'

'Wait.' Dulcie watched as the grey cat trotted into the lobby and then turned, his green eyes luminous in the dim light. 'I think he wants to show me something.'

Ignoring Trista's pained sigh, she stepped carefully after the cat. But if she expected the Russian blue to duck into Roni's office, she was surprised. Even though the office manager's door was slightly ajar, the cat kept trotting, stopping every few feet to glance back at Dulcie.

'He thinks you're chasing him.' Trista's stage whisper revealed her presence. 'He's playing.'

'Maybe.' They'd come to the prop room, where the narrow stairs ran up above the bar. The door was slightly ajar, and the slim cat slipped easily inside, but Dulcie stopped, unsure of whether to follow.

'See?' Trista came up behind her. 'He's just going to his usual haunt.'

'No, he isn't.' A woman's voice – someone inside the room – seemed to respond to Trista's statement, and Dulcie and Trista both froze. As the voice continued, it became clear they had stumbled on to a private conversation. 'I know he isn't ... isn't who he says he is,' the woman was saying. 'But why would he want to hurt her? Wait, what's that?'

Dulcie heard the swift intake of Trista's breath, close behind her, and realized she was holding her own.

'It's just Gus.' A man speaking this time. A man with a familiar voice.

'What is with this cat? I swear he's schizophrenic.'

'He likes you.' The man again, half whispering. 'He likes people. He's a cat.'

'Then why did he attack Amy that time?' The woman. It must be Avila, Dulcie thought. 'Why did he hiss at me?'

'Like I said, he's a cat.'

Dulcie relaxed and turned back to Trista. It was time to go. But as she started to step away, the man started speaking again, even more quietly than before but with an urgency that made her listen.

'Threat.' She was sure she heard that word – or maybe 'threatened'.

'I'm only telling you what I saw.' The voice was growing louder, more frustrated. Could it be Heath? 'I'd seen him with Amy, and now this. And all those questions? I don't like it.'

'You're just jealous.' Avila, it had to be. Which meant they were talking *about* Heath. 'You always have been.'

'No, I'm scared.' The voice was familiar. Could it be Doug? Or Bob? Dulcie couldn't clearly remember what the rotund director's voice sounded like. 'I'm telling you,' he was saying. 'She knows something, and I don't think it's good.'

A hand came down on Dulcie's shoulder and she turned in horror. It was Trista, her face reflecting the fear that Dulcie felt.

'Do you hear that, Dulce?' Trista's voice was barely above a breath now, but Dulcie heard it and nodded in return. '"She knows something",' Trista repeated. 'I think they're talking about you.'

FORTY

'They could have been talking about Roni, too.' Dulcie refused to be frightened, especially now that she and Trista were back outside. 'The way Heath was looming over her.'

'That wasn't Heath.' Trista looked thoughtful. 'I know his voice. I think that was the big guy, Doug.'

'Oh.' Dulcie felt her heart sink. She'd liked the carpenter-actor.

'Well, we should go.' Trista turned to lead the way back to the Square.

'The cops?' Dulcie was willing to take any suggestion at this point.

'No, silly.' The face that turned back to her had an unexpected smile. 'Section!'

It was hard for Dulcie to keep up on the snowy walk. But with more shopkeepers and landlords digging out, it wasn't long before they were walking side by side. Finally, Dulcie broke the silence.

'We have to do something, Trista,' she said. 'I'm not sure what. But we have to do something.'

'Look, I know you're concerned.' Her friend had stopped now and turned to face her. 'And, yeah, it did sound bad. But what are you going to do?'

Dulcie was biting her lip, thinking, when it suddenly hit her. 'Give me your phone.'

'What? Why?'

'Tris, I'll give it right back.'

Her friend handed it over, and Dulcie did a quick search. Sure enough, the theater's website had a director. She found Roni's name listed under 'Subscriptions and Group Sales'. But before she hit the 'call' button, she stopped. What if Heath was still hanging around Roni's office? What if Avila and Doug were within earshot? What if someone else picked up her phone?

A message, however...

Roni, she began to type. *We need to talk.* Dulcie paused. Should she mention going to the police? No, she decided. Roni might simply assume she was overreacting. She should meet with her. Then she could make her case. But how to get her there? Well, there was one subject Dulcie was pretty sure that Roni wouldn't be able to resist. *About Heath*, she typed. *Lala's in the Square @1?* There would be no way for the office manager to get back to her, but if she didn't show, at least Dulcie could have a good lunch. She sent the text and handed Trista her phone back.

'I hope you know what you're doing.' Trista shoved it in her pocket and turned to start walking again.

'All I know is I have to try,' Dulcie said, to the back of her friend's head. 'I've got to do something.'

FORTY-ONE

'I'm sorry. I can't do anything.' Twenty minutes later, Dulcie was getting frustrated. 'The schedule for the midterm was established by the senior teaching assistant. I have to enforce it.'

The sound that followed – part exhalation, part whine – marked her students' dissatisfaction. It also stoked Dulcie's own resistance.

'Come on, guys.' She looked around at the seven students sagging around the table. 'It's not like you don't have more than a month to go. We can do this.'

'But I got a part in my house play.' Keira was definitely leaning toward the whine.

'Congratulations.' Dulcie made herself smile at the girl. 'That doesn't mean you can give up your class work.' She paused, reaching for inspiration. 'There's no reason why the two shouldn't help each other. After all, here we are, looking at themes in literature. And – what's the play?'

'It's the one where the guy wears an ass's head.' Keira was still sulking, but she seemed torn between the urge to pout and to brag. 'You know, the famous one?'

'*Midsummer Night's Dream*?' Dulcie offered. Keira confirmed it with a nod. 'Well, that's great.

We're not studying Shakespeare in this course, but a lot of the themes are the same. Like, the transformative power of love, for example.'

'Like the one URT is doing?' Bronwyn, down at the table's end, had woken up.

'Kind of.' Dulcie didn't want to lose them. 'Though what they're doing is based on Ovid. And, well, they are using a rather loose interpretation of the core work.'

'I heard it was a blast.' Greg, across from Bronwyn, chimed in. 'I was trying to get tickets for this weekend, but they're sold out.'

'Me, too.' Bronwyn leaned in. 'It's like that girl getting killed? That was the best thing to happen to them.'

'I know—' Keira started, but Dulcie had had enough.

'People.' Her stern voice didn't usually carry much weight. Today, though, she put an extra emphasis behind it. 'Quiet, please. You don't know what you're saying.'

Seven pairs of eyes looked up at her, waiting to hear more.

'A young woman's murder is not some kind of publicity stunt.' She saw at least two of them slump back in their seats. She hoped that was because of some belated sense of shame.

'Might as well be.' So much for her optimism. But before Dulcie could gather the words to reprimand the young man who had spoken (Lance, she thought, though he was now looking down at his hands) she had another thought.

'Have you all been trying for student rush tickets?' She looked around the table.

'They're doing those?' Alannah perked right up. 'I didn't think they were.'

'No, is that what's been sold out?' Dulcie looked from the willowy blonde to Greg. He shook his head. 'Not student tickets?'

'They're out of all tickets,' Greg said. 'I couldn't even get on to the website. And when I called they told me, no luck. Sold out for weeks, they said. And I'd promised Elsie I'd take her, too.'

'You're in trouble.' Bronwyn was smiling.

'Enough.' Dulcie slammed her hands down on the table. Something wasn't right. 'Look, it's bad theater anyway. You'd get a lot more out of the text. And speaking of which, since we didn't get a chance to discuss this week's reading, I'd like a two-page paper from each of you on it for next week. That's one-inch margins, double spaced, folks.' She didn't like having to spell this out, but her students had been getting more and more creative with their computer skills. She raised her hand in a vain attempt to silence the chorus of complaints. 'No arguing. Have them printed out by section next week.'

Dulcie could ignore the looks as the students filed out of the room. What she couldn't ignore were the questions plaguing her. Was the URT show really that popular? Could it honestly be sold out weeks in advance?

She shook her head. It shouldn't be a surprise, she figured. Trista, for all her flightiness, wasn't a complete know-nothing. And Chris had certainly enjoyed it – and he wasn't smitten by the handsome Heath. No, Dulcie had to admit, she was the odd woman out here. The show was a hit.

But if it was such a hit, then why was the troupe doing so badly?

Maybe it was an oddity of theater, Dulcie told herself as she packed up her own books. Maybe production costs had run high, or the theater had opened with a deficit. Maybe the denizens of the old bookstore really had cursed the place when they left. Just because it didn't make sense to her, didn't mean it wasn't true. It was another thing she could ask Roni at lunch.

Dulcie slung her bag over her shoulder and pulled on her hat. She was looking forward to meeting the other woman, she realized. Roni was serious, a business woman, but clearly involved in the arts. She and Dulcie might not have as much in common as she and Trista did, at least in terms of background. But it wouldn't hurt to make a new friend. And if the other woman really was in danger, Dulcie had a chance to help her out.

Of course, she realized as she made her way down to Lala's, Roni might not show up. Without her phone, Dulcie had no way of checking to see if the office manager had even gotten her message. Even if she had, she might be busy. She might have countered with another time.

'Bother.' Dulcie stopped short on the sidewalk – and nearly fell over as someone slammed her from behind. It was Heath. It was ... 'What?'

'Sorry.' A tall woman, cellphone to her ear, called as she passed. Dulcie took a deep breath and felt the pounding of her heart begin to subside. Too much had happened recently, and this was merely an accident, the result of her own sudden halt.

The cellphone, though. That was it. She had been flustered and in a rush when she had left the message for Roni. She had borrowed Trista's phone, intending at first to call, but then she had texted, without realizing the obvious. Roni would think that the message came from Trista, not Dulcie.

Well, there wasn't anything for it now. If Roni made it to the restaurant, Dulcie would explain the mishap. It might even give her an entry to ask about the hacking problem.

Dulcie had planned to hold out for a table, once she got to Lala's. No matter how closely they were packed in, a table would be somewhat more private. What she hadn't counted on was the line that stopped her, as soon as she opened the door, of patrons hoping for even a stool at the bar.

'You, come.' Dulcie looked up to see Lala, the hefty proprietress, motioning her over. With a guilty glance at the line, Dulcie made her way up front. 'Here.'

'Lala,' Dulcie yelled up at the big woman. 'I can't. I'm meeting someone.' She looked back at the crowd. 'At least, I think I am.'

Lala looked down at her, her face frozen in thought. For a moment, Dulcie thought she hadn't understood. Or, worse, that she didn't approve. But another nod and a gesture to one of the wait staff, and suddenly another table appeared. Chairs followed and silverware followed, and then Dulcie felt a strong hand on her back, propelling her toward it.

'Why does she...?' The murmuring crowd fell silent as Lala scanned the waiting area. 'Cop,' someone muttered softly.

Dulcie sat, her back to the wall, and felt her face grow red. It wasn't just the heat, which was a welcome change after the frost outside. It was that she had been given the legendary police table: a semi-legal two-top that Lala pulled out whenever an officer came by. But despite the muttering, which had been picked up by the hungry lines, Dulcie was grateful. Particularly when, through a gap in the crowd, she spotted a pale face and glasses.

'Roni! Over here.' She stood and waved. Roni, spotting her, shook her head. 'No, Roni!' Dulcie called again, ignoring the looks of the other diners. 'Please, over here.'

'I can't...' Roni was peering around the restaurant, and Dulcie realized her mistake.

'Roni, that was me. I called you. Sorry.' She rushed to explain. 'My phone – I'll explain, but there's something more important. I'm so glad you made it. We really need to talk.'

'I gather.' It wasn't simply the cold, Dulcie decided. Roni looked pale and tense.

'Roni, are you okay?' It was a silly question, considering what she was going to tell her. Still, Dulcie was relieved when the other woman nodded, eyeing the crowd around them nervously, and shrugged off her coat. 'They're just peeved that I got this table.' Dulcie leaned in. 'Lala knows me. It's a long story.'

243

Even seated, Roni looked positively ill.

'You should eat something.' Dulcie craned her head around, but Lala was already on it. Two wide bowls of thick green soup were placed before them. 'She sometimes decides what you should have,' Dulcie tried to explain. 'She means well. It's pea soup.' She paused, watching the other woman. 'Do you want me to ask for something else?'

'No, no.' Roni seemed overwhelmed by the whole scene, and so Dulcie let her take a spoonful of the fragrant potage before continuing.

'I need to talk to you about Heath.'

It was too much, too soon. Dulcie realized she had overstepped when Roni coughed out her soup.

'I'm sorry. I don't mean to touch on anything personal.' Dulcie handed her a napkin. Everything she said seemed to be coming out wrong today. She waited while Roni caught her breath. She had to warn Roni, but at the same time, it was pretty apparent that the office manager had a crush on the handsome actor, and Dulcie knew from her own experience how vulnerable that made one – and how embarrassing it could be to learn that others knew your secret.

'I know,' she started in again. 'Or, I should say, I'm aware of some things,' Dulcie said. 'Things that maybe I shouldn't, and that I'm sure nobody else is aware of,' she was quick to add. 'And I wanted to talk to you, Roni. You need to know that I've heard some things.'

Roni was staring at her, though with confusion or apprehension, Dulcie couldn't tell. She needed to just come out with it.

'I know you think you know Heath,' she said. 'You think you know who he really is, but I think you may be in over your head with him. I don't think you can trust him.'

'Like I can trust you?' Roni's voice was soft, but its edge was apparent.

Dulcie sighed. Roni was seeing rivals everywhere.

'Please, Roni, I'm not ... I have no interest in Heath.'

Roni seemed to relax at that, leaning back in her seat. She wasn't eating any more of her soup, however, so after taking another spoonful herself, Dulcie decided to try again.

'It's not that I want to get involved,' she said, between tastes. It had been a long morning and Lala's split pea soup was fragrant and warm. 'I sort of couldn't help it. It was just those emails – and then Gus.'

'The cat.' Roni was nodding, as if she understood.

'Yes, the cat. Speaking of him, you've got to find out how he's getting out. It really isn't safe for him. Out there.'

Dulcie looked down at her bowl, the better to scoop up the last drops. When she looked up, Roni was leaning over her own untouched lunch, staring at her.

'What do you want, Dulcie?' The other woman's voice was hard.

'I want him to be safe.' How could Roni not understand? 'And I want you to be safe, too.'

'Point taken,' said Roni, pushing her chair back

so fast she nearly hit a waiting patron.

'Wait!' Dulcie called out. She hadn't had a chance to tell Roni about the virus. But it was too late. The office manager was already pushing her way back through the crowd, leaving her soup to grow cold.

FORTY-TWO

'*Identity is key to both* The Ravages of Umbria *and the fragments in the Philadelphia bequest,*' Dulcie wrote. '*The hidden or obscured identity of the malevolent Demetria in* Ravages *lays the groundwork for the author's essential thesis on the destructive elements of the unequal – or 'disequal' – society of the time. The implied deception in the Philadelphia fragments involves the unnamed nobleman from whom the protagonist, a highborn woman like Hermetria in* The Ravages, *is fleeing.*'

Dulcie stopped typing with a sigh. This was taking liberties. Yes, what she had read implied that the story was going in this direction. She did, after all, have her heroine fleeing and then unburdening herself to the stranger, Monsieur Grey, who offers her a lift.

What she didn't have, she admitted silently to the close and dusty air of the basement office, was any confirmation that the danger the woman was fleeing was a man. Yes, it would fit neatly with the other fragment she had found in the Mildon – the one in which the woman is looking down at the body of some nobleman, a Lord Esteban. But Dulcie didn't have any reason to put those two story fragments together. Nothing except some vague dreams and a bad feeling about Esteban.

She shifted in her hard wooden chair and stared at the blinking cursor. The afternoon light filtered in through the office's one high window, and even now the screen was growing dark. She ought to turn on another light. She ought to erase what she had typed. Dulcie reached for the keyboard again, and stopped herself. No, she decided. She would write it now and see what she could find. If she couldn't connect the fragments by next week, she would revise them. This was a work in progress, after all. Thorpe wanted to see her revising, and if she waited until she had everything nailed down, well, then she wouldn't even begin writing her thesis for at least another year.

'The role of the Stranger is another mystery,' she started typing again. And there she stopped and found herself staring at the bookshelf on the opposite wall, illuminated by an unlikely shaft of sunlight.

Her impression was as intangible as that light – or the dust motes that danced and swirled before her. How could she explain the good feeling she had toward this odd character? A shadowy figure, only really defined by his green eyes, he might be an apparition or a demon. This was a Gothic novel, after all, and seductive demons were as much the rage among women readers two hundred years ago as they were in the twenty-first century.

'The green-eyed Stranger whose carriage offers the protagonist a ride may be seen as a *refuge.'* Dulcie was pretty sure the text referred to 'succor', but she didn't want to disrupt her rhythm to look it up. *'Equally, it might signify temptation; the desire to flee a responsibility or duty.'*

No, she backed up over those words. Dulcie didn't believe that. There was simply too much about the strange man that signaled, or – if Dulcie wanted to get all semiotic about it – signified good. He did come to the woman's aid. He wasn't asking for anything and he only offered advice. He was, Dulcie felt down to her bones, essentially feline. A literary incarnation, in some way, of her own Mr Grey, she believed. And therefore he could not be evil.

'You might be wrong, you know.' Dulcie nearly jumped out of her seat. With Lloyd out leading his weekly junior seminar, she did not expect to hear anyone talking to her. She certainly didn't expect to hear this particular voice saying those particular words.

'Mr Grey?' She resisted the urge to turn around, but felt the reassuring touch of a wet leathery nose against her hand. 'What are you saying?'

'There are many ways to interpret a work of art.' The voice, as soft as fur, seemed to come from close behind her right shoulder. *'One shouldn't stop seeking simply because one has found the first possibility.'*

'You're not telling me that Monsieur Le Gris is bad, are you?' Even as she asked, Dulcie felt her conviction wavering. If Mr Grey didn't identify with the fictional character, who was she to make the connection? 'Is it just that I've missed you?' Her voice fell to a whisper, but her words still sounded overly loud in the small, closed room. 'Have I forced an interpretation out of my own loneliness?'

Something like a purr filled the still air, and Dulcie felt the pressure of a feline head against her hand.

'I've misinterpreted, haven't I?' Dulcie said with a sigh, her disappointment muted somewhat by the presence of her spectral pet. 'The stranger is dangerous. He's bad news for the woman in the carriage.' Silence. 'The stranger could be evil?' Nothing, and Dulcie felt a twinge of optimism. 'The stranger is ambiguous, and I should keep reading?'

The purr again, so loud that Dulcie worried that the grad students down the hall must hear it. 'That's it, isn't it, Mr Grey?' Dulcie started to reach for her laptop and stopped herself. Yes, she had work to do, but more than anything she wanted the feline presence to remain with her, just a bit longer.

The key to identity... ' The voice was growing fainter now, nearly obscured by the rise and fall of the purr. Was that Mr Grey she was hearing, or her own thoughts, already revising the paragraphs before her? *'Identity is key.'*

'I've got it, Mr Grey,' she said out loud. It was him. It had to be him.

'There are many paths in.' She strained to hear him, as the dust swirled and settled. *'Many paths both in and out.'*

Something about his presence, about that purr,

sparked another thought in Dulcie's mind. 'Are you talking about Gus, Mr Grey?' Silence. 'You know, Gus, the theater cat, who I saw outside? I tried to talk to Roni about him. I did, Mr Grey.' A pang of regret that she hadn't been more specific. It wasn't safe for a small animal. Not in a city. Not in winter. 'I'll try again, Mr Grey. I promise.'

All she heard was the purr, and then even that faded away.

FORTY-THREE

'Think of it this way,' said Chris. 'You won't have to worry about turning it off when the show starts.'

Dulcie hadn't even had to ask if her boyfriend had finished with her phone. She had arrived home to find it in pieces on the kitchen table. Apart from wondering how so many components could fit into the small, sleek device, she'd found herself puzzled about how her boyfriend had spent the day – or at least the last few hours. He'd told her that he'd come home around dusk, which at this time of year meant three thirty or so. Although she'd meant to leave herself more time, it was after five by the time she left her office, and already fully dark, and close to six when she'd climbed the apartment's stairs. While she hadn't been able to call Chris to ask about the state of her phone, she'd blithely assumed he'd have gotten to it. After all, he'd said he would finish it once he got home, if not before he left for the day. Plus, he'd been unwilling – or unable – to account for the last few hours,

Granted, the tiny device looked more complicated than Dulcie had ever imagined. She knew she wouldn't have been able to make hide nor

252

hair out of it. Chris had never been flummoxed by complicated electronics before, but she had to wonder if the new technology had overwhelmed him – or if the dark had anything to do with it.

That had been a disturbing thought, and Dulcie had done her best to push it from her mind. Besides, she'd told Chris, she needed to get moving. She and Trista were due back at the theater by seven, at the latest, and she needed to assemble an usher's outfit: all black, like the actors.

Even that was proving troublesome, however. And Chris, with his hangdog look, wasn't helping. At least he'd given up apologizing, for now, and was instead following her around the apartment as she searched for her black sweater. 'It's a pullover.' She checked behind a couch cushion. 'Have you seen it?'

'Is that the one from when we had the pasta accident?' Chris asked, standing behind her. He sounded happy to change the subject, even if the news he was delivering wasn't what Dulcie would want to hear. 'I think it might still be at the cleaners.'

'Yeah, you're right.' Dulcie plopped down on the sofa and jumped back up again. 'I don't have time to worry about this. May I...?'

'Of course.' She didn't even have time to voice her request before Chris turned back to their bedroom. He emerged moments later, holding a black sweatshirt. 'It's not a phone, but...' He stopped. 'Why don't you take mine?'

'No, you're right.' Dulcie held the sweatshirt up. It looked big enough to go on over the blouse and sweater she was already wearing, and so she slipped it on. The result felt a bit bulky, but if she could get her coat on top of it all, she'd be fine. 'I'm just going to the show and then coming straight home. And you're right, I'd have to make sure it was turned off for most of that time anyway.'

'I'm sorry I didn't get back to it.' He followed her into the hall as she pulled on her boots and then her coat, which did fit. 'By the time you get home tonight, it'll be good as new. Promise.'

'Thanks, sweetie.' Dulcie reached up to kiss him – the added bulk made a hug impractical. 'Later.'

He jumped to get the door, and Dulcie added another kiss. He felt guilty, she knew, about not fixing her phone. He didn't have to. After all, she was the one who had unwittingly downloaded the virus. But she was in too much of a hurry, and had too much on her mind, to spend any more time reassuring him. She'd thank him properly tonight, she decided, as she clattered down the stairs and back out to the street.

'Oof.' The cold hit her like a slap in the face as soon as she pushed open their building's front door, and she paused to pull her hat as low as she could. Already, she had wrapped her scarf around her mouth and nose. But there was no protecting that small strip of face that she had to leave bare. At least, if she wanted to see.

She almost didn't have to. Over the course of the day, the sidewalks had been cleared but with the advent of the frosty night, nobody else was on them. But if the paths were clear, they were also slick, as the day's melt had refrozen, leaving a thin layer of ice. As much as she wanted to hurry, she couldn't, and found herself toddling along with her arms akimbo.

'I must look like a demented penguin,' Dulcie said to the night air. The extra layer of Chris's sweatshirt helped keep her core warm. But even with her mittens on, Dulcie's hands quickly felt the chill. And nothing, not even a spectral feline, responded. It was simply too cold.

It was with a sinking heart, therefore, that Dulcie peered down the last block. From what she could see, the URT looked dark. Cursing slightly under her breath, Dulcie wondered if the night's performance had been canceled. Perhaps the call had gone to her non-functional phone. If she had come out in this weather for nothing...

But no. As she got closer, she could see the light in the lobby, and as she step-slid the last few feet, the front door opened.

'Hey, Dulcie!' A large man appeared, holding a shovel. Doug.

He raised the shovel. Dulcie stopped short – and started to skid.

'Hang on.' Dropping his shovel, Doug caught her in two steps. Steadying her on her feet, he walked her slowly to the door, where a bucket of sand waited. 'You okay?' His voice was warm, solicitous.

'Yeah, thanks.' She gripped the door frame in relief. If this was the man she had overheard this afternoon, he was a better actor than she had thought.

'Well, I better get to work.' He grabbed the pail. 'Can't afford to lose any more of our ushers or, god forbid, ticket holders.'

She nodded, still a little shaken.

'I saw you on the list.' He must have noticed. 'You're the first one here. You can check in with Avila.'

With that he stepped back out into the cold.

'Hello?' Dulcie called. Back beyond the lobby, she could hear voices. Tonight, however, she wanted to be careful not to walk in on anyone else's conversation.

'Come on back!' A blonde head popped out of the hallway, and for a moment Dulcie couldn't breathe. Amy. Disembodied. But no, it was simply an illusion. Another actress – Dulcie recognized her from one of the crowd scenes – in the black bodysuit that all the actors wore. Standing in the darkened hallway, her body wasn't invisible. But her light, sunny curls stood out, momentarily distracting the eye. 'The other usher is already here.'

'Oh?' Dulcie followed the bouncing mop to the theater, which was rendered prosaically drab in the house lights. Trista was there, talking to a dark-haired woman: Avila.

'You made it.' Trista nodded to her friend, raising one pierced eyebrow. Unlike Dulcie, she had opted for a black turtleneck and yoga pants and looked more like one of the actors than an usher.

'Tris, Doug said...' She stopped, unsure of how to proceed.

'You saw Doug?' Avila looked up. 'Good. We need to de-ice the walk outside or someone will break an ankle. Here, give me your coat.'

Trista gave Dulcie's outfit a long look. 'You might want to lose some layers.'

'Tris.' Dulcie didn't want to waste any time. 'Doug said I was the first one here. I don't know if that means anything...'

'I came in that side door.' Trista leaned in. 'It was unlocked.'

'Oh.' Avila had returned and was eyeing Dulcie's outfit. 'You're wearing all that?'

'I'll take off the sweater underneath,' Dulcie was quick to offer. 'I was in a hurry, and it's so cold out.'

A quick, businesslike nod. 'The dressing room is back there. You remember? Good.' Avila turned toward Trista. 'So anyway, Trista, when the lights go down—'

Dulcie walked off, leaving the two alone. But any thought she had of changing in privacy disappeared as she neared the dressing-room door.

'Heath!' A black woman, clad only in black tights, was pushing the shaggy-haired actor out the door. If the smile on her face was any indication, his visit hadn't been entirely unwelcome.

'Bye, bye, baby!' Another voice – female – called from within.

Without thinking, Dulcie turned away. She wasn't unduly modest, but she did have her limits. And changing in a co-ed dressing room when none of the other women there were likely to be quite as, well, softly rounded as she was went beyond them.

She looked around quickly, not wanting any of the players to witness her reluctance. The bathroom was back off the lobby – no, the prop

257

room. She didn't need more than a minute to peel off her sweatshirt, shed the sweater and shirt underneath, and have the outer layer back on.

The door to the small utility room was ajar, but the lights were off. Dulcie slipped inside quietly, but left the lights off. Anyone else could walk in. The sweatshirt came off easily: even over her other clothes, it had been a loose fit. The sweater and blouse took a little longer, partly because she had tried to pull them off in one swift move. She had forgotten to unbutton her cuffs and had to struggle a few seconds with the inside-out sleeves, the clothes covering her head. A few seconds' tussle, though, and they came off, leaving Dulcie feeling exposed and rather silly.

'Standing in my underwear in a storage closet,' she thought to herself. 'I wonder if the author of *The Ravages* ever found herself doing this.' But the humor of the situation gave way to the fact that the room was cool – and that the bustle of the theater was growing louder. Reaching for Chris's sweatshirt, she pulled it over her head. In her hurry, back at the apartment, she hadn't noticed, but it smelled faintly of him. A warm, familiar aroma, and she inhaled deeply, pressing the soft cloth to her face.

'Quick, we only have a minute.' Dulcie gasped and froze as the door opened slightly, but the command – a stage whisper – hadn't been directed toward her. Two figures slipped into the room, silhouetted momentarily in the doorway before the door closed again, blocking out the light. Dulcie cringed. If this was going to be a romantic tryst, she would have to find a way to announce her presence quickly.

'What do you want?' Another whisper, this one deeper, answered. A man, Dulcie thought. But not an amorous one. 'I got here as soon as I could.'

'She knows.' The words were so muffled, Dulcie couldn't be sure of them. The sibilant hissed in the dark, like a threat.

It worked like one. Her companion groaned, softly but quite audibly in the close confines of the room. 'She can't know.' The man, agitated, was still whispering, but more loudly. 'That's not ... that's not possible.'

'She does, though.' And then the room fell quiet. So quiet Dulcie could hear her own breath. It was a wonder that they couldn't as well. 'So you didn't tell her?' The woman. She was fishing.

'No, I didn't tell her. I didn't tell her anything.' The man was growing frustrated. Angry. 'You promised me.'

There was desperation in his voice, and then he moved. Whether toward his companion or reaching for the door, Dulcie couldn't tell. Alarmed, she stepped back – on to something soft. Something that moved.

'Mrow!' It was Gus. 'Tsss!' She must have trod on his tail, judging by the way he jumped. The man yelped, and Dulcie fell backward, Chris's sweatshirt flying back up over her eyes.

'What the...?' It was the man's voice, speaking out loud. The door opened and closed with a bang, bouncing back open as the first speaker –

the woman – fled. Dulcie righted herself and pulled the sweatshirt down to find herself face to face with the dashing Heath Barstow.

FORTY-FOUR

'There you are!' Trista grabbed Dulcie's hand as she stood, blinking, in the relatively bright light of the hallway. 'We've got to take our places.'

Dulcie allowed herself to be led back to the performance space, where Trista shoved a bunch of programs at her. She was still trying to make sense of the conversation she had overheard, an encounter that had ended with Heath Barstow staring at her, a look of shock or horror on his face, before he had bolted from the room.

'Sure,' she said, taking the programs. Trista was talking to her, something about the seat numbers and protocol. Dulcie half listened as she glanced over the programs. The classical source material, she knew from her own experience, was given a brief paragraph in the folded sheet. The rest of the write-up consisted of a discography, as well as the brief – and somewhat fatuous – bios of the actors involved.

Heath Barstow: Apollo, Hercules, Tony Manero. The head shot of the lead looked so different from the face in Dulcie's memory. In the tiny black and white, he positively glowed, his hair streaming out around him in all its leonine glory. Who had he been talking to – and about whom?

261

Avila Circule: Diana, Muse, Girl on Train. Clearly, the handsome actor didn't discriminate in his affections. The dark-haired Goth girl was only supporting cast.

Amy Ralkov: Aphrodite, Medusa, Stephanie Mangano. The name of the dead girl caught Dulcie off guard. She'd forgotten that the new-comer – *'A Tech junior, majoring in applied sciences and advanced computing'* – had handled such major roles. Aphrodite even had a solo.

'Hey, Dulcie,' Avila called out with a smile as she raced by, carrying a tray. Dulcie responded automatically and watched as the actress ascended to the elevated tables over by stage left. That's where she and Chris had sat – and where they'd been served by Amy.

If Avila was taking over Amy's waitressing duties, did that mean she had also assumed her roles? And, if so, was that reason to hurt her?

'Dulcie!' Trista's tone wasn't as friendly, and Dulcie looked up. Her friend was leading a party of four over to the floor, but another group was waiting. Behind them, the line stretched back into the lobby.

'Sorry, folks.' Dulcie put on her best smile as she walked toward the waiting foursome. As she led them in, she saw Doug carrying out folded chairs.

'Who gets those?' She grabbed Trista as they both converged on the line. Doug was setting up the chairs on the edge of the dance floor.

'Overflow,' Trista said over her shoulder, as she reached for an older couple's tickets. 'The

262

ones marked with an X.'

'Overflow?' She took the next group, a party of six.

'We requested a banquette.' The woman sounded snippy.

'Yes, of course.' Dulcie led them over to stage left. Avila was setting up a wine bucket and champagne flutes. 'Your waitress will be right over.'

'Crazy, isn't it?' Avila followed her back down to the bar area.

'They've added extra seats?' Dulcie asked in response.

Avila nodded. 'Ever since, well ... Amy?' And she headed off to the bar.

Dulcie mulled this over as she welcomed the next party. On one level, it was downright ghoulish. People were actually choosing to come out to see a play because one of the players had been killed. On another, she was grateful. Anything that gave the arts a boost was a blessing. And, in a way, it was a fitting tribute.

Three students. 'Hey, aren't you a teaching assistant for Pope and Spenser?'

Dulcie smiled and nodded, leading them to the overflow section.

'Ushering.' The one who had recognized her smiled. 'That was smart.'

'It's good it's so busy, huh?' Dulcie asked. She had made a point of running into Avila again, even though she had to pretend to misread a ticket to do so.

'Really.' Avila had a full tray of what looked like martinis, but was still managing a smile.

263

Dulcie stopped the party she was leading, so that the dark-haired girl could place her tray on a table. 'This has got to help the bottom line, huh?' She kept her voice low as Avila placed the drinks.

'Dunno.' The tray went back up as Avila pivoted to the next table. 'Have to ask Roni, I guess.'

Her smile, Dulcie noticed as she seated her party, was looking a little strained. Was that because Avila had been the other party in the closet? The dark-haired actress had been friendly enough when Dulcie first ran into her, but that had been a while ago. She and Dulcie had both been running around since then, seating people and serving drinks. Dulcie hadn't seen Heath anywhere in the room: as the lead actor in the musical comedy, Heath was above waiting on tables. But he had to be somewhere nearby. If Avila had run into Heath on one of her rounds across the room, and he had told her that Dulcie had been privy to their conversation, that might account for the tightness around her smile. Or it could simply be the weight of that tray.

Roni. Maybe she was key. Dulcie picked up another party and thought about the bespectacled office manager. She'd never gotten a chance to tell her about the latest email problem. And since emerging from the prop room, she had a new concern – maybe the office manager had been the woman they'd been talking about. But Trista had grabbed her before she could get back to the theater office, and Dulcie hadn't seen the office manager around. If it had been Avila in the prop room, that was not a problem. The dark-haired girl hadn't had a chance for anything more than the most hurried conversation since the front doors had opened. And Heath wouldn't do anything, now that he knew Dulcie had heard him plotting. Would he?

The lights started flashing, and Dulcie froze. Was it an alarm of some kind? No, she realized as Trista turned toward her with an exaggerated sigh. The seating was complete. The last drink orders were being delivered, and the show was about to start.

FORTY-FIVE

'Yo, Medusa!'

Dulcie stared, aghast, as Heath, in a white three-piece suit, waved at a sequinned dancer in an oversized shock-blue wig. Either the troupe was improvising as it went along, or she had managed to block large parts of *Changes* from her memory.

'Tony!' The wig, complete with sequinned snakes, looked unwieldy, but the squeal that emerged from beneath it definitely came from Avila. And either she really was thrilled at the opportunity to jump from the balcony into Heath's disco arms, or she was a better actress than the one who had immediately preceded her on to the stage – a satin-draped Annette, who had hit the floor with a thud and a conspicuous flash of light, 'transformed' into a singing, dancing tree. Circus training, Dulcie remembered. That wig, however, proved to be a handful. Literally, as Avila's arms went up in a gesture that seemed designed to hold it in place.

'I love this part,' Trista leaned over to whisper. The two ushers were seated by the entrance on a black bench the bartender had pulled out for them, once the theater door was closed. 'The whole place is about to explode.'

266

'Right.' Dulcie tried to sound non-committal. She did remember the dance-floor number, as 'Tony' and 'Medusa' hustled under swirling lights. Some kind of sparklers went off as the cast all joined in – that had to be the explosion Trista was talking about. Already, from her vantage point at the back of the room, she could see the cast quietly taking their places. It was a neat bit of trickery: the black outfits rendering the dancers nearly invisible. From here, she could see the edges of their white satin shifts, ready to be thrown on at the downbeat.

Avila had been one of those dancers, Dulcie remembered. The lead role had been Amy's. The pretty student hadn't been recognizable under that wig – blue snakes? – but the program had made the casting clear. As the interminable love duet went on, she found herself wondering again if such a step up would be worth killing for. Despite her dismissive words, Avila certainly seemed fond of the male lead.

'Who you are is who you want to be...' Dulcie could hear Trista singing along. *'Be who you want to be is who you are...'*

Well, her friend hadn't been a poetry major. And the tune was catchy. Besides, Dulcie now recalled, this number led into Gus's appearance. After the number's flashy conclusion, the cat's solo tightrope walk was a brilliant bit of staging – the only kind of follow-up that would keep the audience's attention.

Dulcie looked up at the bar overhang. That's where Gus would be waiting. If he was willing to perform tonight, that is. Dulcie wondered if the mishap in the prop room had thrown the sleek feline off. Maybe he needed his beauty rest before appearing. Or maybe her misstep would have woken him, gotten the sleek Russian blue up in time to make his big scene.

Leaning forward on the bench, she stared up into the dark. Was that a movement? A bit of grey, checking out the crowd? No, she couldn't be sure.

'You know, you know, I know you...' Trista's singing had subsided to a hum as the song itself wound down. Only a few voices could be heard: the women in black, lining the walls, and Avila, up on the stage.

'I know you. You know I do.'

Trista snorted, and Dulcie looked up. Her friend had her hand over her mouth, suppressing, Dulcie suspected, a laugh. It was too late: a snicker rose from the audience. A distinct chuckle could be heard stage left, and Dulcie remembered. This was supposed to be a moment of silence. The chorus had done its job, building to a subtle, eerie peak. That last note – the one they had all held – was it. Those voices were supposed to fade away, leaving a big dramatic pause before the explosion of sound and color, when all the dancers would magically 'disappear' and Gus would take his solo turn.

Only Avila had flubbed it. Maybe it was that she was new to the part. Maybe it was that wig, which covered enough of her face that she probably couldn't see Bob, the director, partially visible behind a mirrored screen stage right, frantically gesturing for her to stop.

Maybe, Dulcie thought, with a twinge of sympathy, it was that Avila had gotten carried away. The song she was singing, *a cappella* now and ever so slightly off key, had to do with true love – how lovers perceive each other's true identities behind 'life's masks'.

'I know you!' Avila's wobbly voice rose to the song's climax, only four bars behind the rest of the cast. Dulcie bit her lip. This was going to be worse than embarrassing. Heath, who a moment before had been frozen in confusion, was now glowering, his handsome face suffused with rage.

'You know I do...'

Only from where Dulcie sat, it didn't look like Heath was glaring at Avila. The off-key Medusa had stopped now, one hand steadying that oversized wig. This was the moment before the explosion – the big bang that would now, Dulcie feared, sound like an anticlimax. And Heath was staring off-stage – at the director, Dulcie realized. He wanted to make sure that Bob knew Avila was responsible for the debacle, not the show's leading man.

'It's not her fault,' Dulcie whispered to Trista. 'These things happen—'

Boom! The glitter bomb exploded, showering the audience with mylar confetti. And then, through the sparkle, they saw it: a slash of grey, like an asteroid, shooting toward the stage.

'Gus!' Dulcie cried out. The cat had launched himself, not from the top of the bar and not on to a walkway of any sort, but off the balcony, stage left, flying like a missile across the stage and down. 'No!'

Her yell was echoed by another shriek, as the cat landed on the screen, claws extended. For a moment he hung there, green eyes ablaze. Then he bounded off, knocking the screen to the floor, and revealing Roni, not even in costume, standing there, exposed.

FORTY-SIX

'She's never been afraid of cats before.' Trista was talking to the director.

'I wasn't afraid *of* the cat,' Dulcie repeated for the umpteenth time. 'I was worried *for* him.'

She shouldn't have screamed. She realized that as every face – including that of the utterly unfazed Gus – had turned toward her. Not that she'd gotten a chance to apologize. A heavy hand, descending on Dulcie's shoulder, had spun her around and propelled her from the auditorium. It was Bob, the director, his moustache bristling with rage. Trista had followed, though voluntarily or not, Dulcie couldn't tell. Now the friends stood out in the hallway while the show continued in the theater behind them.

'Dulcie...' Trista's tone was supposed to quiet her down, Dulcie knew that. But the volume of the show in the theater behind her had only increased since the interruption. If anything, she thought, she and Gus had provided the one moment of true drama. It was an uncharitable thought; one she shouldn't share. But really, and at this point her thoughts would out, here she was being treated like a criminal, when all she had done was show concern for...

'Dulcie!' Trista grabbed her arm. It might as

271

well have been her mouth, Dulcie suspected: the force and intent was clear. But as Dulcie turned to protest her friend's unjust attempt to muzzle her, she bit her own tongue. Heath, still in his white three-piece suit, was standing behind her, looking a bit flushed.

Dulcie jumped. 'You!'

'Me?' With his large head craned forward, the actor looked like a giant bird. 'What happened? Everyone wants to know.'

'Nothing.' Trista started to step between them, but Dulcie had already recovered. With one outstretched arm, she held Trista back. It was time to face the man responsible for Amy's death.

'Nothing happened,' she began, feeling the weight of each word. 'Has happened. Yet.' Heath might be bigger than she was, but Dulcie would not be intimidated. 'I was worried about Gus. That was a big jump. But now I understand.' She paused as the realization dawned on her. 'He wanted to show me something. He wanted me to see whom you were talking about.'

From Heath's intake of breath, she knew she had hit on something.

'And now I know.' Dulcie paused for dramatic effect. 'It was Roni. Poor Roni.'

'What?' Heath was doing his best to feign confusion, but Dulcie was on to him. 'Oh, you know how she feels about you. You have to. But you couldn't count on that keeping her quiet, could you?'

'Roni?' Heath's voice was so strained, it nearly cracked.

'Roni.' Dulcie held his gaze.

'Roni?' Behind her, the director asked the question. This made Dulcie glad. If Gus's daring leap had made one thing clear, it was that the time had come to make her findings public.

'Roni,' Dulcie repeated, her voice firm.

'Um, Dulcie?' Trista, to her right, was tugging at her sleeve. 'It's Roni.'

'I know it's Roni.' Dulcie kept her eyes locked on Heath's deep blue ones. She wouldn't let him look away. 'That's why I had to speak out.'

'Speak out about what?' Dulcie knew that voice. She turned.

'Roni!' She reached to embrace the office manager, but Roni stepped back.

'What are you talking about?'

'I'm talking about Heath,' Dulcie began. 'I know you like him, but he's not who he seems.'

'No ... you can't know.' Roni's voice sounded strained, strangled even, and Dulcie's heart went out to her. 'You don't really know.'

Dulcie shook her head sadly. 'I'm sorry, Roni. I've had my suspicions and before the show I overheard him talking about you.'

'About me?' Roni's question was barely audible.

Dulcie nodded. Poor girl, she thought. She's in shock. 'He said things that might be construed as threatening. And, well, he was involved with Amy...' She didn't need to fill in the blanks. Roni was staring at her, mouth open. So, she noticed were Trista, Heath, and Bob – whose moustache was positively quivering.

Heath spoke first. 'Are you nuts or something?'

273

'Now, hang on here.' The portly director wasn't far behind. 'Are you accusing Heath of something here?'

'Yes.' It was time to be clear, and Dulcie was going to say so. Only just then, her gaze was captured by a movement – a grey movement. Gus, the theater cat, had emerged from the auditorium and was twining around Heath's ankles, purring loudly enough for all assembled to hear.

'Gus?' Dulcie didn't understand what was happening. The cat wouldn't be feigning affection, would he? And he couldn't be wrong.

'Okay, that's enough.' Bob grabbed her upper arm. 'Let's get you out of here.'

'Wait.' Trista stepped forward. 'Hang on a minute. Dulcie?'

Trista turned, and Dulcie realized all eyes were on her. She wanted to tell them what she'd heard. What she believed had happened. But Gus was staring up at her, too. His green eyes held hers, and his purr was only growing louder.

She shook her head. 'I don't know,' she said at last. 'Maybe...'

Trista pulled her aside, and out of the director's grip. 'As you'll recall, my friend hit her head – because of your street prank. And she hasn't taken legal action, but really, considering the way you run things here...'

'Okay, okay.' Bob backed up, hands in the air.

'Heath?' A woman's voice called from the auditorium door. 'Heath, you're on.'

'Wait.' Dulcie wasn't sure what to ask, but she knew the conversation wasn't over yet.

'Dulcie.' Trista put her hand on Dulcie's arm.

'Let him go.'

Heath took a step toward the door. 'Heath!' The soft voice called again, and he turned to go. But as he reached the door, he turned once again. His face, Dulcie thought, was no longer handsome. It was full of fear.

FORTY-SEVEN

'What was that about?' Trista hustled Dulcie toward the coatroom. 'No, never mind. Tell me once we get out of here.'

'Wait.' It was Roni, trotting after them. 'I'm ... I'm sorry about all of that. I feel like I'm to blame.'

'No.' Dulcie turned to the office manager, who had gone even paler, if that were possible. She also looked frightened. 'It's not your fault,' Dulcie tried to reassure her.

'I feel like I've missed things. Maybe wanted to miss things. Maybe I...' They'd all been talking quietly, once again aware that a performance was taking place in the adjoining auditorium. But now Roni's voice had become even softer, and her last words – addressed to the floor – were inaudible.

'Roni, it's okay.' Dulcie pulled away from Trista to comfort the other girl, who leaned into her with a sob. 'Trista.' Dulcie looked over her shoulder as she wrapped her arms around the crying girl. 'Do you mind?'

'Hey, no skin off my back.' Trista stood watching them for a minute. 'I've had enough excitement for a while.'

Dulcie watched as her friend retrieved her coat

and headed toward the door. Then, her arms still around the dark-haired girl, Dulcie spoke as gently as she could. 'Would you want to talk, Roni?'

'Uh huh.' The other girl nodded and, head still down, led Dulcie back to her office and unlocked the door. 'I've been trying to be more careful,' she explained, blinking back the last of the tears.

'That's smart.' Dulcie didn't want to say anything about closing the barn door too late. Instead, she followed the office manager into her small sanctum and took a seat in the guest chair.

'I confess, I've been scared.' Roni sat behind her desk. It was an oddly formal arrangement, but the tiny office didn't have a couch. 'I mean, I haven't wanted to say anything, but, well, Heath has been acting really odd. You know?'

Dulcie nodded. She did know.

'I mean, he's an actor.' Now that Roni had opened up, it seemed like she had a lot to get off her chest. 'So, I don't think you can believe anything he says. But women do. I think, well, I'm not sure...' She paused.

'You don't have to say any more.' Dulcie didn't want to make it hard on her.

'No, I do.' Roni nodded, her mouth set in a determined line. 'I don't know who started it, but I think ... maybe...' Dulcie was about to break in again, but Roni kept talking. 'I think he and Amy were behind the whole hacking thing.'

'What?' That wasn't what Dulcie had been expecting.

'I'm almost sure of it.' Roni was nodding, gaining courage from her own words. 'She was

277

studying computer science, you know?' Dulcie nodded, but kept quiet. Roni's unfortunate verbal tic didn't require confirmation. 'I think she broke into our system for some reason. In fact, I saw her here, late one night. She was with Heath. That was before I started locking the office.'

'And you think...' Dulcie wasn't sure how to phrase the question. It seemed like a distinct possibility that the couple might have ducked into the tiny office for privacy, rather than any more nefarious reason.

'I *know*.' Roni must have had the same suspicion. 'She was leaning over my keyboard. Typing.' She paused, as if she was having trouble remembering. Or, no, Dulcie realized, because recalling the scene out loud was too painful. 'And Heath – well, Heath saw me first. He must have heard me, because he turned and said my name. He said, "It's not what you think. She's found something." But he was lying.'

'You think she was behind the hacking?' Something wasn't adding up. 'But the timing—'

'I don't know.' Roni cut her off. 'About that, I mean. I do know she'd gotten into our bank account.'

'Did you tell anyone?' To Dulcie, this would have been obvious, but Roni only shook her head.

'I should have, I know. But Heath came up to me after.' Roni ducked her head, but Dulcie could still see the blush that crept up into her face. 'He went on about how Amy was just a student, a nobody. That I shouldn't get her in trouble. That she didn't matter.'

278

'And the money?'

'He said he'd get it back.' Roni's voice had fallen to a whisper. 'That he'd make Amy give it back. That's why I think...' She swallowed. 'I think he was trying to do that. Maybe they fought...'

It all made too much sense. 'You've got to tell the police.' Dulcie leaned over the desk, but Roni shrank back. 'It was bad enough when it was just the money. But you think maybe Heath...' Dulcie paused, unsure how to ask. 'Maybe Heath was the one who hurt her?'

Roni was nodding, her misery clear in her face. 'He's been looking at me funny since then. I mean, I don't know anything for sure, but...'

Her voice, trailing off, convinced Dulcie. 'I'll go with you, if that will help.' Roni looked up, and Dulcie reached over the desk to take the other girl's hand. 'There's a detective I know. He'll understand why you didn't come forward before.' Even as she said it, Dulcie doubted that she was telling the whole truth. 'Well, he'll be easier to talk to,' she amended her words. 'We'll go first thing tomorrow.'

Roni took a deep, shuddering breath. When she let it out, Dulcie felt she could see the tension flow from her. So much so that the applause she now heard almost seemed to be for her. Only Roni's startled glance at the door brought her back to the reality: *Changes* had finished its second act. Already she could hear voices as the audience filed into the hallway.

'Look, I better go.' Dulcie didn't want to run into either Heath or the director. 'Do you want to

279

come with me?'

Roni shook her head. 'I should stay. I would normally be here when the show is done.'

'Makes sense,' Dulcie agreed. 'Don't let on that anything is different.' She stood and peeked into the hallway. Only the public, as far as she could tell. 'Do you want to meet me there?'

'No, it'll be close to midnight, and I've got to open up tomorrow, no matter what.' Roni managed a weak grin. 'After I open?'

Dulcie didn't like it, but she could understand the office manager's logic. 'Well, okay,' she said. 'How about I come by tomorrow at ten?'

'That will work.' Roni had pulled herself upright and was already facing the computer. 'And Dulcie?' She turned to see her visitor out. 'Thank you.'

FORTY-EIGHT

Despite a blast of wind that took her breath away, Dulcie felt warmed as she hurried out into the night. She'd done a good deed tonight. Despite disrupting the performance, she'd helped a friend. Or, if not a friend just yet, someone not that different from herself.

Roni already seemed like a new woman: her suspicions must have been weighing on her. Plus, Dulcie's own suspicions had been confirmed. But as she made her way down the block, that cozy feeling began to fade. Some of it was the cold. Even with her scarf up around her face, Dulcie could feel her cheeks going numb, and on these icy sidewalks, she couldn't even run to warm up.

Some of it was worry. Had she done the right thing, letting Roni stay at the theater? She wouldn't be alone, Dulcie knew that. But still ... Dulcie sighed. At least in the theater, it was warm and light. Out here, everything looked strange. Although the snow was still fresh enough to be mostly white, its icy crust reflecting the street lights, the drifts and plowed-up snow made for strange shadows that turned the familiar walk into something eerie and new. Even the colors were different – silver, almost.

Or blue – blue-grey – kind of like Gus, with his soft, shadowy coat. Even the way the shadow moved, ducking around a pile of snow as a lone driver slowly made his way down Mass Ave, was reminiscent of the cat. Which, come to think of it, got to the heart of her unease.

Why had Gus been so friendly toward Heath?

It could be nothing, Dulcie knew. Although her natural bent was to attribute greater powers of discernment to any feline, it was possible that Gus was no more perceptive than – well, than Roni had been. Besides, as she had seen, Heath worked hard to endear himself to people. And he could be charming. In fact, Dulcie had liked him, despite herself, when they first met.

Another car went by, moving slowly on the icy road. It was funny how quiet the city could be, Dulcie noted. That car might as well have been going 'shush' as it passed, its lights throwing those strange, blue shadows. Once it was gone, Dulcie could hear herself breathe, the sound amplified by the wool swathed around her head.

She reached a corner and had to haul herself over the ridge of plowed snow. At least, she thought as she grabbed the icy upper edge for support, others had been here before her. A rough step had been dug out, large enough for a bigger foot than hers, and then, on top, a slightly flattened place.

Was everyone taller than she was? With an effort, she pulled herself up and paused, considering how best to dismount. Earlier pedestrians had probably simply stepped down from here, but the distance was a little too great for

Dulcie to feel comfortable doing that. And the surface of the street – with its mix of snow and salt – looked grimy, as well as treacherous. Still, there was nothing for it, and Dulcie let herself down carefully.

On the other side of the street, she had to reverse the process, though at least she was climbing down on to a well-shoveled walk, the snow parted to make a channel all the way to the end of the block. On each side, the snow had been piled waist high. Beneath her, she noticed, the bricks looked scrubbed, shining under the street light.

Which she was suddenly staring straight up at, as she lay on her back on the icy bricks.

Dulcie had slipped so quickly, she had barely been aware of it happening. Just a quick rush of air and her world had turned upside down. If not for her coat and the thick wool of her hat, she realized as she sat up with care, she might have been seriously hurt. As it was, she'd had the wind knocked out of her and one ankle seemed a little sore. Standing took an effort, but with nobody else around, at least she'd been spared embarrassment.

Back on her feet, she vowed to tread more carefully – especially where the more prosaic concrete gave way to Cambridge's iconic brick. One block further, and she was moving at a snail's pace. The fall had made her timid, plus her ankle was beginning to throb.

'This is crazy.' Dulcie reached into her pocket. She'd call Chris – or call a cab. But her pocket held nothing more than a wad of tissues. Her phone was still back at the apartment and, possibly, still in pieces. Helplessness and the growing ache in her ankle were making her angry. Bad enough that Chris kept disappearing on her. If he wasn't going to keep his promises...

'Hello?' She turned and staggered a bit as her boots slipped on the ice. 'Is someone there?'

Nothing. It must have been an icicle falling. A clump of snow finally succumbing to gravity. A rat.

She toddled on a bit farther. It was half a block before a patch of ice stopped her in her tracks. Anxious about falling again, she grabbed on to the shoveled snow that lined the walk, its crusty surface cold but solid enough, and gingerly stepped on to its edge, trying her hardest to work her boot into the snow. Another step, again avoiding the slick red brick. Another.

That sound again. 'Hello?' She spun, barely catching herself as her feet slid out from under her. 'Who's there?'

Nothing, and in truth her heart was now beating so hard she couldn't tell what she had heard. Maybe her awkward moves had knocked some snow into the street. Maybe another pedestrian only a little further back was also trying to navigate the treacherous walk.

Didn't anyone put salt down any more? Sand?

The next stretch was a little better. Paradoxically, someone had gotten lazy with the shovel, and the resulting mix of hard-packed snow was uneven, but easier to traverse. Soon Dulcie would hit Central Square. Not long after that, she'd be home. And if Chris hadn't fixed her phone, she would ... Well, she would just be grateful that he was working on it.

'I don't mean to be too demanding, Mr Grey.' The street light above seemed to glow with a blue halo. Beyond it, she could see the moon, gleaming full. 'It's just that I don't always know what's going on with Chris any more.'

She spoke out of habit and because it was comforting. This afternoon, she hadn't taken full advantage of her spectral pet's visit. Tonight, out alone in the oddly quiet city, she could use the company – as well as any advice her feline friend could give. 'Am I asking for too much?'

Walking with baby steps across another slick patch, Dulcie found herself thinking again of Gus. The theater cat had definitely intended to show her something, of that she had no doubt. But if his plan was to expose the true object of Heath's anger, then why cozy up to the actor afterward? Could the Russian blue have been trying to disarm Heath? Was he so dangerous that he would take out his rage against a cat?

'Gus was outdoors this morning,' Dulcie murmured to herself, remembering. 'I thought that Doug let him out, but maybe it was Heath.' Deep in thought, Dulcie didn't hear the footsteps coming up behind her. 'Gus saw what happened the night Amy was killed. If Heath thinks Gus is a witness, he could be dangerous.' She caught herself and almost laughed. Who was she kidding? Heath *was* dangerous.

'Dulcie?' The voice – a man – was right behind her.

At the sound of her name, Dulcie spun around.

This time, she felt herself falling – flailing – grabbing at the air. She saw the street light spin – the sky. And then strong arms were grabbing her, pulling her to her feet. Holding her steady as she blinked in shock. And found herself face to face with Heath Barstow.

FORTY-NINE

'Heath!' Dulcie jumped back in fright, pulling herself free of the actor's strong grip. Immediately, she felt herself start to fall again.

'Dulcie, please.' He grabbed her, holding her upright. 'Be careful.'

'Me? You're warning me?' He had let go of her, and she stepped back – a bit more cautiously this time. Keeping her voice low and calm, she stared at the man before her. 'What do you want, Heath?'

'I need to talk to you.' From the way his brow knitted, Dulcie would have thought he was the one with the throbbing ankle. 'I need to,' he repeated.

'That's why you've been following me?' She worked to keep the alarm out of her voice, playing for time. If only she had her phone.

Heath nodded vigorously. 'I needed to wait till you were alone. At the theater, I – well, I couldn't talk.'

Dulcie took another step back, reaching into her pocket. No phone, but she found her keys and made a fist around them. If she had to, she would fight. 'I'm not sure what we have to talk about, Heath.' Another step. 'Roni and I are going to the police first thing in the morning.'

287

Why, oh why, had she not insisted they call Rogovoy immediately? Roni had been squeamish, for sure, but Dulcie could have pressed her. At least Roni was still at the theater, where she would be safe.

Or not. Heath was shaking his head. 'No, she won't,' he was saying. 'Roni won't go to the cops.'

Dulcie's blood ran cold. 'What did you do to her?'

'Me?' He had the audacity to sound shocked. 'I didn't do anything. I just know she won't. You have to trust me.'

That was the last thing Dulcie was prepared to do. However, she did want to keep him talking. 'Well, we'll get back to that.' It was the best she could muster. 'What did you want to talk to me about, Heath?'

'Don't...' He shook his head, some of those long locks escaping from his knit cap. 'Look, there are things you don't know about me.'

Dulcie held her breath. Was he going to confess?

'But it's not what you think – not what you said.' He took a step toward her, a strange look on his face. *A man turning into a wolf* ... The words sprang into Dulcie's mind.

'I'm not that guy, and Roni knows it.' Heath was still talking. 'She's the one who...' He stopped and bit his lip.

'She's the one who saw you and Amy,' Dulcie finished the sentence. 'She saw Amy at her computer. Maybe you helped her. Maybe you even forced her to do it.'

'No, that's not what happened.' Heath rubbed his face with a gloved hand. 'Yes, Roni came in and saw us. Amy was at the computer. At Roni's computer. But Amy wasn't doing anything wrong. And I—'

'What?' Dulcie waited for his declaration of innocence.

'I wouldn't hurt her. I would never have hurt Amy.'

That wasn't what she had thought he would say. In fact, everything about it – the syntax, the phrasing – was wrong. 'You're not being honest.' The moment the words were out of her mouth, Dulcie regretted them. She shouldn't antagonize this man. She should agree – and get out of there.

'No, I'm not.' He looked pained. 'I ... look, there are things I can't tell you. But I would never have hurt Amy. You've got to believe me.'

Again, he was using the conditional. And so, no, she didn't trust him. But she nodded, the better to placate the man before her. 'Yeah, okay,' she said. 'Amy was acting alone. Maybe you didn't even know what was going on. But now Roni is involved.' To her surprise, he nodded, his mouth set in a grim line. 'You've got to stay away from Roni, Heath. Promise me that.'

'I wish I could.' His voice had fallen to a whisper. 'That's what I wanted to talk to you about. I need you to understand why I...' He stopped, mouth open, and Dulcie found herself wondering if he was expecting a prompt. 'She's making me do things.'

'Roni is.' Dulcie took another step back. This

289

was creepier than she expected, and she needed to get away.

'She's not who you think she is.' Heath stepped toward her. 'I mean, I'm not either.' Another step, but Dulcie was backing up steadily now. 'But Roni knows things.'

'And that's why you need to keep her quiet.'

'Yes.' He looked positively relieved. 'You understand!'

'I understand that you murdered Amy Ralkov.' Dulcie gripped the keys in her fist. 'And now you're planning on silencing Roni, too. Permanently!'

'What? No!' Heath reached for her, but Dulcie was waiting. Whipping her fist from her pocket, she slashed at him – keys extended. With a shout, Heath recoiled and slipped, his feet flying up into the air as the actor fell on to his back.

'Dulcie!' He struggled to get up.

'Stay away from me!' Dulcie began backing up, too afraid of falling to run. 'Stay away from Roni, too!'

He was on his feet. He was coming closer. Larger and more agile than she was. The street was lonely. Quiet. Deserted.

And then they heard it – low at first, and rising, it split the night. As eerie as those strange blue shadows, and as clear. The howl.

FIFTY

Scrabbling like a scared cat, Dulcie pulled herself over the wall of snow into the street and took off.

'Dulcie, wait!' Heath called.

She didn't; nor did she look back. The loosely packed snow on the street's edge squeaked and shifted as she ran, but at least it gave her traction and she was a block and a half away before she dared look back. Heath was not behind her. She strained, but could make out no movement under the street lights.

Briefly, it flashed through her mind that perhaps he had hurt himself in his fall – hurt himself more than she had, anyway, she amended. Her ankle felt red hot, but she could still walk. Perhaps he hadn't been reaching out to grab her as much as trying to steady himself.

For a moment, she wondered if she should go back. But, no, that was crazy. She might have just escaped from a killer. She would call the cops as soon as she got home – unless, no, none of the storefronts were open at this hour, if they opened at all today.

Besides, she thought as she limped along, there had been that strange howl. Now that the adrenalin was wearing off, she had to wonder what she had heard. The wind had been strong all night, blasting up from the river. She had heard it rattling street signs and moaning as it forced its way through the slats of a bench. Besides, the city was unusually free of traffic tonight. Maybe, in the absence of other sounds, the whistle of the wind had simply been exaggerated, amplified by her fear into something more threatening and wild.

After all, if there really had been something threatening out there, wouldn't Mr Grey have come to her aid?

'You would have, wouldn't you?' She looked up at the moonlit sky, pausing for a moment on the street. 'If something were really out there?'

A blast of wind threw up a whirl of snow, the crystals dancing before her.

'Mr Grey?' She shifted her weight off the bad ankle as she watched the swirl rise up and subside. In the back of her mind, a memory echoed: *'You have to listen, Dulcie.'* But what did that mean? That she should have paid more attention to the howl? Or that it wasn't a howl at all?

'Whatever.' She turned away from the sparkling snow devil and began to trudge down the street again. The adrenalin gone now, leaving her exhausted as well as in pain. By the time she reached her corner, she was barely thinking, putting one foot in front of the other automatically, desperate to get home. To get out of the cold. The next blast of wind caught her full on, and she ducked her head, leaning in. This time, she could hear it moan, a sad and lonesome sound that only served to dramatize her thoughts. She had been scared and, worse, hurt. A man had threatened her, and then, perhaps something more. And she had been alone. Nobody, not even her special spirit friend, had come to her aid.

The cold was overwhelming now, chilling her even through her layers of wool and down. Where her face was exposed, the skin stung as if burnt, and when the wind picked up again, it felt like a slap. Head down, Dulcie kept on. Four more blocks. Three. Two.

It was the wind, she told herself – that moaning constant wind – that was forcing the tears from her eyes. Tears that froze even before they left her stinging cheeks.

FIFTY-ONE

'Dulcie!'

At the sound of her name, Dulcie spun around, ready to jump. When she had first gotten up to their building, minutes before, she had felt near to collapsing, the stairs up to the apartment barely surmountable. She had made it up to their flat, but that was the last of her strength.

'Chris?' She had called as she staggered in, too numb and tired to worry about her boots or the loose snow they had tracked in. All she wanted was to be held, to be comforted. 'I'm back!'

She'd been greeted by silence. Even Esmé, it seemed, had abandoned her, and she'd just stood there.

'Dulcie!' When the door burst open behind her, she didn't know what to expect. But before she could even formulate a response, Chris had her in his arms, kissing her and calling her name.

'I was so worried,' he said finally, after he let her go enough to remove her coat. 'I've been looking for you.'

'Looking?' She let him take her scarf and hat and then sat to remove her boots.

'Trista called and told me what happened.' He pulled his own boots off and reached to help with hers. 'She felt bad that she'd left and wanted to apologize. She said you'd stayed to talk to the office manager but didn't want to wait. It's cold out and it's late – and I knew you didn't have your phone.'

'I had a scare.' Here, with Chris, it was easier to dismiss. 'I – ow! I twisted my ankle.'

By the time he got her boot off, they could both see why: her ankle had swollen and was hot to the touch. But despite Chris's repeated pleas, Dulcie refused to go to the emergency room.

'What are they going to tell me? That I've sprained it?' Taking Chris's shoulder, she hobbled over to the sofa. 'Let me just keep it elevated, and we'll see how it is tomorrow.'

'You should have it X-rayed.' Chris tucked a pillow under her foot, and went to make cocoa.

'Tomorrow...' Dulcie had almost acquiesced when her memory kicked in. 'Bother. Chris? Did you manage to finish working on my phone?'

'Just about.' He came back in, and then stopped. 'Why? Who do you want to call at this hour?'

'I need to call the police.' Lying on the sofa, with an afghan tucked around her, as she relayed what had happened, the whole encounter sounded less threatening. 'At the very least, I should talk to Rogovoy,' she said, when she had finished. 'Roni and I are going to talk to him first thing tomorrow.'

'But you still want to call now?'

She nodded. 'I have his personal numbers – his desk and his cell. If I can leave him a message, he can be there to meet us.'

'Oh.' His face fell, and Dulcie jumped in.

'I promise, I'll take a cab. And if my ankle still hurts, I'll go to health services right after.'

'It's not that, Dulcie.' He looked up, a hangdog expression on his face. 'I wanted to make sure I'd gotten the worm off your phone, so I had to wipe it clean.'

'Clean?' She envisioned a muddy device.

'Clean.' He nodded. 'Your memory – your directory – is gone.' Before she could complain, he jumped back in. 'But I may have some good news for you, too.'

'Yeah?' Somehow, she wasn't sanguine.

'Yeah.' He was nodding. 'The worm? It wasn't breaking into anything. It was a diversion program. A cache, of sorts.' She shook her head. 'It didn't steal anything per se; it was waiting for you to type information in. That's why it was connected to the ticket offer. If you went for it – you know, typed in a credit card number – it would copy your number down. Passwords, too.'

'Wow, do you think Amy designed it?'

Chris shrugged. 'She could have. It's a neat bit of programming, but not overly complicated. Basically, it works because nobody suspects it's copying down the info.'

'Copying it, huh.' Dulcie shook her head, puzzled. 'I feel like there's a question I should be asking, Chris. I just can't place it.'

He laughed, but his voice was sad. 'One question? Try a million. Why would she do it? If nothing else, she was still a student. If the acting thing didn't work out, she could finish her degree, make her money legally. And why rip off a theater company she was part of?'

'That's it.' Dulcie wasn't quite sure, but it felt right. 'The theater company – I just got that email last night. It was sent after she died. So she either had an accomplice or we're barking up the wrong tree.'

Chris was waving her off. 'No, not necessarily. The email could have been generated automatically. You know, every day or two days, once you're on the list. At least until you opt out.'

'Either way, it's not any reason to kill someone.'

'No, sweetie,' said her boyfriend. 'It isn't.'

FIFTY-TWO

'Twas not the jostling of the coach nor the headlong rush of the great steeds, their eyes white with fright as they surged and scream'd into the night that made her head spin so. No, the wild Fear that tore at her, sparking the wildest Imaginings in the dark and fatigued corners of her mind, came not from the rush of the road – nor the lurch and tilt of their Vehicle as it careened along that rocky Road. 'Twas the Stranger himself, so calm and so preternaturally still e'en as her glov'd Hands grasped the cracked and faded leather of the seat. 'You are not whom you Seem,' she cried, her very Voice lost amid the jangle and bustle of their frantic ride. 'And I who had been warned – counseled by your very words – have Fallen into Error at your hands.'

'Not I,' the Stranger cried, and made to Leap across the dark'ning Void. 'My Warning is Misread!' Outside, the Horses screamed as Night flew swiftly by.

Dulcie woke, startled by this latest development – the Stranger evil? Was he about to attack? No. She shook herself. This was a dream, not reality. Not even, she made herself acknowledge, some-

298

thing she was likely to find in the Mildon fragments. This was a creation of her subconscious, piling together the harrowing events of the last week and her own fears from the night before.

Still, the nightmare, vivid as any waking adventure, had left her with the conviction that she had stumbled on something important. So important, in fact, that after checking the clock, she realized she needed to contact the police immediately. Her ankle was still tender, so she grabbed her phone and hopped into the kitchen. If she no longer had his private number, she would call the university police.

'Detective Rogovoy, please.' She spoke softly, so as not to wake Chris. If only the detective was at work this early.

'Ms Schwartz. Why am I not surprised to hear from you again? Didn't we have an agreement?' The gruff greeting would have scared Dulcie, if she weren't used to the university detective's ways. As it was, she ignored his unmannerly greeting and dove right in.

'Detective, this isn't about theories any more. I have some leads for you to share with your colleagues.' She spoke as clearly as she could while keeping the volume down. 'I believe I have information about what Amy Ralkov was doing that may have gotten her killed, and I know who her accomplice was.'

'You what?' Even for Rogovoy, this was loud. 'You know how that poor girl got herself murdered? What do you think this is, Ms Schwartz? Some kind of parlor game?'

'No, I just—' She didn't get a chance to finish.

299

'That poor girl didn't get *herself* killed.' He sounded genuinely angry. 'She was murdered. Someone stabbed her – in the neck. The skin is soft there, and whoever did it by luck or skill hit an artery. It wouldn't have been hard to do, physically, Dulcie. But it was still a brutal act of violence. Not something she did to herself. And not – definitely not – something you want to get involved in.'

'I didn't...' She caught her breath, grateful now that she hadn't wasted his time with the tool box or the pinking shears. 'I didn't mean that, Detective. Only that I may have found something.'

Only the sound of breathing let her know he hadn't hung up. She worked to clear her head of the images he had put in it. Amy's throat, that tender skin...

'She was studying computer sciences, right?' Dulcie asked, her own hand straying to the underside of her chin. 'Well, there's something hinky in the theater emails – a virus program – designed to steal people's financial information when they buy tickets. And the theater has been losing money, and—'

'And you think she created this virus?'

'I do.' More heavy breathing. Dulcie felt her own pulse. It wouldn't have taken much.

Another pause. 'Why would she do that?'

It was the same question she had asked only the night before. His next one, however, surprised her.

'How do you know she didn't discover it? Maybe she was killed to cover it up?'

'Because she was seen.' Dulcie realized with a

sinking feeling that she was condemning the poor girl's memory. 'Someone witnessed her at the box office computer.' In the pause that followed, she tried to remember everything Heath had said. 'And, well, I think her boyfriend kind of confirmed it.'

'The so-called star, Heath Barstow?'

Dulcie nodded, before realizing that she needed to articulate her response. 'Yeah, I think he might have been involved too. He might even have, well ... He says he didn't. But he confirmed what the office manager said.'

'And he's Mr Reliable.' Before Dulcie could respond, the gruff detective broke in. 'Look, Dulcie – Ms Schwartz – I need you to listen to me. This is an active police investigation. There are elements here that you aren't aware of, and you can't keep inserting yourself in here. I'm glad you called me, rather than the city cops. But, really, please just let it drop.'

'I can't.' Dulcie found herself looking up at the clock.

'Excuse me?' The growl was back.

'I told Roni – she's the office manager – that I'd go with her this morning to talk to the cops. I thought I'd take her in to talk to you, but I wanted to make sure you were there first.'

A grumble like thunder came over the line. 'You thought you'd take her in?'

'She's scared.' Dulcie thought back to the scene she had witnessed the night before. 'She might be in danger.'

'Look, you've done the right thing, okay?' Rogovoy didn't wait for an answer. 'You called

301

me. Now, please just leave it.'

'But...' He had to understand. She was acting as a friend.

He didn't. 'Look, Dulcie, I know you mean well. But really, kid, this is serious. Now go make a snowman with that nice boyfriend of yours, okay?'

'Okay.' The line went dead.

'What's that about?' Chris came into the kitchen. 'No coffee?'

'I wanted to talk to Rogovoy first.' He nodded and reached into the cabinet for the filters. 'He told me to stay out of it.'

'I'm not surprised.' He measured out the beans. 'But you told him about the worm, right?'

'Yeah.' She nodded. 'Hey, we should tell Jerry and Trista. Jerry bought tickets before we got comped.'

'Oh, hell, you're right.' He turned from the coffee, then turned back. 'He won't be up for a few hours.'

'I'll see what I can find out from Roni.' Dulcie tried to hide her limp as she returned to the bedroom. 'Maybe she can access the email list.'

'I thought Rogovoy said to leave it alone?'

'There's nothing to leave. I'm not doing anything.' Dulcie pulled on her warmest socks. 'But I'm not going to stand her up. That girl needs a friend.'

FIFTY-THREE

Dulcie didn't want to lie to Chris. Saying that her ankle was 'perfectly fine' was a bit of an exaggeration, that was all. And although it meant she had to turn down his offer to wrap it, she figured her boot would offer enough support as she trudged back into the Square. It wasn't like she was going to jog anywhere: today the sidewalks were a little more cleared of snow, and more of them had some kind of anti-skid grit scattered across the icy bits. But slick patches remained and more than once Dulcie found herself leaning on the snow to the side of the walk for support. Two days in, the snow pack had developed an icy crust, too, but that only made it more banister-like as she made her way down the street.

At least she had her phone back, and once she was again hands-free she dug it out of her pocket to see that several voicemail messages had piled up. These would help her rebuild her contact list, she told herself as she hit play.

'Dulcie – you've got it all wrong.' Lucy was, as usual, talking as if they'd been having an ongoing conversation. 'I know you've been working hard at this, dear. Your rising moon has been shadowed by the trine of Mercury, which I am sure has made the past few days particularly *trying.'* Dulcie looked down at the phone, her gloves making it a little tricky to hit 'delete'. *'But you're wrong about his identity, dear. Please don't let yourself be fooled.'*

It had to be coincidence. There was no way Lucy could know about her dream. Dulcie thought back to their last few conversations. Yes, she had probably told her mother about her latest paper. Maybe it had even been earlier. Since she had begun her thesis, five years ago, she had been intrigued by the anonymous author of *The Ravages*. Not only was it great fiction, it was a pioneering work of feminism. When she had found political writings that clearly used the same literary devices, she felt validated in her interpretation of the novel – and closer to giving the author a name. With the journal entries and the new novel fragments of the Philadelphia bequest, she was closer still. She knew it. Surely, she had chatted about something that had so consumed her.

But her mother had said *'his* identity'. Not hers. And while Dulcie could not be sure, she had always acted on the assumption that the author of *The Ravages* was a woman, one of the unheralded 'She-authors' who built the Gothic genre.

Was it possible that her mother knew that right now, at this point in time, she was dealing with another question of identity? That she was debating whether that one mysterious character, Monsieur Le Gris, was actually a villain? Was in some way related to the evil lord – the one who, it seemed, had imprisoned the heroine of this new book? She had always associated the enigmatic stranger with her own Mr Grey, not only because of his name but because of his sudden appearance – showing up with advice just when he was most needed. Had her prejudice blinded her to the reality of what was a fictional character? Surely, she hadn't said anything to her mother about Le Gris.

No, she shook her head. It had to be coincidence.

At any rate, she now had the number for the arts commune on her phone again. She'd touch base later, she told herself, before moving on to the next message.

'Ms Schwartz?' It was Thorpe. *'I don't believe I'll be able to make it in today.'* Of course, he had called her Friday morning before their proposed meeting. *'But I will be working at home, so if you would send me your pages I will do my best to get to them.'*

Well, maybe the delay had done her a service. Yesterday morning, Dulcie hadn't had pages for him. When she got through with Roni, she would send what she had written in her office. There was one more message, from a few hours later. *'Ms Schwartz.'* Thorpe again. *'I understand the desire to procrastinate, but I really do not appreciate having my time wasted. Contact me immediately or expect to face disciplinary action.'*

Dulcie paused, considering. The morning wasn't as cold as the day before. Still, did she really want to stand here, on the street, explaining herself to her adviser? A police cruiser drove by – in the direction of the Square – and she decided. No, she'd call Thorpe afterward and explain. First, she had an appointment to keep.

FIFTY-FOUR

'Dulcie, I can't,' Roni repeated, her voice strained.

Five minutes later, Dulcie had reached the URT and been happy to find it open. Cast members she vaguely recognized were chatting by the door, and Roni had grabbed her as soon as she stepped into the theater lobby, pulling her into her office. 'I'm sorry,' said the office manager, 'but I just can't go right now.'

'You have to.' Dulcie didn't understand. 'It's not safe for you otherwise.'

'But we have a matinee today.' Roni looked over Dulcie's shoulder. She'd left the door ajar, and the lobby beyond was filling up with the cast and crew. 'I'm sorry; I'd lost track of the days. And I'm also trying to get through all of our ticket records. You know, get rid of that bad email before more of our patrons are infected by that virus.'

'But what about...' Dulcie dropped her voice. 'Heath?'

Roni shook her head. 'He didn't show up today. We've lined up a cover. You know, an understudy. So I'm fine here.'

Dulcie would never understand theater folk, and the noise wasn't helping. She leaned back to close the door, determined to push the office manager further, and stopped herself. Gus was standing in the doorway, looking up at her with those deep green eyes. He was trying to tell her something, she was sure. The question was: what?

'Wait, Heath didn't show? Are you sure he's okay?' Dulcie thought back to their confrontation. Had she left an injured man out in the cold?

'Oh, Heath?' Dulcie turned to see Avila pushing the door wide. Gus must have scampered off. 'Probably had to touch up his roots or something. Roni? They need you at the box office.'

'Coming.' Roni turned toward her keyboard and began typing furiously. 'Let me just finish this.'

Avila stepped out, and Dulcie followed. 'I'm serious,' she asked the actress. 'Have you heard from him? Has anyone?'

'Aren't you sweet?' Avila smiled at her. 'Don't worry, Dulcie. We call it "matinee-itis". I mean, who wants to do two shows in one day? I bet he'll show up miraculously cured in time for the big Saturday night show. I mean, it's not like he's going anywhere else.'

'Well, probably not.' Dulcie mused over the possibility that the blond-haired actor had fled.

'Check it out,' said Avila, inclining her head toward the ticket window where a line had formed. 'I think we're here for a while.'

Before Dulcie could follow up, her phone had rung again.

'There you are!' Despite the noise in the lobby, Dulcie recognized Suze's voice. 'I've been try-

308

ing to reach you.'

'Did you message me?' Dulcie glanced down at her phone. What else had been lost when Chris had cleaned it? 'Or email?'

'Figured I'd just keep trying to reach you in person.' Even through the din, her friend sounded harried.

'Is everything okay?' This wasn't like Suze.

'What? Oh, yeah. Just crazy busy.' From the pause that followed, Dulcie got the sense that her friend was multitasking even as she spoke. Sure enough, she could hear Suze's voice, muffled by a hand, speaking to someone on her end. A moment later, she was back. 'Sorry, Dulce. I figured I'd keep trying till I got you in real time.'

That was nice. 'My phone's been out of commission,' she explained.

'Hope you didn't catch anything.' Noise on both ends. Dulcie figured her friend hadn't heard her properly.

'No, I'm fine,' she said. 'It's my phone that was out of order.'

'Yeah, I heard. Hang on.' When Suze came back, her voice was both louder and more clear, and Dulcie realized her friend had had her on speaker phone. 'I meant, I hope you didn't have anything cached. You know, saved.'

'Well, actually, Chris had to clean out my directory when he rebooted me.'

'Oh, that's nothing then.' Suze didn't seem to understand the gravity of the problem. 'I'm just glad you didn't have anything of yours taken. And, hey, now you have my office number again.'

'Yeah.' Dulcie didn't quite follow. 'So what's up?'

'Besides wanting to touch base with my former roomie?' Dulcie waited. Suze would have left a message if that were the case. 'I wanted to see if you'd had any more run-ins with the law.'

'Actually, I was hoping to talk to the cops today. Voluntarily,' she added, before Suze could ask.

'About your phone?' More noise on the line.

'No,' said Dulcie. Suze must be distracted. 'About the murder. You know, the girl at the URT.'

'Oh, of course.' The line grew quieter. Suze must have closed her office door. 'The city is handling that, right?'

'Yeah, I think so. But we're going to talk to Rogovoy.' Dulcie turned to face the wall, hoping to block out what sounded like an argument about exchanging seats. 'Sorry, Suze. I'm right by the box office here. I'm in the URT now. But, yeah, Roni the office manager is coming with me.'

'I don't know, Dulcie. I wish you weren't involved in this.'

'I'm just helping out a friend, Suze.' Dulcie was warmed by her concern. 'And, hey, maybe I'll get some free tickets out of it.'

What Suze said next was obscured by loud greetings, as a new party came through the door. 'What?' Dulcie put one hand over her ear.

'I said, there's no such thing as a free ticket, Dulcie!' Suze was yelling. 'They always get you one way or the other.'

'Yeah, you're right.' Dulcie was itching to tell her friend about the night before, but not while standing in the URT lobby. 'Talk soon.' She got off the phone and turned to see Roni standing behind her.

'Sorry, I didn't mean to eavesdrop.' Roni looked around. 'I was hoping you were still here.'

Dulcie felt her spirits lift. 'Can you get away now?'

Roni shook her head. 'No, after the matinee, maybe,' she said. 'Can you come back – around three?'

'Yeah, I should be able to.' Dulcie paused. She knew how hard it was to go to the cops. 'And Roni? You're doing the right thing. Don't let Heath get to you.'

'I won't, Dulcie.' Even as she said it, her eyes darted around the room. 'And thanks.'

Out once more in the cold, Dulcie considered stopping by the health services. Standing in the lobby, she'd been able to take the weight off her swollen ankle, but walking once again made her very aware that something was wrong. It couldn't be broken, surely, or else she wouldn't be able to walk on it at all, she figured. But with each step, she found herself wincing.

'Hey, Chris?' She'd gotten his voicemail, but talking to that took her mind off the pain. 'I think maybe you were right.' A beep alerted her to an incoming call. 'Is that you?'

She clicked over.

'Ms Schwartz, there you are.' It was Thorpe. 'I've been trying to reach you, you know.'

'I know, Mr Thorpe, I'm sorry.' Dulcie stepped badly and felt a searing pain go up her leg. 'My phone's been out of order.'

'And your computer has been out of order, too?'

'No, though it did have a virus.' She began talking before she realized he hadn't meant to voice concern. 'But I have those pages for you. I can send them over.'

'Too little, too late, Ms Schwartz.' His vehemence startled her. 'If you had simply left your paper for me, I would have it read by now.'

'Yes, Mr Thorpe.' She'd started walking again, which made talking a bit difficult. But even as she threaded her way carefully down the cleared path, she started to do her calculations. 'If I get out of the health services in time to meet Roni, I could come by around four,' she said.

'Four?' Thorpe sounded incredulous. 'Do you actually have pages written, Ms Schwartz?'

'Yes.' So she hadn't for their first meeting. But since then, she had been writing.

'I don't see why you can't simply drop them off sooner then.'

'But, Mr Thorpe...' She stopped walking. Sometimes, it was easier not to fight. 'Sure,' she said. 'I'll be by within fifteen minutes.'

As she hung up, she realized that she'd missed a call. Chris must have gotten her truncated message.

'Hey, sweetie. No! Esmé, stop it! What is it?' Dulcie could easily visualize the cat leaping for Chris's hand as he held the phone. 'Sorry, she's demanding attention again.' Dulcie thought she could hear a perturbed mew. 'Anyway, you're probably down at the police headquarters now. Um, don't know if you want to bother, but when you get out, you might want to talk to the office manager about another matter.

'Turns out, that girl Amy never ended up charging Jerry for the tickets he got for Lloyd and Raleigh. She had to change the number when you and Trista got those comps, and the paperwork never went in. So Jerry owes the theater. But at least his credit info is secure. Anyway, he says if you can tell them that he'll come by with cash that would be great. What is it, Esmé? Man, Dulce, this cat is out of control.'

Chuckling, Dulcie put her phone away. She'd treat herself to a nice long chat with Chris once she got through with Thorpe. Odds were, she'd have to wait at the health services for someone to look at her ankle, and she'd call him back then. And if he indulged in an 'I told you so', well, that would be a reasonable price to pay.

By the time she reached the little clapboard, she was limping badly.

'Oh, Dulcie!' Nancy saw her coming through the door and ran to meet her. 'What did you do to yourself?'

'The ice,' she said as she collapsed into a chair. 'I'm sorry.' She looked back toward the door. 'I've tracked in all sorts of snow.'

'Don't you worry about that.' Nancy took Dulcie's hat and looked down at her feet. 'Do you want help taking your boot off?'

Dulcie shook her head. 'To be honest, I'd be afraid that I wouldn't be able to get it back on.'

313

'Of course.' Ever practical, Nancy went back into her office, returning with an armless wooden chair. 'Here, let's elevate it.'

'Thanks.' Maybe it was Nancy's motherly concern, but Dulcie could have sworn her ankle already felt better. When Nancy returned with one of her own mugs filled with sweet, milky coffee, Dulcie was sure she was healing. If only she didn't have to face her adviser, up the stairs.

'Thanks so much, Nancy,' she said at last, as the warmth of the hot drink sank in. 'I don't suppose that Mr Thorpe would be willing to come downstairs to meet with me?'

'I would think it would be the very least he could do.' Nancy smiled at her, hovering, and Dulcie found herself smiling back. The secretary had a way of phrasing things that made everything seem gentler and more humane. She could easily imagine the balding adviser grumbling about having to relocate for the meeting, but she appreciated the sentiment nonetheless.

'I'll go get him,' said Nancy. 'Oh, but first things first. You've gotten some mail.'

'Mail?' Dulcie watched as Nancy ducked back into her office. On any other day, she'd have risen and followed.

'Something from a journal, I believe.' Dulcie almost jumped up at that, ankle pain or no ankle pain. But just as she was testing the arms of the chair to see if she could raise herself up, Nancy reappeared. 'Here we go.'

It was a thick envelope and the return address was from a box office in Chicago. Holding her breath, Dulcie tore it open.

'*Dear Ms Schwartz,*' she read. '*Pursuant to our editorial meeting of January the thirteenth...*'

'It's a contract,' she read. 'University of Chicago is interested in one of my proposals. They want to publish part of my thesis in an upcoming book. But, wait...' She fished in the envelope for the remaining loose sheet.

'What is it, Dulcie?' Nancy's eyes were wide with anticipation.

'They're talking about notes, as if we'd discussed the article already.' She skimmed the letter and went back to the top.

'Maybe they mean they discussed the article among themselves,' said the secretary. 'To give you some guidance before you wrote. That wouldn't be a bad thing, would it?' Nancy was picking up on her concern. 'Perhaps it might make things run more smoothly.'

'Well, yes, I guess.' She was looking up at the secretary, but she was thinking of her laptop – and the computer virus. 'But they say they sent them already. If those have gotten lost, how many other responses have I missed? And where have they been going?'

'Maybe Mr Thorpe will be able to shed some light?' Even Nancy's famed optimism sounded strained. 'At any rate, I'll see if I can fetch him.'

While she climbed the stairs, Dulcie pulled her laptop out and opened it. To her relief, it started right up – and the pages she'd written for Thorpe, at least, seemed to be there. With a quick keystroke, she sent them to the printer in Nancy's office and then she started to read.

What she found filled her with dismay. The

pages she'd been so proud of, back in her office, looked speculative now – more wishful thinking than scholarly. What had she been thinking, gassing on about the stranger in the cab? How much of this was material she had actually found in the new pages, and how much was taken from her dreams?

She skimmed another page, her heart sinking as she read. Maybe Thorpe was right: she was spinning her wheels. It was time to settle down and write. She would stop researching new material and make use of what she already had. If she applied herself, she could have her thesis drafted by spring.

The sound of steps on the stairs only firmed her resolve. Steeling herself, she looked up to greet her adviser, who was descending the stairs, a pile of journals in his arms.

'Mr Thorpe,' she said. 'You ... I...' As she paused, looking for the right words to admit what felt like defeat, he nodded toward her boot.

'Ms Schwartz.' The balding scholar looked more pink than usual, and Dulcie wondered if he had a cold. 'Ms Pruitt tells me you've met with a mishap.'

'It's nothing serious, but thank you. And I wanted to say...' Dulcie slid her boot off the chair, only to notice the puddle of ice melt that had accumulated on the seat. 'Oh, dear.'

'Never mind, Ms Schwartz.' Standing there, he seemed to grow even pinker. He placed the journals on the floor.

'I can go up to your office.' Dulcie was worried. 'I just needed to rest it a bit.'

'No, no, please.' Thorpe waved her down with a bird-like gesture.

'Well, at least let me get my pages.' She started to stand, nodding over to the printer in Nancy's office as she braced herself on the chair's arms. 'Because, Mr Thorpe, you were right.'

'Never mind that.' More fluttering and Dulcie, startled, collapsed back into the chair. 'Don't bother with those pages.'

'But ... my chapter?' Only now did she realize that the nervous hand gestures and, most likely, the pinkness in Thorpe's extended face augured nervousness of some sort. 'Mr Thorpe,' she asked, growing concerned. 'What is it? What's going on?'

'It seems your paper has stirred up a bit of attention.' More fiddling. Dulcie realized she was holding her breath. 'Including the offer of a contract from Chicago, I hear.'

'Yes.' She hadn't thought Nancy the type to gossip, but perhaps she had thought she was doing Dulcie a favor, passing along her good news to the acting chair. 'Though, I seem to have mislaid...' She paused. Better not to let Thorpe know that she had lost a letter.

'Here they are!' Nancy, with what sounded almost like real enthusiasm, handed over Dulcie's pages. 'Mr Thorpe, would you like me to get you a dry chair?'

'No need, no need.' The adviser dropped the pages on to the damp seat. 'In fact, I have other work for Ms Schwartz to focus on.'

With that, he reached down for the journals and handed them over to Dulcie. 'These are the latest from the press at Chicago,' Thorpe said. 'I recommend you start with the one on epistolary prose under Hamilton. In fact, why don't you open to the editor's page now?'

Thorpe was actually singing by the time he took off for lunch. For a moment, Dulcie feared he would even invite her, but the balding scholar caught himself in time. 'Ms Schwartz, you should get to work,' he'd said instead, as he wrapped a wool muffler around his neck. 'Don't let a little thing like a sprained ankle slow you down.'

'Like he knows anything about it.' Dulcie couldn't help but grump as she reached for where she had dropped her own hat and coat.

'Do you want me to call you a cab?' Nancy popped out of her office, her face showing her concern. 'Or an ambulance?'

'It's not that bad.' For Nancy, Dulcie could summon a smile. 'In fact, my ankle's feeling better.' She stood, gingerly testing it with her weight. 'Maybe I just needed a rest.'

'Or a counter irritant.' Nancy's comment was offered so softly, Dulcie doubted for a moment that she had heard it. After all, she had begun to suspect that the secretary and the department chair had more than a professional relationship.

'Don't get me wrong,' Nancy must have read all this on her face. 'Mr Thorpe is a kind and honorable gentleman. But he does have his little enthusiasms.'

'That's one word for it.' It helped to air, but Dulcie knew better than to unload entirely on the secretary. 'Well, at least I'll have another publication to my credit.'

Nancy smiled at her, pleased by her attempt at optimism. 'We're all lucky to have you, dear.' Nancy reached around to arrange Dulcie's collar in a particularly motherly touch. 'Mr Thorpe in particular.'

Dulcie stepped outdoors with a sigh of relief that might have been audible by the river. Despite Nancy's kindness, she had begun to feel suffocated in the little office as her adviser's excitement sucked all the oxygen out of it. No, it wasn't his excitement, she decided, as she hobbled slowly down the stairs. It was his complete and utter disregard of her priorities. Her thesis. Her – yes, she might as well admit how she felt – author.

'And have you lost your own vision?' The voice took her by surprise, and she stopped, looking up in the air.

'Mr Grey?' She had reached the sidewalk, which she tested carefully with her uninjured foot. The air was cold enough so that even at midday, a thin sheen of ice covered the brick, making it shine like a freshly waxed floor. It was pretty, if treacherous, but some careful buildings and grounds person had scattered sand here, making the walk a little easier.

'Have you not been seeking a name?' The voice was warm as always, like a gentle breeze in the frosty day, but Dulcie thought she detected a gentle mocking. *'An identity, for yourself.'*

'I've been trying to uncover the author's

319

name.' As soon as the words were out, Dulcie knew she had to admit another truth. 'And yes, a name for myself. But this project with Mr Thorpe, it's not going to do either.'

A chuckle, or was it a purr? And Dulcie was hit by a sudden memory: Mr Grey, back when he was still a cat of flesh and fur, crouching in the kitchen she had shared with Suze. He had been so intent, so still, that the room-mates had become worried. Did they have mice? Was it some kind of horrid bug that had so entranced the little hunter? Or had it been a figment of his feline imagination, some play of dust or the light that had drawn his attention to the crack in the molding by the fridge?

'You didn't catch anything there, did you?' she asked the air. Surely, the memory had come from him. 'Are you saying that I'm like that? That I'm trying too hard?' Nothing. 'Mr Grey?' The mid-day sun glinted off the heaped snow, glittering like diamonds.

FIFTY-FIVE

As inconclusive as they were, Mr Grey's words had mollified Dulcie, even if she couldn't have explained exactly what they meant. After all, he had clearly intended to show her something. And he had visited, which was a comfort.

If only he could have kept her from slipping on the ice last night, she thought as she made her way down the walk. She had been overly hasty, she could tell now, in turning down Nancy's offer of a cab. With each step, her ankle became more aggravated, and she was limping by the time she reached Mass Ave, the weight of her bag on her shoulder growing with each step. Well, only a few more blocks to health services. Once her ankle was wrapped, she'd head the other way back to the URT.

If she ever got there. She was moving slowly now, and as her speed decreased so too did her sense of well-being. Like the stab of pain that made her gasp each time she put her weight on her left foot, doubt was cracking her earlier calm.

Why *hadn't* Mr Grey been there, last night? Not just to help her when she slipped, but when Heath had threatened her?

Maybe, she told herself, this was a sign of faith. Mr Grey believed in her – believed in her ability to take care of herself, no matter what she faced. In truth, she had gotten away from Heath and gotten home safely, despite banging up her ankle. And, in truth, she had begun to believe that the grey spirit was slowly leaving her, weaning her away from her supernatural protector. It wasn't as if she didn't have Esmé in her life. And Chris.

What was going on with Chris, anyway? He had also been MIA last night, arriving home after she did. Could he really have missed her on the same path they always took into the Square? Her initial suspicion was just too horrible. Chris couldn't really be some kind of, well, werewolf. Could he? But if not, then what were the other options? She didn't – couldn't – believe he was seeing someone else, but how could she know for sure? Jerry probably didn't question Trista's loyalty, either. If it were drinking or drugs, his work would be suffering.

And if Thorpe really did keep on monopolizing her time, how was she ever going to complete her thesis?

Dulcie was so preoccupied by these thoughts that she didn't see the woman barreling toward her.

''Scuse me!' Dulcie turned in time to see a large woman, made larger by her hot-pink parka. 'Coming through!' Hemmed in by the walls of snow, Dulcie knew she couldn't get out of the way, and instead leaned into the bank to let her pass.

'Thanks!' The woman was gracious enough to yell as she passed, but the move – the fast turn –

had aggravated Dulcie's ankle more. If she could just get up to that next set of storefronts, she decided, she would step inside, call Chris – and if she couldn't reach him, she'd call a cab. She was done with the heroics.

The end of the block was in sight when her phone rang again. For a moment, she ignored it. She needed to sit down. Then it hit her: if this were Chris, he could meet her. She fished her phone out and answered quickly.

'Hello?'

'Dulcie!' The voice was familiar, but rushed and breathless.

'Roni?' The scene back at the theater had been chaotic, but not that bad. 'What's up?'

'I should have listened to you.' The other girl's voice sounded muffled, and Dulcie realized that she must be talking with her hand over the receiver. 'Where are you?'

'I just left the office,' said Dulcie. Maybe it was the cold, but she didn't understand.

'The police?'

'No, my department. English and American Lit—'

She didn't get a chance to finish. 'Good. Oh, Dulcie, you were right. Can you come back? Like, now? Everyone's left the theater and I'm alone in my office. Heath is here and he's acting crazy. Dulcie, I'm scared.'

'I thought he was out sick?' Even as she said it, Dulcie remembered: the actor had been a no-show. No reason had been given. 'Never mind,' she interrupted Roni's sputtering response. 'Have you called the police?'

323

'He thinks I've already gone to the police!' Roni's voice had dropped to a panicked whisper. 'I don't want to make him angrier.'

'If he's already angry—'

'Please, Dulcie.' Her voice was little more than a hiss. *'Please!'*

'But...' It was hopeless. Dulcie was used to dealing with logical minds. Roni might be a bookkeeper, but she'd clearly been infected by the dramatic way of thinking. She'd been planning on accompanying the office manager to speak with Detective Rogovoy anyway. Her ankle was tender, but it could wait.

'Okay, I can be there in about ten minutes.' She tested her ankle. No, she wouldn't be able to go any faster.

'Thanks, Dulcie.' Already, Roni sounded calmer. 'The front door is still unlocked, I think. I'm staying in my office.'

'See you soon.' Tucking the phone away, Dulcie began to hobble. As she walked, she thought about calling Rogovoy. Maybe he would be able to meet her and they could pick up Roni together. Better yet, he could go straight to the theater. Dulcie wasn't sure if she really believed the dark-haired girl needed protection. She did need reassurance, however.

As Dulcie walked, she realized she'd developed a rhythm. The packed snow on either side functioned as a kind of railing, and she found that if she walked with her arms slightly akimbo, she could lean on the frosted surface as she passed. It was awkward, but it was faster than her previous limp. It also meant that her hands were occupied with moving her along, so that by the time she had her phone out and Rogovoy's number ready to go, she had arrived at the theater – five minutes earlier than she had expected.

For half a second, Dulcie weighed her options. In the back of her mind, she could hear Suze. The voice of reason, Suze would tell her to be careful, which meant she should call Rogovoy. Then again, Suze would also tell her not to get involved with the police without proper representation, and although Dulcie was confident that the university detective would not treat her unfairly, she had also been reminded repeatedly that this was not his case. If she and Roni went into his office to have a chat, that would be one thing. But if she called Rogovoy from the theater – the crime scene – might he be compelled to notify the state cops?

What if she were able to get Roni to come out of her office? If she called Rogovoy and told him they were on their way, that surely would be a different matter entirely.

Not that she would be foolhardy. Dulcie held her phone in her hand, her thumb on the call button, as she reached for the theater door. It was locked. With a sigh of regret, she backed up from the university police number and went to incoming. She found Roni Squires' number and hit 'call'.

'Dulcie, where are you?' The office manager picked up on the first ring. 'Are you coming?'

'I'm right out front. The door's locked.' She paused. 'Why don't you come out to meet me, and we can go to the police.'

'I ... I can't.' Roni sounded breathless. 'He's here, in the theater. Can you come get me?' Dulcie started to object. If Heath was on a rampage, she didn't want to put herself at risk. 'I promise, I'll call nine one one if I hear anything,' said Roni. 'But maybe we can just sneak out.'

'But I can't come in, Roni.' Dulcie was getting frustrated. 'I called because the door is locked.' Panic was making the office manager less rational than usual.

'The side door – that's our stage door.' Dulcie remembered the unmarked entrance that Doug had used. 'He must have come in that way. Please, Dulcie,' she entreated, before Dulcie could object. 'We'll go out together. I'm just so scared.'

Grudgingly, Dulcie agreed. 'Give me two minutes, Roni. I'm moving slowly here.'

As she made her way to the side of the building, Dulcie thought once again of calling Rogovoy. 'Am I being stupid, Mr Grey? I should just call him, right?'

She didn't really expect a response. She knew the answer, but she ducked down the side of the building anyway, hoping for privacy and some shelter from what had become a bitter wind. The side door, she could see, was slightly ajar, and she kept her eye on it as she once more reached for her phone.

Dulcie...' It had to be the wind. She didn't really expect an answer to her question, but as she maneuvered the phone, clumsy in her gloves, she heard it again. *'Dulcie.'*

Against her better judgment – knowing it would be futile – she looked up. There! A movement, over by the door. A shadow in the line of darkness growing, as the door opened ever so slightly. A paw appeared, reaching out as if batting at the frosty air.

Gus! That neat paw, cloaked in silver fur, couldn't belong to anyone else. As Dulcie watched, the furry appendage reached around, claws outstretched in an attempt to gain traction on the painted surface. A dark leathery nose appeared, pushing through the crack. The Russian blue was slowly forcing the heavy door open.

Dulcie limped down to the door as quickly as she could, determined to stop the theater cat before he could slip out the side door. Hobbled as she was, she would be no match for a determined cat once he got out the door.

'Gus! No!' Green eyes gazed up at her, unblinking and inscrutable. The paw reached out again, and Dulcie ducked down, extending her own gloved hand. She meant to push the eager paw back inside, and then quickly close the door. But before she could, Gus had grabbed her, his claws hooking into the soft wool and pulling the glove half off her hand.

'Kitty!' The movement – or maybe it had been Dulcie's startled cry – spooked the cat. He tugged at the glove, desperate to free it, and only tangled it more. The eyes that now looked up at Dulcie were wide with terror.

'Hang on.' Dulcie reached to unhook the claw, which was now extended far enough to show its fleshy base.

'Naow!' Gus pulled, frantic now.

There was nothing for it. With one hand immobilized by the panicking feline and her bag sliding down the other, she opened the door far enough to lean in. Stepping inside, she scooped the cat up. As the door shut behind her, Gus appeared to calm down, and without further ado, she freed him from his woolly shackle.

'Mrrup?' The feline asked in a conversational tone, sounding for all the world as if he hadn't been desperate with fear only moments before.

'You wanted to get me in here, didn't you, Gus?' Dulcie wasn't serious, at least not totally. Surely the cat had been trying to get his claw free, rather than maneuver her into this back hallway. Still, it was nicer to be inside the warm building, with a cat in her arms. And she could still call Rogovoy, as soon as she put Gus down.

'Dulcie?' She started at the sound of her name – but the voice belonged to a woman, and she looked up to see Avila, in a black leotard, poking her head around the corner. 'What brings you here?'

'This little guy.' Awash in relief, Dulcie hefted the cat up. Clearly, Roni wasn't alone in the theater, and she was glad she had another excuse for what could be interpreted as sneaking in through the stage door. 'I saw this guy trying to push his way out. I guess the door wasn't latched.'

'Gus, you silly boy.' Avila backed up as Dulcie stepped forward, and Dulcie remembered her aversion to the silver feline. 'How did you get that door open?'

'I don't think he...' Dulcie paused. Could Avila dislike the Russian blue enough to have wanted him to run away? She looked down at the cat in her arms. 'You didn't open that door, did you, Gus?'

'Oh, Heath probably left it unlatched.' Avila waved off her earlier question as she turned to walk back into the main theater. 'You coming?'

'Yeah, thanks.' Dulcie began to limp after her, curious. 'So Heath is here?' At this point, she didn't trust Roni's perception.

'Showed up just as the matinee was letting out. Of course.' The actress turned and fixed Dulcie with her dark eyes. 'And I swear, his hair is a few shades lighter than it was last night.'

She turned and kept walking, which freed Dulcie from having to answer. But as Dulcie followed the petite actress through the back hall-way, she found herself breathing more easily. Clearly, Avila didn't consider Heath to be a threat. If anything, she seemed to be losing inter-est in him. Which only made Dulcie wonder at Roni's fear.

'Avila?' Dulcie called. She had fallen behind, due to her limp, and reached the open theater area just as the actress was about to exit via the door to the lobby. 'May I ask you some-thing?'

'Try me.' The actress turned, the leotard's low-cut back revealing the muscles in her shoulder.

If she was going to ask, it had to be now – before she was near to where Roni might over-hear. 'Do you think that Roni might be a little...?' Dulcie hesitated. She didn't want to be rude. 'A little biased about Heath, sometimes?'

Avila smiled, her dark eyes straying to the disco ball suspended overhead. 'Yeah, well...' A pause. 'That's what happens when you take guys like that seriously.'

'You think he was joking?' Dulcie toyed with the idea as she absently stroked Gus. Could the super-serious bookkeeper have misunderstood something she had heard?

'Not joking, per se.' Avila shrugged. 'She's not a theater person. I think it must be hard, sometimes, to understand how we are. I mean, I didn't think she'd stick it out. I thought, for sure, with her background, she'd get another real gig.'

'Oh, no. She hated her old job.' Dulcie shook her head. To an actress, all corporate work probably sounded the same. 'She told me that the only useful thing she got out of marketing was knowing how to work up a spreadsheet.'

'Whatever.' Avila leaned on the auditorium door, about to push it open. 'I'm just glad she got our computer systems up and running.'

'You might need a real IT person, I'm afraid.' Dulcie wasn't going to spill the beans about the virus, but surely people inside the company must know. 'Someone else with some serious programming skills.'

Avila turned. 'But that's what Roni did.' The door creaked open behind her. 'Programming.'

Dulcie must have frozen. Must have clutched the cat in her arms in shock. There was no other explanation. Because just at that moment, Gus yowled and, with a powerful kick, leaped from Dulcie's hands. Dulcie turned to see the cat, fur on end as he flew across the room, disappearing under a cocktail table. Behind her, Avila gave a startled cry. And just at that moment, the room went dark.

FIFTY-SIX

'Avila!' Dulcie called out. 'Where are you?' That last cry – half gasp, half strangled scream – had been unnerving, but Dulcie was going to remain calm. 'Did a fuse blow?'

She was greeted by silence. Even the cat seemed to have disappeared, and so, with her hands out before her, Dulcie took a halting step into the theater, toward where she had last seen Avila.

'Are you there?' Dulcie called out into the silent theater. The actress was afraid of cats, she reminded herself. Plus, she had been leaning back against the auditorium door. She must have been startled when Gus had jumped. It must have opened behind her. Dulcie took another step. She must have fallen backward, into the hall from the lobby. Maybe she had hit the light switch. Maybe even hit her head.

'Avila?'

Nothing. Dulcie had never realized before how dark a windowless room could be. Avila must have hit her head. Maybe even now she was lying in the hallway, unconscious. Bleeding.

What was that? The question blasted through Dulcie's mind even before she could figure out why. Then she heard it – again – the barely there footfall of someone who was being careful not to

332

be heard.

'Gus?' The word slipped out, more a wish than an actual question. And although she knew with the calm part of her mind that she was speaking at barely above a whisper, that one syllable sounded as loud as a shot. Dropping her voice further, a breath more than a whisper, she tried once more. 'Mr Grey?'

Another step. Closer. Another, and her hope died. That sound was not, Dulcie realized with a shudder, the quiet footfall of a cat.

She couldn't breathe. Didn't dare. There – behind her!

'Who's there?' She spun around, only to land hard on her bad ankle. 'Oh!' The pain shot up her leg as she collapsed, falling sideways and knocking into something hard – a chair – the metal legs tripping her up as she fell to the floor.

Whoever was there must know where she was. Must know, she realized as her heart pounded, that she was lying there. Unable to flee. She willed herself to be still, to be silent.

She could hear breathing now. She closed her eyes.

'Yaoow!' The cat's cry sounded unearthly in the dark, and Dulcie sat up, staring.

'Oh! Ow!' A woman – close by – and then another yowl and a hiss. The clatter as another chair went down.

'What the...?' The lights came on, so bright that Dulcie started back, covering her face with her forearm. 'Avila, is that you?'

She looked up to see Heath, standing by the auditorium's main door. His hand was on the light switch, and he was staring at her, his handsome face unreadable.

'Dulcie! Oh, thank god.' Roni suddenly was by her side, holding her and at the same time cowering behind her. 'Heath was after me. But you're here. You made it.'

'Dulcie?' Heath looked dumbfounded. 'Wait – Roni?'

'I said I would.' Dulcie let the office manager help her to her feet. 'It went dark...'

'Come on.' Roni was pulling at her arm. Pulling her toward the back of the stage. 'We've got to get out of here. It's Heath. He's here. He knows we know. He'll kill us both.'

'Dulcie, no!' The actor started toward them, staring at Dulcie as Roni pulled at her arm.

'Come on!'

'Wait.' Dulcie pulled away, balancing carefully to protect her sore ankle. Things were coming together. Only why would...?

'Harvey Brenkham!' It was Avila, standing in the entrance to the auditorium. Eyes blazing, her muscular arms outstretched as she bore down. 'What the hell are you playing at with those lights?'

'Watch out, Dulcie!' Heath yelled. 'She's got a knife!'

FIFTY-SEVEN

What happened next, happened in a blur. Despite the house lights, Dulcie found herself reacting by instinct – moving before she could see, acting on what she knew to be true.

Avila was strong and she was fast. But Dulcie was faster. Willing herself to ignore the pain, she swung herself around, flinging her bag. With her laptop for ballast, it connected – hard – and she went over after it. Avila landed on top of her, forcing the breath out of her, and for a moment, Dulcie saw stars.

Then the clatter of metal on the hard floor, chairs and tables thrown to the side, and Heath was there, pulling Dulcie to her feet. She turned, looking for her bag and saw it – several feet away – lying beside a sharpened letter opener.

Avila was standing, legs apart and ready to attack. But as Dulcie watched her, she relaxed, the fierce expression fading from her face.

Roni wasn't getting up. She wasn't a threat any longer. Dulcie's bag had knocked the office manager for a loop, and now she lay blinking up at the three of them, finally at a loss for words.

'Roni Squires,' said Dulcie. 'You've hurt your

335

last innocent victim.' And with that, she fished her phone out of her pocket one more time and called the cops.

FIFTY-EIGHT

It took several hours for everything to be sorted out, and by the time Roni had been taken away in handcuffs, Dulcie was exhausted. The state cop who had been the first to question Dulcie had done his best to be polite – at least she believed he had. But she couldn't avoid the feeling that he viewed her as a nuisance. A dabbler even.

'I didn't know they were looking into everyone's background,' Dulcie complained softly to Avila and Heath. 'Or that they'd put together the identity theft with Roni's old job and were watching her.'

The three were seated in the auditorium, drinking the coffee that one of the cops had sent out for. Gus was grooming at their feet. 'What got me was that Roni was talking about the hacking – about the worm – as if I'd warned her,' Dulcie said. 'But I never did get a chance to tell her more than that I thought the company was accidentally spamming people. And then, she said she'd been in marketing, when Avila said she did IT, and that she was new to the company. Those seemed like minor fibs, at first, but it all started to add up.'

'I'd heard her say that, too,' said Avila. 'About

337

being new here. I figured she just didn't want you to know that she knew Harv— Heath, here.'

'It's okay, Avila.' Heath should have looked relieved. After all, he'd been the one who was being blackmailed. Instead, he looked deflated. 'You can call me Harvey. By curtain time, everyone is going to know anyway.'

'Sorry, hon.' Avila put a hand on his arm. A friendly touch, Dulcie figured. Nothing more. After all, not only was the newly blond actor the laughing stock of the theater world, but he had also been complicit in the cover-up of a murder. Dulcie didn't know if he'd face charges. She did know that Avila was too smart and too talented to be dragged down with him.

'But can I ask you something?' Avila asked. 'Why did you run? Why change your name?'

The actor looked up, his eyes sad. 'After the whole thing in New York. You know, *Hamlet*? I felt cursed. I really felt that line about, you know, "the blasted Heath".'

'That's *Macbeth*.' Avila's voice was gentle, but the actor's head dropped even lower. 'It's okay, honey,' she said. 'We know what you mean.'

'Miss Circule?' One of the uniformed police had come over. 'May we ask you a few more questions?'

'Sure.' Avila got up to follow the young cop and Gus followed behind. As Dulcie watched, the silver cat rubbed against her ankles and, almost without thinking, Avila reached to pick him up, pulling him into her lap as she sat to give her statement. They made quite a couple, Dulcie thought: both lithe, both more muscular than they first appeared. Was that why Gus had wanted to protect Avila, chasing her out of Roni's office that time? Had the theater cat tried to do the same with Amy? They had clearly found each other now, Avila's former aversion seemingly forgotten as she cradled the Russian blue in her arms.

'It's the circus training,' Heath said softly. 'She's light on her feet.'

'You knew what I was thinking?' Dulcie turned back to him, grateful that he hadn't been able to read the other question going through her mind.

'It's part of the training, you know.' The ghost of a smile played on his lips. 'Knowing what different emotions look like, how thoughts play out on our faces.'

'Is that how you found out about Roni?' Dulcie had to ask.

He shook his head. 'No, I was too stupid. Too full of myself. It was Amy.' He paused, swallowed. 'Amy saw how hurt Roni was, when she found out she and I were involved. Amy went to talk to her – and saw something on her computer. None of the rest of us would have known what it meant. It was just Amy's bad luck.'

'But you knew.' It wasn't a question. 'I mean, you know what happened after.'

Heath nodded. 'I suspected. Amy tried to explain it all to me, about how people's information was being copied or whatever. But I didn't want to hear it. I was a star again,' he said, choking up. He paused and cleared his throat. 'I didn't want to rock the boat. And, well, then Amy told me that Roni wanted to talk with her, and Amy was good with that. Said it was all going to be straightened out. I think she thought Roni was going to confess, was going to go to the cops with her after the show.' He paused again, the weight of all that had happened bearing down. 'And then, well...' His voice was almost gone. 'It was too late, wasn't it?'

They sat quietly for a moment. Heath looked smaller, somehow. Even with his newly dyed hair, the golden luster was gone.

'How did you know?' Heath asked, finally. The question was open ended, but Dulcie figured that the actor had really only one remaining concern.

'It was a combination of things, really.' She said, as gently as she could. 'Everyone kept talking about how good you are, but that you would never go anywhere else. *Could* never. That was a big clue.' She decided not to mention the dye job, or the obvious attempts to bolster his self-importance. For all she knew, that was true of all actors. 'And I would have suspected Roni long before, only you had vouched for her. So I had to assume she had something on you.'

He nodded and looked away.

'Mr Barstow?' Another officer was walking toward them. 'It is Mr Barstow, isn't it? You're going to have to come with us now.'

'Yes.' Heath answered with a little more force than necessary. He turned to Dulcie with an apologetic smile as the police officer led him away. 'I'm sorry. I put you at risk.'

'Don't worry about it,' said Dulcie. At least she would have a story for Trista. And he had been called away before he could ask her about Gus.

FIFTY-NINE

'He warned me, Chris. I know he did.' Dulcie was sitting on an examining table in health services, catching her boyfriend up on all the things she couldn't tell the cops. 'He made sure I saw what I needed to, but then when I was in danger, he tripped Roni up.'

'Or she stepped on him.' Chris smiled indulgently.

'You think that just because he isn't Esmé or Mr Grey—' She stopped speaking as the doctor came in.

'As I thought, nothing's broken.' With a click, she called up the images of Dulcie's left ankle. 'But you should know, sometimes a sprain is just as bad.'

Dulcie held her tongue as the doctor wrapped the ankle and sent her off with a set of crutches and a matching list of proscribed activities. As Chris helped her into her coat, however, she realized she had to speak.

'You know what this means, right?' She looked up at her boyfriend. 'I'll need you to be around at night, at least for a while.'

'Of course,' he responded, his brow wrinkling. 'Why would you even question that?'

'Well, it seems like you've been disappearing

at night a lot.' She paused, unsure how to proceed.

'I guess old habits die hard,' he said with a smile. 'But I can change my ways for a while at least. As long as you don't expect me to start acting like Jerry.'

She looked up at him, confused.

'You know, chasing you around like you're some femme fatale.' He held the door open as she hobbled out, swinging her injured leg. 'Don't get me wrong – he loves that stuff and Trista plays up to it. But it's not me.'

'I would never...' Dulcie didn't know what to say. 'I didn't mean...'

'Anyway, from what the doc said, you'll be up and about in a month, for sure. Then we'll both be able to get out more.'

'Chris?' That timing – one month, a full lunar cycle – there was something in it, she was certain. She should follow up. But Chris had gone ahead to hail a cab and was now waving from the other end of the plaza, a smile as big as the moon on his sweet, pale face.

SIXTY

'Spin me a tale about Seeming, and I shall answer with my own.' The Stranger spoke with a voice as soft as summer fog, and yet still could he be heard. 'We are none of us merely what we would Seem. We are all of us more, and thus burden'd by what we may Bring. 'Tis our Curse, and yet also our Blessing. Would you not agree, my Lady?' In the shadowy Night, his very features seemed to grow and soften, as she dashed away the Tears that threatened to pour forth, her Heart's water, though whether of fear or of Relief, she would be loath to say. 'If some of us fare brighter under the Moon's fair luminescence, would you have us called out in Light of Day? Would you have us Depart from you, while your own Secrets hold you back?' 'No, I would not.' She whispered to the Wind, her voice a secret Promise to the Dark. 'I would have you stay, be what you will.'

By Monday, Dulcie had accepted the inevitable. Although she had hobbled back to campus eagerly after receiving Griddlehaus's call, she would have to put aside this latest intriguing fragment of text. The Philadelphia bequest had waited more than a hundred years; it could wait a while longer.

As she made her slow way over to the departmental offices, she steeled herself. All weekend, Thorpe had been emailing and then texting her – using his new-found skill to urge her to get started on the Chicago article. This morning she was due in his office to discuss what he insisted on calling their 'joint strategy,' a phrase as confusing as it was ominous.

She was going to have to come clean. Whatever notes Chicago had sent her had been lost. Whether they had been deleted when Chris had cleaned her phone, or simply swallowed up by the postal service, she might never know. What she did know was that she would have to contact the editors, and hope they had kept a copy of their comments. And before that, she needed to tell everything to Martin Thorpe.

'Mr Thorpe?' She had made it up the stairs and, dropping her bag on the floor, stood in front of his open door. 'I have to make a confession.'

An hour later, Dulcie's head was spinning. On one hand, she had never expected Martin Thorpe to be so enthusiastic about her research. On the other, she felt she had let herself be co-opted in a way not even her former adviser, who had a penchant for stealing his student's work, had managed.

'This will be a marvelous opportunity for you,' Thorpe had exclaimed, pacing around his office. 'Having an article in Chicago will put us both up for the Candlewick Prize.'

'But, Mr Thorpe...' She had to tell him.

'You do know what this means, don't you?' She had never seen him so excited. 'We'll both be up for one of the biggest prizes in academe when this comes out.'

'Wait, I have to ... what?'

'The Candlewick. Which even the dean's committee must recognize as a signature honor.' He was on his toes now. 'You know Bullock won the Candlewick the year before he was named department chair, don't you?'

She stopped, his words sinking in. 'Wait, we both will be up for it?'

'Yes.' Thorpe motioned her into the guest chair before, finally, taking his own seat. 'Don't you know? The journal expects us both to work on this project, faculty adviser and degree candidate. It's their way.'

'Great.' Dulcie forced a smile. It was a change to see the dour man so elated. And here she was going to have to spoil it. 'As long as they don't mind—'

'Here, we've already gotten notes.' He poked around on his desk until he found a stack of pages neatly clipped together. 'I grabbed these as soon as they came in, but you might have Nancy make you a copy.'

'Notes? But...' Dulcie reached for the packet. Sure enough, the journal's logo topped the first page. 'I thought they'd sent these to me.'

'Well, technically, they may have.' Thorpe looked down at his desk, and Dulcie thought he might be blushing. 'But of course anything that comes to the department falls under my bailiwick, and I recognized the address, and so...'

He began to scribble on a yellow legal pad. 'We'll have to start with Hamilton, of course. Have you found any evidence that your author, that *Rampages* one, knew him? No? Well, you'll have to get to work then, won't you?'

'I...' It was no use. She let him continue.

'Yes, yes, that will all be very good.' He kept writing. 'I'm thinking of calling it "The Federalist Femme".'

'But, Mr Thorpe,' she broke in finally. 'Don't you want me to focus on my thesis?' She made herself say the words. She could return to the Philadelphia bequest afterward, as a postgrad. It might be possible. 'I thought you wanted me to finish it. To narrow my scope and write, so I'd be ready to defend this spring.'

'Narrow? Nonsense!' Thorpe barked. 'Now is not the time to talk about narrowing anything, Ms Schwartz. Not at all.'

He must have seen the shock that stopped her questions, because he continued in a more subdued voice. 'This may in truth occasion a delay in the ultimate presentation of your dissertation. But such a credit can only burnish your reputation and add further luster to your thesis when it finally is ready to defend,' he said, warming to the topic. 'The truest graduate students are the foot soldiers of research!'

SIXTY-ONE

Count it as a gift, Dulcie. The email from Professor Showalter couldn't have come at a better time. Slightly stunned, Dulcie had hobbled home, grateful for the slight thaw that had left the sidewalks damp but wider and easier for her to maneuver on crutches.

Still, it had taken all her strength to get back and up the stairs. Now she sat at the kitchen table and read the note that had come in response to her own panicked missive, sent after her meeting with Thorpe.

The Chicago Avatar is a prestigious journal, Thorpe is right about that, and not all change is necessarily bad. This will buy you time to do your real work. Please tell me more about the new fragment when you are at leisure. All best, Renée Showalter.

'Not all change is necessarily bad,' Dulcie read out loud. 'What do you think of that, Esmé?'

'Mrup!' With a leap, the plump cat deposited herself in Dulcie's lap and began to knead.

'Of course, now that Thorpe actually cares about my research, he's going to try to take credit for it.' She stroked the cat's back as she spoke. 'I guess that's better than rushing me

347

through it.'

'Rushing through what?' Chris appeared in the doorway, his arms full of paper bags. 'We have time for dumplings, I hope?'

'I do.' Dulcie smiled up at her boyfriend. 'But don't you have plans?'

'Only for dinner.' He placed the bags on the table. They smelled great. 'Don't get up, I'll get the bowls. How'd the meeting go?'

'You wouldn't believe it,' she began.

'Tell me,' he said. 'I've got all night.'

By the time the dumplings – and the soup and the greens and the noodles that Chris had deemed essential accompaniments – were done and they had all retired to the sofa, Dulcie had brought her boyfriend up to speed.

'Sounds like your old adviser, all over again,' he said when she was done. 'Trying to home in on your research.'

'Yeah.' Full and warm and cuddled against Chris, Dulcie didn't find the idea quite as offensive. 'I'm going to have to be on my guard.'

'But this means you'll have extra time to do your own work, right?' He stroked her hair. Esmé, meanwhile, was purring at Dulcie's feet.

'Yeah, it just seems a little daunting.'

'You can do it, Dulce.' Chris's voice was growing softer. Either that or she was falling asleep. 'What is "seems" anyway?'

''Scuse me?' she asked, or thought she did. The sound of Esmé purring grew louder.

We are what we would be.' She was answered by a different voice, deeper and riding on that

348

purr. *'We needs go through many changes.'* Dulcie closed her eyes and thought of Chris and Suze. Of a world of make-believe and illusion, and a silver cat. Of Trista and of her dear, departed friend, Mr Grey. *'As we are so many things. The world is wide, little one, and full of love. All is possible, if you will only try.'*